LIE DENY REPEAT

WHO'S DECEIVING WHO?

SUSAN WILKINS

For Sue Kenyon, who makes it all possible.

PROLOGUE

He's going to kill her. The realisation sweeps through her body like a howling wind. How does she know? It's an eerie sensation. And she resists it. The very idea is absurd, isn't it?

His eyes are diamond hard as he tilts his head and gives her that roguish smile. It could almost be a come-on, a precursor to sex. The smile is to lure her. To throw her off guard.

Time slows from a trickle to the spiralling descent of each individual grain of sand.

Is this how it ends? His choice. His decision. Has she lost all agency completely?

Her lips part to speak, but no words come. What do you say? Do you beg? Do you bargain?

Her heart thumps in her chest.

She's underestimated his rage. His spite and need for vengeance. As he steps forward, the smile fades. His eyes narrow to dark pinpricks of fury. He blames her. He's making it her fault that he has to do this.

She glances around. For a way out? For a weapon?

Will it be quick? Will it be painful?

A deep and visceral compulsion to survive kicks in. She'll fight. She'll claw the eyes from his face. Tear his flesh with her teeth. If she can just get past him and make it to the door...

She balls her fists. But her voice must beguile and seduce. Make him remember how connected they are, and what it feels like when they make love. She must rescue him from the terrible rage that's consuming his reason. He can't be this man. She must make him see that.

'Listen,' she whispers. 'Let's just try and—'

He seizes a hank of her hair, twisting it round in his hand and yanks her towards him. The brutality and shock of it paralyses her. She gasps, but before she can scream, he clamps his hand over her mouth.

1

Monday, 8.15pm.

Dr Cheryl Woodward's gaze skates across the columns of figures on her laptop screen. This is the only time she has to scrutinise the data, when the lab is quiet and everyone's gone home. Her office has a small window. The slatted blinds are open even though it's dark; a raw February night, moonless with a watery glimmer from the LED lights in the car park. But she's oblivious to the world outside, to everything but the data and the work.

As she scrolls, her brain analyses the numbers from the latest batch of experiments. They look promising.

Do they really? Or is she fooling herself?

Promising is not good enough. What she needs is a definitive sign, some small confirmation that they're on the right track. It could be another blind alley. This kind of scientific research can be slow and frustrating. You create a theory and an experiment to test it. That fails. You try again. And again.

Wanting something to be true doesn't make it true.

Science has to be rigorous; it must be based on evidence. She learned that as an undergrad, and now she teaches it to her students. It has to be their mantra, she tells them. What she doesn't tell them is what it's like to be the head of a major biotech lab in a global race to be the first and the best. This work could save lives. She doesn't tell them about the burden of expectation. Talking up a possible breakthrough hoping to raise the investment to make it happen. That's the gamble. She doesn't mention that.

The phone on her desk vibrates. She glances at it.

Xan.

She feels a rush of guilt as she answers.

'Sorry, sorry, sorry!' she says. 'I lost track.'

Her husband chuckles. 'Did I say anything?'

'It's been manic today. A faculty meeting that lasted two bloody hours. I just wanted to look at the latest test results before—'

'Cheryl,' he says. 'It's your birthday.'

She doesn't need reminding. Her fortieth; a milestone she'd prefer to ignore.

'Do you realise,' she says, 'that Marie Curie won her first Nobel Prize when she was thirty-six?'

'And do you realise,' he says amiably, 'that I'm standing here surrounded by an army of science nerds. Your friends, your colleagues and your fans, not to mention our potential investors, who are all getting legless on champagne at our expense? The thing that's missing is the star of the show, the birthday girl.'

'Darling, I'm so sorry. I know you've gone to a lot of trouble.'

He laughs. 'Husband of the year, I'd say.' He's teasing, but there's an edge to it.

He is entitled to be annoyed.

'You are,' she says. 'You're amazing. And I'm closing my laptop and I'm on my way.'

'You can show me your full appreciation later,' he says. 'In the conventional manner.'

His suggestive tone gives her butterflies. Nine years of marriage and two kids have all but killed their sex life. But for her, he's still the hottest man in the room. And it's not just the looks. His charm is effortless. She takes life too seriously, she knows that. She worries; about the work, progress in the lab, about the kids, about the climate, about her age. But he always makes her laugh. He's the extrovert to her introvert. She's yin to his yang. All marriages involve compromise, but theirs works. Mostly. He loves her. She must keep telling herself that.

'I will. I promise,' she says coyly.

'It's a date.' He hangs up.

As she slots her laptop into her bag, she tries to remember where she put the set of lacey underwear he bought her the Christmas before last. Probably at the bottom of a drawer somewhere. And will she even get into it? She's feeling bloated and pre-menstrual and has the start of a headache.

But Xan is doing all this for her. Okay, she hates parties. But she must meet him halfway. It's only fair.

Earlier in the week, she tried to talk him out of it.

'C'mon,' he said. 'It's two birds with one stone. A big do. The perfect opportunity to showcase you to potential investors.'

Showcase!

It makes her sound like a fashion brand or a stand-up comedian, not a serious scientist.

She walks out into the dark corridor and the lights come on automatically. The geek in her loves this; such a simple piece of technology. Even when the place is deserted, she's comfortable. She'll never admit it, but a childhood fear of the dark lingers. However, anxiety, like everything else, is a question of mindset. What she needs to do now is adjust her mindset.

The party will be fine.

Launching a biotech start-up is a complex business. She understands her husband's argument. If they don't grab the opportunity and exploit the commercial potential of her work now, someone else will. It's all about timing. She wants it. Of course she does. And she wouldn't even be in this position if it wasn't for Xan. He's the one with the conviction that they can make this happen. He knows what he's doing.

And he's doing it for her.

They were still living in the States when Cheryl got offered the chance to come back to Cambridge and run her own lab. Xan said go for it. It was too good an opportunity to turn down. He put his own ambitions on hold. His career was going great guns. He'd worked his way up through several Silicon Valley tech start-ups. He's a brilliant businessman, oozing confidence and charisma. If they'd stayed there, he'd be CEO of his own outfit by now. But he gave it up for her, followed her back to the UK and stayed home with the kids.

She's heading down the corridor to the lifts and her phone pings to tell her that the cab she's ordered is waiting outside. Glancing down, she clicks an acknowledgement, which is why they almost collide.

'Oh my god—'

Cheryl's eyes dart upwards towards the voice. Panic seizes her and she lurches backwards.

'I'm so sorry, Dr Woodward!' says the looming figure as it settles into a recognisable form. One of her post-doctoral researchers?

'Kayleigh!' she gasps. 'What the hell are you doing here?'

Kayleigh is big and sporty; maybe a rower? Cheryl can't remember. Twenty people in the lab, how's she supposed to know them all?

The researcher towers over her. 'I'm so sorry, Dr Woodward,' she mumbles, raising her palms.

She's told them all to call her Cheryl many times. But most insist on Dr Woodward. Why?

Cheryl takes a breath.

'Why are you here?' she says sharply. 'Lurking around.'

'I thought you'd be at the party,' says Kayleigh.

'I'm just on my way,' says Cheryl.

Her mind scoots back to her various conversations with Xan. Didn't he say he was inviting everyone who works for her in the lab?

Calm down.

'Didn't you receive an invitation?' says Cheryl.

'Yes, but… well, I didn't… I'm not very…'

'Fine with me if you don't want to go,' says Cheryl. 'To tell you the truth, I'm not that keen myself.' She forces a smile.

Kayleigh smiles back. Timid, tentative. 'No, it's not that. I was just finishing something,' she says. 'I might pop in later.'

They stare at each other awkwardly. Boss. Subordinate. Kayleigh must be five ten at least, but she's hunching her shoulders to look small.

'Good,' says Cheryl briskly. 'Right, I should go. My husband's annoyed enough as it is. And he's gone to a lot of trouble.'

The researcher is staring at her blankly.

Too much information.

'Come if you can,' she adds. 'If you feel like it.'

The researcher nods.

Cheryl walks away. She presses the call button on the lift and the doors open. She steps inside.

That's a relief.

2

Monday, 9.20pm

He wanders like a wraith through the freezing fog. Close to the river, it's pitch black. Pools of light gather round the street lamps along the path. He knows he must keep moving. His fingers are numb; his limbs stiff and slow. The cold bites.

Keep going. One foot in front of the other.

It's a struggle. His mind coasts, drifting between thoughts. When he was a boy, his mother let him sleep out in a tent in the back garden. The tent was green and flimsy, but he had a sleeping bag. He wishes he had a sleeping bag now. He had to abandon the last one. Some kids pissed on him when he was sleeping in a doorway. It was soaked through, too rank even for him.

Now all he has are the clothes he stands up in. T-shirt, hoodie, dirt-encrusted jeans. The jacket is torn and lets in the rain. But the boots are still good. Real Doc Martens. He got them from a charity, a bit big, but with newspaper stuffed inside, they do the trick most of the time.

But not tonight. He can't feel his toes. Once he saw a bloke with frostbite. His toes were black.

One foot in front of the other.

He can see his own breath. It's like smoke coming from his nose. When he had his glasses, they used to get steamed up. But the glasses are long gone. The world's a blur. He can't see people's faces, which is good.

Last time he was in the hostel, someone nicked his scarf. When he was little, his mother would say: be a good boy, don't forget your scarf. He was a good boy, wasn't he?

The only good thing about the cold is there are fewer people about. Less hassle. Who would be out here on a freezing night like this if they didn't have to be? His stomach rumbles. It's hours since he's eaten. He found more or less a whole burger in the bin outside McDonald's. It was still warm.

He was a good boy, wasn't he? His mother often said so. Sometimes, if he tries hard, he can still picture her face. But she worried about him so much. That little green tent, his cosy sleeping bag, if only he still had them.

One foot in front of the other.

His bones ache; the cold devours him. He's lost weight. Soon there'll be nothing left. He's lightheaded and oh so weary. In front of him on the path, there's a bench, enveloped in a halo of light. Would it be such a bad thing to sit for a moment and rest? Just take a few minutes out.

He sits.

Summer is much better. The bins are overflowing and he can sleep under the trees, hidden away on the river bank, away from prying eyes. It's the one good thing about Cambridge, the river. The place is full of tourists, but he doesn't beg. This bloke he met, the bloke with the toes, told him he was a fool. You could make good money guilt-tripping the tourists. Enough for a few cans. Enough to score some gear.

Be a good boy, his mother said. And he was a good boy, wasn't he? Not a beggar. He always did his best; she knew that. He's drifting again. The back garden was so green and full of flowers. His mother loved flowers. She could grow anything. Sometimes she let him help her, help her with the weeding. And in the house, she had lots of plants. She let him water the plants. You're such a good boy, she would say. Always so helpful.

Suddenly, he feels a hand gripping his shoulder. His stomach lurches. He's being attacked.

There's a voice. It seems to come from far away.

'Alright mate,' it says. He opens his eyes. There's nothing left for them to rob. Maybe his boots? The man standing in front of him, looming over him, is large. And a blur. He cowers away. The blows, the pain, let it come quickly.

But the man says, 'You don't want to be out here tonight, mate. It's too cold. You know the church, the one in Christchurch Street? They're running an all-night soup kitchen. You need to get up there, get yourself some hot food. And they've opened up some extra places in the night shelter. You hearing me, mate?'

He realises he's closed his eyes. He always does that when he's waiting for the first blow. The man shakes his shoulder. He looks up again. A uniform? The man is a cop. There's another one, a female, standing behind him. She's talking into her phone. The man turns to her and says, 'I dunno, he's pretty much out of it. Perhaps we should take him in.'

'The Sarg'll love you,' she says.

'Yeah, well, I don't wanna come back in the morning and find a stiff. Let's take him up the church.'

The cop takes hold of his arm and hauls him to his feet.

'Come on, sunshine,' he says. 'Work with me here. Let's see if we can find somewhere inside for you tonight. Is that okay with you?

The words drift through his head. He says nothing. The cop is pulling him along. He doesn't care. He doesn't care about anything anymore.

3

Monday, 9.35pm

The country house hotel is a couple of miles outside Cambridge. It's a Georgian mansion, Bath stone covered with ivy and twinkling with lights in the icy February darkness. The taxi drops Cheryl at the front door.

As she totters into the building, she worries about the dress. Blue has never been her colour. She should've stuck with the grey. It's too short; she feels exposed. And the heels; she hates wearing heels. Okay, as a small woman, she needs a couple more inches in height. But she can hardly walk in the bloody things; she must look ridiculous.

The concierge directs her towards the ballroom where the party is taking place. The double doors stand open. Two glittering chandeliers dominate the room. White-gloved waiting staff move between the guests with trays of champagne and canapés.

What the hell is this costing them?

She hovers in the doorway. The hum of conversation is

mesmerising, but it makes her feel excluded and small. Her impulse is to turn tail and run. This is why she hates parties.

Mindset.

She takes a deep breath and focuses on walking into the room without breaking an ankle in these damned shoes.

Heads turn, smiles, greetings. The odd familiar face.

Why are there so many people?

Xan has been on the lookout and heads across the room to rescue her.

'You look fantastic,' he says. 'And blue is definitely your colour.'

'I feel like a turkey wrapped for Christmas,' she says.

He laughs. Xan is always laughing. He finds all sorts of things funny. Perhaps this is why so many people enjoy his company. He has a fund of jokes and a sharp wit.

He takes her hand and gazes down into her eyes. 'Listen to me,' he says. 'You are brilliant. One of the most talented scientists of your generation. Half the people here already know that. And the others soon will. So there's nothing to worry about.' He raises her hand to his lips and kisses it. 'This is your time to shine, Cheryl. Enjoy it.'

Looking up at him, she's almost tempted to believe it. Why else would such a gorgeous man have married a boring little swot like her? But the doubt still plagues her. She knows she's clever, but it's never felt that much of an advantage. In the lab, in her own domain, she's fine. But situations like this make her feel like a teenager.

She catches sight of her sister, Lorna, across the room, chatting away. There's a smattering of colleagues from the university too.

'You see there are some friendly faces,' says Xan.

He can read her mind. He understands. And he's doing all this for her.

Cheryl smiles. 'I'm sorry to be so late. I know you've gone to a lot of trouble.'

He grins. 'This is only part of it. You can't have a birthday, especially not a fortieth birthday, without a special surprise. I hope you're ready for this.'

Not expensive jewellery again.

She wishes he wouldn't spend money on useless stuff that's going to live in a drawer for most of the year. Her engagement ring is a one point two Carat diamond which she has to take off and lock away when she's working.

But she smiles.

He leads her across the room towards the corner, and with a conjuror's flourish, he points to a triptych of display boards. 'Ta-dah! We now have a company name and a logo. Acanthis Biotech. What do you think?'

She stares at the glossy designs. This is out of left field. He's set up a company, before they've even discussed it?

Too soon.

He's grinning at her. 'I hope you're pleased?'

The work is not ready. How can she be pleased?

'I'm… amazed,' she says. 'I don't know what to say.'

She scans his face. The smile is fading; he knows her too well. She's no good at pretending. He can see her disappointment. Right now, even some ridiculous overpriced rock would be preferable. She casts around for something more to say. The logo appears to be a kind of abstract bird?

'Nice logo,' she says. 'Why a bird?'

Now his gaze is fixed on her, monitoring her. 'I thought you'd like it. It's from Greek mythology. Acanthis was transformed into a bird. And we're going to soar.'

'I hope so.' she says.

He frowns. 'Cheryl, I know what I'm doing. You need to trust me.'

He's staring down at her, solid and immovable, and his annoyance is surfacing. She doesn't want a row, not here, not in front of all these people. But this isn't fair, and she won't be railroaded.

'How are we even paying for all this?' she says.

He huffs. 'Let me worry about that.'

'But I do worry.'

'It's an investment. You spend money to make money.'

She adopts a more conciliatory tone. 'This company thing. I just wish you'd talked to me about it.'

'Why?' he says. 'So you can say no before scurrying back to your lab?' He folds his arms, closes his eyes. He's reining himself in.

Cheryl notices her sister glancing in their direction. And she's not the only one. The power couple having a spat; that'll delight some of her less sympathetic colleagues.

Xan sighs. His face is full of contrition. 'I'm sorry,' he says, 'that was uncalled for. It's just that, putting all this together…'

She reaches out and clasps his hand. Let them all look. She doesn't care. 'No,' she says. 'I'm the one that should be sorry. I arrive late. Now I'm behaving like a child. You're entitled to be pissed off.'

He smiles. 'You have to believe in yourself. I do.'

'I know.'

This is the great thing about her husband, upsets are gone in an instant. Now he's beaming, and those gorgeous blue eyes are full of love.

'I'm not trying to put pressure on you to deliver,' he says. 'That's not what this is about. I want to make your life easier. Get you out of a pokey university lab with a ridiculous teaching schedule and stupid faculty meetings, into a state-of-the-art facility, where you'll have fifty top-notch researchers to support you. We'll hire the best in the field. I'm just trying to give you the space to do what you do best.'

Gazing up at him, her eyes brim with tears. She's tired and pre-menstrual. That's why she's being so reactive.

'I know,' she whispers. 'I'm sorry.'

But his gaze skips over her head. He's smiling at someone across the room. She turns to see.

A young woman is strolling towards them. Tall and slender as a gazelle with a mane of golden hair, she exudes style and poise. Xan is watching her approach, and that look flickers across his face. Half smile, half what? Desire?

Long time since he's looked at her like that.

It all happens in a nanosecond but sends a shaft of envy zinging through her.

'Here's someone I want you to meet,' says Xan.

The woman can't be more than twenty-five. She's offering her hand to shake. Her nails are long and immaculate. They wouldn't survive like that in the lab for five minutes, thinks Cheryl. And her dress is grey and chic, not a ridiculous, shiny blue like wrapping paper.

'This is Hannah Blakeney,' says Xan. 'She's a senior associate with HDZ Venture Partners.'

Cheryl tries to concentrate. She has to wipe her nose with the back of her hand. Venture Partners means money. The vital seed capital they'll need to get the business up and running. Xan keeps banging on about this.

Hannah has a wide, toothy smile, and she displays it to full advantage. 'I am so happy to finally meet you, Dr Woodward,' she says. 'Your husband's been telling me about your work. Oh my god, we are so excited.' She rolls her eyes, like a contestant on a quiz show who's just won the star prize. Her long silky fingers grasp Cheryl's small lab-roughened hand.

She smells of something pungent and expensive that certainly didn't come from Boots.

So smug!

The feelings erupting inside Cheryl are absurd. Intellectually, she knows that. But she can't stop them. Her mind skitters back to school days. The cool girls were all some version of Hannah, and always tall. They got the attention, and they certainly got all the boys. Small glass-wearing nerds like Cheryl never got a look in. But that was then, and this is now, she reminds herself. Treat her like a student. She's no older than the postgrads who work in the lab.

'It's lovely to meet you too,' Cheryl says with a regal smile.

Think Queen Victoria. She was short. And powerful.

'And that brings me to my real surprise,' says Xan. 'But I'll let Hannah explain.'

'We just want to hear more,' says Hannah. 'My firm has three hundred million under investment. We focus on start-ups in the very initial stages. Biotech is a tricky field. But we're the experts, and we know the real deal when we see it. I called my boss and I told him. We must get in here, put down a marker before anyone else. He agreed.'

A marker? What's she talking about?

She beams. 'We'd like to offer you fifty thousand in seed capital, to show we're serious, and so we can move this forward as a team.'

A team?

Cheryl glances at her husband. His face is flushed like an excited schoolboy. He laughs. 'I'd call that serious, wouldn't you, darling?'

Cheryl is stunned; a mixture of elation and fear floods through her. But Xan is right. Of course he is. This is good.

It's just that having it foisted on her like this has thrown her on the back foot.

'Well, yes. Thank you,' she manages to say. 'That's amazing.'

'Oh, and happy birthday,' Hannah adds.

Xan grabs flutes of champagne from a passing waiter. He hands them over and takes one for himself.

'To Acanthis Biotech,' he says, raising his glass. 'Going public in three years and making billions.'

Cheryl's head swirls with a maelstrom of conflicting emotions. She raises her glass aloft. The chilled liquid has created condensation on the glass. It's slippery in her fingers.

Hannah is looking down at her and grinning.

Fifty grand sounds a lot to just *put down a marker.*

But Xan knows what he's doing. He can handle these people, can't he? This is his world.

She wants to be excited. She is excited. It's time to be bold and not let her anxiety get in the way. Her husband is right.

Mindset.

'Sorry,' she says. 'You must think I'm an idiot, Hannah. I've wanted this for so long. But this will give me the freedom to do the work the way I want to do it. And I am grateful.'

She raises her glass to chink against Hannah's. But the slender flute slides from her fingers, crashes to the polished wooden floor of the ballroom and shatters into a thousand pieces.

4

Monday, 10.45pm

Hannah Blakeney scans the room. It's been a surprising day. Not at all what she expected when she walked into the office this morning. She didn't expect to end up in a sedate country house hotel on the outskirts of Cambridge. But she's feeling pleased with herself. And rightly so.

It's a weird gathering; the awkward fusion of a corporate bash with a birthday party, and in a room that looks more like an overpriced wedding venue. But she suspects Xan Woodward is doing this on his credit card. A Monday night in February? He probably got a cut-price deal.

He's middle forties, lean and wolfishly hot. And he gazes right at you; cornflower blue eyes, but the lashes and hair are dark. A bit of a Celt in there somewhere? He probably looks even better under his well-cut suit. How he and his mousy little wife got together is a mystery. Her dress is awful. She's a bag of nerves and she looks like she just wants to run out of the door. Hard to believe she's the scientific brains in this outfit.

Hannah's day had started early at a desk in London, with a strong coffee, trawling through proposals for half-arsed apps from spotty teenage nerds. She was feeling tetchy and bored.

Since she transferred over from her uncle's private equity firm to HDZ, they had given her all the dross. At the time, getting into venture capital felt like a smart move. It was a macho environment; her uncle had warned her about that. Like many places in the City, it paid lip service to diversity and nothing more. And she was the new girl in this testosterone swamp. Her so-called colleagues made no secret of the fact they were running an office sweepstake on who could screw her first. A bunch of cocky, mostly public schoolboys with the emotional intelligence of gnats. Once she got her teeth into a project with real potential, she'd leave them standing. She looked like a girl, but she was ruthless. She could play as dirty and vicious as any man. She'd grown up with three brothers, and she knew how to compete in this world. And how to win.

Just after lunch, her boss, Nat, called her into the office and said he had something in Cambridge he wanted her to check out.

'What do you know about biotech?' he said. He was munching his way through a messy burrito. Sauce dripped down his chin.

Sod all, basically.

She had a first in economics. School biology had given her the creeps. Videos of people dissecting sheep's eyeballs and frogs that were still twitching. Gross.

She gave him her best smile. 'New frontier. Very exciting. It's where we should be.'

He looked at her and sighed. Did he realise she was blagging it?

'I've read loads about it,' she added.

And she was a fast learner; he knew that.

He wiped his mouth with his fingers. 'This is a lead Freddie's come up with.'

Freddie Turner was the current blue-eyed boy. The youngest associate to make partner.

'He's got a background in biological sciences.'

Bloody typical.

Freddie also had slicked back hair, bulging eyes and a wide mouth. He was undoubtedly related to a frog.

'But he's in Germany chasing a new vaccine start-up. And this can't wait.'

'I can handle it,' she said, as if it was no big deal.

Yes!

He gave her a sceptical look and drummed his fingers on the edge of his glass desk. She waited.

Self-assured, enthusiastic, but not too eager.

She crossed her legs for good measure. A discreet amount of thigh to remind him she had assets Freddie the frog lacked.

'Okay,' he said. 'Let's do it. But keep me in the loop.'

'Obviously,' said Hannah with a serene smile.

'And don't fuck it up. I don't want to pay over the odds. Seventy grand max. Freddie has contacts in Cambridge who say this Dr Woodward could be ahead of the pack.'

Hannah read the briefing paper on the train from London. It sounded outlandish. Making human organs with a 3-D printer, using the patient's own cells. Really? How? Half an hour googling revealed that there were a dozen labs worldwide working on this. It was red hot. A bladder had been created, and it worked. More complex organs like the liver, kidney or heart were proving difficult. But once someone cracked it, there'd be a gold-rush. Freddie was not wrong. There was serious potential here.

She got off the train in Cambridge at four o'clock that afternoon with a plan. There were two founders. Dr Woodward turned out to be the wife; she was the scientist, but her husband was the business ninja. She rang Xan Woodward's number. He'd got Silicon Valley peppered all over his CV, which suggested, once you stripped out the bullshit, he'd have some connections. She needed to head off any competition.

He replied with a text and a smiling emoji, saying he looked forward to meeting her at the party. So she FaceTimed him, and when he saw her actual smile that did the trick.

They met before the party in the hotel bar. She had to prove to Nat she could do this, and she knew she'd only get one shot. What would it take to reel him in?

She soon discovered that Xan Woodward had genuine charm. His mobile features were rarely still and he liked to talk. All she had to do was sip her gin and let him display his peacock feathers. And they were fine feathers. But she'd always had a weakness for older men; especially if they were tall and gym-fit and could wear a tuxedo.

Maybe a daddy thing?

'After uni I was restless,' he said. 'I went travelling. Started on the east coast, kept moving west. And by the time I got to San Francisco and saw what was going on there, I knew what I wanted to do. In the end, I was there for fifteen years.'

'Wow,' she said. 'You're practically an American. Explains the cool, transatlantic accent.'

He grinned. Preening himself.

He liked flattery. But who doesn't?

'I thought about staying,' he said. 'Could have. Part of me

wanted to. But I like a challenge. And the work that my wife is doing has certainly provided that.'

'She sounds an amazing woman,' said Hannah. 'I can't wait to meet her.'

'Yes, she is,' he replied. But he continued to gaze straight at her. It wasn't intrusive or leery. But she felt the frisson. A delicious pheromone buzz.

A few things crossed her mind at that point. Was he coming on to her? It felt like it. Ordinarily, a one-night stand with a guy she's picked from an app wouldn't faze her. But this was business. She didn't want to come over as unprofessional.

Intriguing.

'Can I be honest?' he said. 'I've had five offers of seed capital. But they're all from the States. Cheryl would prefer a London-based firm. Like yours. HDZ has a brilliant reputation. And it's her birthday.'

Hannah called Nat from the women's toilet.

'Five offers?' he said. 'Cheeky sod. That's absolute bullshit. He's trying to play you.'

'I know that,' she said. 'What do you want me to do?'

'Sounds desperate Offer him fifty, no negotiation. Freddie can pick it up when he's back.'

'Okay,' she said. But it rankled.

Freddie the frog.

The Woodwards were excited about the offer. Obviously. At the party, she mingled and chatted. A couple of other VC firms were represented. They'd come for a sniff too. They soon realised she'd gazumped them. Nat should give her some credit for that. Was she just going to hand over to Freddie?

Now it's getting late. She considers her options. Get a cab to the station, train to London. Job done. Leave it to Freddie.

Nothing lost. Nat would be pleased with her. She'd done what he told her to do. And she hadn't fucked it up.

Or what? One thought keeps niggling.

This one's mine. Just go for it.

As she gazes round the room, she feels a growing reluctance to walk away. Moments like this, choices are made which define your life. Success or failure? Win or lose? She's been with the firm a couple of months, and she knows nothing about biotech. But what if she can persuade Xan Woodward that he'd much rather deal with her? Make him insist upon it. Create a bond. Cut Freddie out of the loop.

Guests are drifting away. Most of those left are pissed thanks to the free bar. Dr Woodward herself has disappeared. Odd little woman. They didn't come over as the happiest of couples. Chalk and cheese.

Hannah has been observing them both through the course of the evening. They remained in separate clusters. Dr Woodward went into a tailspin of embarrassment and apologies when she dropped her champagne flute. After that, she stuck like a limpet to a sharp-suited woman with a dykey haircut and horn-rimmed glasses; apparently her sister, who's a lawyer.

They left together shortly after ten thirty.

But Xan Woodward stayed. It's obvious he enjoys the role of genial host.

Hannah sips her mineral water. She's been careful to keep her wits about her. Okay, she's clueless about biotech. That doesn't matter. She's smart enough to blag it. In the end, this is a people business. Careers and fortunes depend on a network of personal connections. These can take years to build.

But who wants to wait years?

The tailenders are getting rowdy. Woodward is in the

thick of it; he's definitely a party guy. He's by the bar, jacket off, glass in hand, at the centre of a group of men, laughing.

Worth a bit of a risk? Hell yes. Nothing to lose.

Hannah straightens her dress, tosses back her hair, and walks towards them. Xan Woodward turns and looks at her. He grins.

Wow! There it is again. That pheromone hit.

No reason business can't be fun too, is there?

'Hey,' he says with a wave of his hand. 'Here she is. The woman who makes dreams come true.'

She scans him. He tilts his head, gives her a quizzical look. As courtship dances go, it's brief.

But she gets it. He's drunk enough. Loose enough. Hungry enough.

And if she says yes, it's game on.

5

Monday, 10.49 pm

A dismal night. Patches of dense freezing fog interspersed with the harsh glitter of headlights hurtling towards them out of the murk. Cheryl sits in the passenger seat of her sister's car, staring out of the window. It's disorientating, which matches her mood.

'What bloody awful weather,' says her sister, from the driver's seat.

Cheryl's just relieved to have escaped and to be cocooned in the cosy capsule of Lorna's Fiat 500 electric as it purrs cautiously along the dual carriageway leading back into town.

'Do you think there's something wrong with me?' says Cheryl glumly.

'Why? Because you don't like parties.'

'Maybe I'm agoraphobic?'

Lorna glances at her. 'Was it that bad?'

'Or perhaps I'm just a miserable, ungrateful cow,' says Cheryl.

Her sister chuckles. 'When he called me and told me what he was planning, I reminded him about the party thing.'

'What did he say?'

'It's her fortieth!' Lorna mimics his booming male voice surprisingly well. 'How can she not have a party?'

'I missed not having the kids there,' says Cheryl. 'I'd rather have spent my birthday with them. And you, of course. Just a small family dinner.'

Lorna pulls up at a set of traffic lights.

'Jordan's fourteen. I don't see why Xan couldn't have included him,' says her sister.

'He said it wouldn't be fair on Sasha. Told the kids it was a grown-up thing. To be honest, I think Jordan was relieved.'

She imagines her son at the party, lurking in a corner, scrolling on his phone. In the last six months he's shot up, becoming lanky and distant, with the first hints of a downy beard on his chin. He's morphed into a secretive teen, who refuses to communicate with her. She understands puberty; the chemistry, the hormones, the biological turmoil he's experiencing. But she still misses her little boy.

For the first five years of his life, it was just the two of them. She was a single mum and struggling to finish her doctorate. It was tough until Xan came along. He'd rescued her, married her and made her little boy his son. At the time, she couldn't believe her luck. And she still can't. Jordan adores him. She's envious of their relationship; her son is far more likely to respond if Xan asks him to do something. But she always wanted Jordan to have a good male role model in his life, and now he does.

The lights change to green. The car glides forward.

Cheryl senses the tension in her sister. She knows what's coming. It's the discussion they always have.

'Y'know…' says Lorna.

'Don't!' says Cheryl, holding up her palm. 'Not on my birthday. Please.'

'Okay,' says Lorna. 'Sorry.'

They drive on in silence.

Which is worse.

Now she feels bad. Since they were children, Lorna has been her rock. Cheryl was eight when their mother died. Their grief-stricken father couldn't cope and dispatched both girls to boarding school. And without her big sister, Cheryl would never have survived.

Cheryl heaves a sigh. 'I know what you're going to say, but I do stand up to him,' she says. 'I know you think I don't, but I do.'

'I thought we weren't talking about it?' says Lorna.

'The problem is he doesn't always listen.'

'The problem is he hears what suits him,' says Lorna. 'I see he's gone ahead and set up the company. He told me within three years you'll be going public and you'll be multi-millionaires.'

Cheryl tries to ignore the snippiness in her sister's tone. Xan and Lorna live on different planets. Her sister's always had strong political views; going on demos, getting into rows with people. She's a family lawyer, and much of her work is pro bono, working for clients who rely on food banks. To her, excessive wealth is immoral. All billionaires are villains.

'I know the money doesn't matter to you,' Lorna adds. 'The work you're doing is brilliant and important.'

Here we go again.

How is it she always ends up here? Stuck in the middle of the argument between her husband and her sister?

Cheryl sighs. 'Look, you're right,' she says. 'I don't care about being rich. But proper investment means a bigger, better equipped lab and faster progress.'

Now she's siding with Xan.

'You like being an academic,' says Lorna. 'Will you still have enough time for all your teaching?'

Probably not.

'Xan says it's all about timing. He's worried someone else will get there before us. And he could be right.'

Lorna reaches through the darkness and squeezes her hand. 'If you're not ready, you shouldn't do it.'

How does she know?

'I owe him, Lorna. He gave up his career for me. And he knows about this stuff. I'm a scientist, a lab rat. I don't understand business. He's obsessed with making this work.'

'Obsessed is right.'

She doesn't understand.

'He just wants me to be successful. He's doing it all for me,' she says.

Lorna doesn't reply.

She knows she sounds defensive.

'Well,' says Lorna. 'As long as you're happy.' The tone carries the full weight of her disapproval. But her sister's handled too many divorces. And she's a lesbian. She tends to assume most heterosexual relationships are rubbish.

The little car pulls up outside the house.

'Want to come in?' says Cheryl.

'I won't. Early start,' says her sister.

'Thanks for the lift.'

A peck on the cheek. Cheryl gets out. She has her key ready, but knows her sister is keeping a watchful eye until she disappears into the house. It's unnecessary; the neighbourhood is safe. Edwardian villas, most of them tastefully renovated and brought back to single occupancy.

But that's Lorna. Always expecting trouble.

Cheryl unlocks the front door and gives her sister a wave. As Lorna drives off, she steps into the elegant hallway.

She loves this house. It's the best place she's ever lived. When she and Xan first looked at it, she was sure it was too expensive. Loads of original features. Polished wooden floors. The sleek, airy kitchen with bi-fold doors onto the garden is straight out of a design magazine.

They'd just returned to England from the States. It was quite a shock, more so for Xan. He'd given up his job. All they had was her income from the university. Cheryl was worried how they'd manage financially. But he was blasé about it. And full of plans for new businesses he was going to start.

'You spend money to make money,' he said.

'How?' she said. She hated being in debt. Even a few hundred on her credit card made her feel guilty. The house was beyond their means at that point, she was sure of that.

But he disagreed. He went out and got a loan at a very competitive rate. And now here they are in this beautiful home.

She ditches her heels at the front door and pads upstairs. That's when she notices her daughter's light is still on. Sasha is only eight, and Cheryl told her husband that they should hire a babysitter for the evening.

He'd brushed this aside. 'Jordan is perfectly capable of looking after his sister.'

Really?

She knows even before she knocks on her son's door, he'll have his headphones on and his mind in cyberspace. The last thing he'll be thinking about is his little sister.

She checks on Sasha first. Her daughter is sitting up in bed reading a book. She looks up and smiles as her mother enters.

'Goodness me,' says Cheryl. 'Do you know what time it is?'

'I just wanted to get to the end,' says her daughter. 'It's the exciting bit. The fight with the dragon.'

Cheryl perches on the side of the bed, strokes a lock of dark hair out of her child's eyes. They're so blue, like Xan's. Cheryl is glad that Sasha loves to read; so unusual nowadays, most kids spend all their time on their phones. But although she has her father's looks, she has more of her mother's nature. She lives in a world of her own. And Cheryl worries about that. She's far too shy. Other kids seem to unnerve her.

'Well, the dragon will be there in the morning,' she says. 'Now it's time for you to snuggle down and get some sleep.'

Sasha smiles and closes her book. She's still a child, still compliant and happy to be cuddled. Unlike her teenage brother.

'How was your party?' says Sasha.

Tedious,' says Cheryl. 'I'd much rather have been at home with you and Jordan.'

She pulls up the duvet, tucks it under her daughter's chin and kisses her forehead.

'Now go to sleep.' She turns off the bedside light.

'Can Daddy come and tuck me in, too?' says Sasha.

'He's not home yet. Now go to sleep, darling. It's still a school night.'

Jordan's door is shut. She'll deal with him once she's out of this awful dress.

She goes to her own room, dumping her coat and bag, reaching round to tug at the zip. Tucked in her coat pocket, her phone buzzes with an incoming text. Pulling it out, she looks at it.

Xan.

Sorry darling, it's going to be a late one. Don't wait up.

I'll see you in the morning xx

Cheryl peers at his message. Sounds innocuous, but she's been here before. The words hit like a punch in the gut, knocking the breath out of her.

No! Not again. He promised.

Disturbing images cascade through her brain.

Stop! Focus.

She can't. It's her bloody birthday! He should come home to her. The last time this happened, he made her a solemn promise. A drunken mistake, he said. It wouldn't happen again. It meant nothing, he said. But if that was true, why do it? She has no reason to be jealous. That was his line.

But who? Not VC woman who's giving them the money?

Pushing that thought away, she steps out of her dress and hangs it up. Strips off her underwear; the fancy lingerie she'd worn just for him.

For after the party. What a fool.

As she flings it into the laundry basket, she glimpses her naked body in the mirror on the back of the wardrobe door. Two children, sagging belly, the scar from a Caesarian. It's the body of a forty-year-old woman who works all hours and doesn't have time for the gym.

Not what he wants. And who can blame him?

She unfolds her pyjamas and puts them on. The anger is fizzing inside her, deep down in her gut. Sleep is going to be impossible, so she gets the laptop out of her briefcase, climbs into bed and opens it.

Mindset.

There are a few more stats from the latest experiment that she should go over. Her eyes are sore. She's been wearing her contacts all day. She should take them out. But this will distract her, just for half an hour or so. Then she'll take a sleeping pill.

6

Monday, 10.52pm

The soup tastes good, it's full of beans and tomato. As he clutches the cardboard cup with both hands, he can feel the warmth of it seeping through to his frozen fingers. The cops brought him here. He didn't resist. What would be the point? They were only doing their job.

The woman in front of him has a kindly face.

'Go on,' she says. 'Take a hunk of bread, too.'

He reaches out and picks up a piece of bread. One reason he prefers to avoid people is this. He doesn't want to see the pity in their eyes. He knows what they're thinking, and he knows what they're wondering. How did a young guy like him end up like this? He wonders it himself. He has no answers. Out there in the cold, his mind has slowed. Thoughts drift through his head. Crazy thoughts. Sometimes he wonders if he's losing his mind. It feels like that.

He takes his soup and bread and heads for the far corner of the room. Away from the others. The stinking old dossers with vacant eyes. It's taken a long time for him to accept that this is who he is. He's one of them. A down and out. A homeless person. The shame of it eats away at him as much as the cold.

Most days he hangs out in the doorways of empty shops. But people still pass him by. And he hears what they say.

'They're all just junkies. Look at them. It's pathetic. Why can't they pull themselves together and get a job?'

Occasionally, someone will come along who tries to give him money. He refuses it. Shakes his head, turns away. He'll take stuff from the charities because he has no choice. But individual people? He knows what his mother would've said about that. She'd be disappointed in him. He's disappointed in himself. How did it come to this? He's not sure he knows.

More crazy thoughts. Voices in his head.

February can be the worst time of the year. The nights are long, Christmas is a memory, and everyone is feeling cold and mean. You spend a night in a shelter, and you can guarantee you'll get robbed. Or some alchy will go ape-shit and beat you up, just because he can.

Last summer, while he was sleeping, someone stomped on him and broke his wrist. He went to the hospital. They patched him up and called a social worker. The social worker asked lots of questions. What drugs are you on? He said he couldn't remember.

They found him a rehab place. He was there for two days. They shaved his beard and cut his hair. Three meals a day, which was glorious. Roll ups were allowed, but no booze and certainly no drugs. It wasn't a bad place, but he knew he couldn't stay. He was there under false pretences. They didn't understand. If drugs could fill the void in his soul, then he'd be taking them. Getting off his face was not an option. He had to bear the raw pain. Every day. Every hour. This is his penance.

Mother would understand that.

Suffering is what he deserves, but it also keeps him alive. Once he lets go of that, he knows he may as well throw himself under a train.

The voices will tell him when.

But that day will come. He knows that too. And he's already picked out the perfect spot.

7

Monday, 10.58pm

Detective Sergeant Jo Boden climbs out of the squad car. Duty cover for CID on a miserably cold February night wouldn't be most people's choice, but she's saving for a mortgage on a flat and happy to get the overtime.

The multi-storey car park is a concrete, brutalist structure in the middle of town and uniform have already cordoned it off. There's an ambulance parked on the road at the bottom of the out ramp; two paramedics are waiting beside it with their gurney. The PC with them walks forward to meet her.

'Well,' says Boden. 'What have we got?'

'Dead when the paramedics arrived,' says the PC. 'Nothing they could do.'

'Body still in situ?'

'Yep.' He wipes his nose with the back of his hand. He's shivering. Too much standing around.

Boden gives him a sympathetic smile. 'What the bloody hell were they playing at on a night like this?'

'Car park's largely empty, no one about. Suited their purpose, I guess. The other lad's in the back of the ambulance.'

'He's alright?'

'In shock. He dialled 999.'

'Okay,' says Boden. 'Let's see the body first.'

The PC nods. He scoots round the exit barrier and heads towards the steep concrete ramp which leads to the floor above. At the bottom of the ramp, a battered metal shopping trolley with a broken castor lies on its side. Boden looks up the slope. Near the top, the corpse lies in a crumpled heap. All she can see are jeans and an expensive trainer.

The PC waves his hand vaguely upwards. 'Looks like he was riding in the trolley. Came round the corner at speed. Front wheel hit the curb. He was catapulted out of the trolley and slammed into the wall head first. Bit of blood on the wall. Paramedic reckons his neck's broken.'

Boden nods and sighs. 'A stupid prank gone wrong?'

'Looks that way.'

'Just the two boys?'

'Not sure. There might've been others who ran off.'

'Okay.' Boden plods up the ramp. It's rough, pitted concrete with darkened tyre tracks. After several steps, her thighs burn. She pauses to take a breath. The PC is beside her, easily keeping pace, which makes her feel old. She needs to run again. Or get back in the gym.

'Bit steep,' he says.

'Yep.' She pretends she's stopped to take a pair of blue vinyl gloves from her pocket. She pulls them on.

He reaches the body first. Points to the concrete side wall. 'Probably hit it there, bounced off. You want forensics?'

'Yeah, we'll need that for the coroner.'

He moves away to make a call.

She squats down and carefully pulls back the hood to reveal his face. Ginger hair, skin smooth as a baby, just a kid. His eyes are fringed with long, sandy lashes and closed as if he's taking a nap. Someone's son. She extracts a phone from his jeans pocket and bags it. No other ID.

Standing up, she turns to the PC. 'Cordon all this off for forensics. I'll tell the paramedics they can move him. I'm going to talk to the other boy.'

The slope is easier going down. She speaks to the paramedics first. Brisk and businesslike. No one likes dealing with dead children.

In the back of the ambulance there's a boy swaddled in a foil blanket. He has auburn hair, head dipped forward and a stunned look on his face. As she climbs in to join him, he starts like a frightened rabbit.

'I'm Jo,' she says. 'I'm a police officer.'

The boy blinks at her a couple of times. Grey eyes full of fear. 'Is he… dead?' says the boy. 'They told me to stay here.'

'Yes,' says Boden. 'I'm afraid he is.'

His chin puckers and trembles. He's trying to be a man.

'Was he your friend?' says Boden gently.

He stares at his feet—another pair of expensive trainers—and nods.

'Did you see what happened?'

The effort of containing his tears is choking him.

Finally, he splutters, 'We were making a video.'

'A video? So you were filming him in the trolley?'

Another curt nod.

Boden's heart sinks.

'To put on social media?' she says. Now it makes sense. A ridiculously dangerous piece of daredevilry to gain followers on social media.

Tears and words erupt from him. 'We took it in turns to

ride the trolley… but I'm better at filming than him. I don't get it. We've done it loads of times. Scoot it round the corner, jump in. Once it picks up speed, you just have to keep it straight…'

His voice trails off.

He looks up at her with the puzzled eyes of a child. 'I'm sorry,' he says.

'I think you're in shock,' says Boden. 'So I'm going to take you home.'

He shakes his head savagely. An attempt to erase the horror?

'I just don't get it,' he says. 'He's fallen out loads of times. Me too. It's no big deal.'

He wipes his face with the back of his hand.

'What's your name?' says Boden.

He sniffs. 'Jordan… Woodward.'

'How old are you, Jordan?'

'Fourteen.'

'What's your friend called?'

'Ben Whiston.'

'Anyone else here with you tonight?'

He shakes his head. 'Just me and Ben.'

8

Monday, 11.20pm

Cheryl's gaze drifts over the figures on the spreadsheet. Nothing's going in. She has her laptop propped up on a pillow in front of her. Her brain skitters between thoughts. It's not as if her husband's infidelity is anything new. But, after the last time, he promised her. She tries to rationalise and look at it objectively. Some men are like this, aren't they? It's just sex. Doesn't mean he doesn't love her.

But on her birthday?

The casual cruelty of it stings. She forces her mind back to the spreadsheet. Glances across at her phone. Nothing more from him. There won't be. He'll turn up in the morning, bright and breezy, with some elaborate tale. It'll be full of details: who said what, how much they drank, how he'd crashed out on someone's floor. He knows how to convince; he's an accomplished liar.

Does he take her for a fool?

The short answer is he does. And that's why it's so hard

to let go of her anger. She can feel the toxicity of it, in her chest, in her throat. This is her body's mechanism, created over millennia, for protecting her from harm. It's telling her to take action. But where will that get her?

If she challenges him, they'll just row. He'll front it out. Accuse her. Tell her she's always ridiculously jealous. Why doesn't she trust him? Why doesn't she believe him? She knows his technique: attack is the best form of defence. And that's how it will end, him stomping round the house full of righteous indignation. The kids upset. Her trying not to cry.

She hates these kinds of arguments. They're toxic in themselves. The backwash can last for days. It fills the house. And Xan is obdurate; he'll stand his ground and stick to his story. The more she questions him, the more stubborn he becomes. It's easier to give in.

The weak little woman? Is this who she's become?

But there's a choice; if she wants their marriage to survive, and life to return to normal, and the house to be calm, and the kids to be happy, she has to back down.

Getting out of bed, she draws the curtains back. The garden is full of dark silhouettes shrouded in mist. It's a cold night. But she's safe and warm in her own home. This is what matters; her beautiful home and her beautiful children. And it matters to him too.

He's under such pressure, he needs to cut loose. Jealousy is pointless; it only causes her misery. Maybe she should just accept that he's different from her. He needs his fun, but he'll come home. He always does. That's the rational way to look at this.

. . .

At first, she thinks the noise is coming from outside. It's disembodied and distant. But then she realises it's the doorbell. The doorbell is ringing.

Xan!

He's forgotten his key! He's home! A bit the worse for wear, probably. But he wasn't lying.

She doesn't bother with a dressing gown. She runs downstairs barefoot. Flicks the light switch on in the hall. The bell rings again.

Stupid, stupid! Of course he wouldn't. Not on her birthday.

She opens the door with a welcoming smile. Then freezes in shock.

Jordan? Why is her son out there on the doorstep when he should be upstairs in his bed?

A woman is standing next to her son, and she's holding out something in front of her.

'Detective Sergeant Boden,' she says.

'Jordan?' says Cheryl. 'What the hell is going on?'

He can't meet her eye. His face is gaunt. He looks wretched. She reaches out to him.

'Oh, Jordie…'

But he slides past her into the house and bolts up the stairs.

'Can I come in Mrs Woodward?' says the woman.

'Dr Woodward,' says Cheryl

'My apologies,' says the woman. 'Can I come in and explain?'

'You're the police?' says Cheryl.

'Yes. DS Boden.'

'Of course. Sorry. Come in,' says Cheryl, standing back from the door.

Jordan has disappeared. His bedroom door slams shut. But Sasha is standing at the top of the stairs.

'Go back to bed, Sasha,' she says. 'I'll come up in a minute.'

She leads the police officer down the hall and into the kitchen, giving herself a few vital seconds to gather her thoughts. It's clear that her son was not in his bed, or even in the house, as she thought.

Why didn't she check? She always checks.

And he's in some kind of trouble.

Turning the light on, she faces the police office. No uniform. Didn't she say she was a detective?

'I'm sorry to have to tell you this,' says the police officer. 'Jordan's friend, Ben Whiston, was killed this evening.'

'Oh my God!' says Cheryl. 'How?'

'It seems that the two boys were involved in an elaborate stunt that went wrong.'

Cheryl listens in disbelief. She can't speak.

Jordan was involved?

'They were at the multi-storey car park in town, riding a shopping trolley down the ramp, and filming it for social media….'

Cheryl struggles to focus on the words the police officer is saying. But why was Jordan even out? She told Xan they should get a babysitter. The girl two doors down is lovely; she'd have been happy to do it.

'….tried to ride it at some speed down the ramp. It seems likely that the wheel of the trolley hit the curb…'

Cheryl forces herself to look the police officer in the eye. She seems so calm. Just another job to her.

'… hit the concrete wall head first. Paramedics declared him dead at the scene….'

Cheryl's brain is screaming. *It could've been Jordan.*

'… investigated further, but it seems most likely to be a tragic accident. A teenage prank that went wrong.'

She stops talking.

What did she say? It will be investigated further?

Cheryl feels giddy. She slumps down on a stool.

'Take a deep breath,' says the detective.

Cheryl tries to, but her pulse is racing. 'I don't know what to say. I just got home. I didn't even know he was out.' She's gabbling.

Breathe.

The police officer is watching her. They have that look. Blank, but not blank. Is she being judged? Of course she is. How could she not know where her fourteen-year-old son was? That's what the police officer is thinking.

'Would you have an address for Ben's parents?' says the cop. 'I didn't want to upset your son any further by asking him.'

What's that supposed to mean?

Cheryl dithers. 'Oh, umm,' she says. 'I've got it on my phone. I'll have to go and…'

'Of course. Take your time. I'm sure this is quite a shock.'

'Yes. And I feel so bad. I really had no idea…'

'Teenagers like to impress one another on social media,' says the cop. 'We see it in a number of forms. Unfortunately, in this case, it's had a particularly tragic outcome.'

'I just can't believe that Jordan would…' she tears up. 'Sorry. I'm so sorry! Ben's parents. You need to… oh my God… I'll get the address.'

'Thank you.'

Cheryl scurries out of the kitchen and heads for the stairs. She can feel the cop's eyes boring into her from behind. She knows what the woman's thinking. This is all her fault.

And it is. If her marriage was solid, if they were a happy family, if she'd been at home tonight, where she should've been, none of this would've happened.

She's let her boy down. Let him down badly. And she can't bear it.

9

Tuesday, 2.55am

Cheryl sits on the stairs with her phone beside her. For the first half hour after the police officer left, she kept calling Xan. His phone was off. The calls went to voicemail. She tried to stay calm, but panic was engulfing her. She left several frantic messages.

Why wasn't he here?

Between making the calls, she looked in on her son. Jordan was curled in the foetal position on his bed. Cheryl knew he was pretending to be asleep. She stroked his forehead. It was an age since he'd even let her touch his hair.

'Jordie, this isn't your fault,' she whispered. 'It's going to be alright.'

He didn't respond; his eyes remained shut.

She covered him with a blanket and left the room. When she needed Xan, where was he? Out screwing some bloody woman!

Sasha was hovering in her bedroom doorway.

'Is Jordan in trouble?' she said.

'No,' said Cheryl. 'There's been a terrible accident. But he wasn't hurt.'

'A car accident?'

'No,' said Cheryl. 'His friend Ben got hurt. But Jordan did the right thing. He called an ambulance. Now I need you to be a good girl and go back to bed. We'll talk about it in the morning.'

'Who was that woman?'

'She's a police officer. We'll talk about it some more in the morning.'

'Where's Daddy?'

'He'll be back soon. Come on, let's get you back into bed.'

It took her another ten minutes to settle her daughter. She looked in again on Jordan. He hadn't moved. But his breathing had changed to a slow, steady rhythm. Now he was asleep.

She went down to the kitchen and poured herself a glass of white wine. Cheryl has never been a drinker. It was more of a displacement activity because she didn't know what to do.

How on earth could this have happened? How did she get so diverted from the things that mattered? Her children. Her precious boy.

Why didn't she check Jordan's room when she came home? She meant to. But then she got the text from Xan. It distracted her. Made her forget about her son.

She sat at the kitchen counter and drank the wine. Calling him every five minutes wasn't going to work. Staring out at the misty garden, she composed a text. How could she even explain this?

Ben is dead, but it could've been Jordan.

In the end, she kept it simple: *Jordan in trouble. Police have been round. Please come home.*

After that, she sat on the stairs and waited. She's been there ever since.

It's 3.05 when she hears Xan's key turn in the lock. The front door opens. And he stands there. Behind him in the street, an Uber drives away. His jacket is crumpled, his shirt only half buttoned, and he has a stricken look on his face.

'What the hell has happened?' he says. 'Is he alright?'

'Not really,' says Cheryl. She gets up and walks down the stairs towards him.

'What do you mean?' says her husband. 'Is he hurt?'

'He was out with Ben Whiston. Some kind of teenage prank. Ben is dead.'

'What?' Xan shuts the door behind him. 'My God! But Jordan's okay?'

'Physically. Yes.'

'What on earth were they doing?'

'A police officer brought him home. She said that it was a stupid stunt that went wrong. And they were filming it for social media.'

'What kind of stunt?'

'Riding a shopping trolley down the ramp in a multi-story car park,' says Cheryl. 'Jordan was filming it. Ben was in the trolley. He got thrown out. His head hit the wall and he broke his neck, they think.'

'Jesus wept!' says Xan, raking his fingers through his hair.

'Where were you?' says Cheryl. 'I've been phoning and phoning, Xan. Where the hell were you?'

Xan pulls off his jacket and flings it over the newel post. 'That's not important now. Where is he? In his room?' He's about to head upstairs.

'Leave him,' says Cheryl. 'He's asleep.'

'Are you sure he's alright?' says Xan. 'He's not hurt in any way?'

'He just watched his best friend get killed,' says Cheryl. 'He called the ambulance. I think he's in shock. Sleep's the best thing for him.'

Xan is pacing. He can't stand still.

'You're probably right. But what do we do now?' he shakes his head. 'What did the police say?'

He strides off towards the kitchen. She follows.

'They're treating it as an accident,' says Cheryl. 'The detective who brought Jordan home says they'll want to talk to him. In our presence, obviously. But they'll need to write a report for the coroner.'

Xan has his hands on his hips. He slaps the marble counter. 'Bloody social media! Have you spoken to Ben's parents?'

'No, of course not,' says Cheryl. 'The police officer was going round to tell them. I had to give her their address.'

Xan stares at her. His eyes are full of sorrow.

His voice cracks. 'It could've been Jordan, couldn't it?'

'I know,' says Cheryl.

They stare at each. Both at a loss. Xan gets a glass from the cupboard, goes to the sink and fills it with water. He gulps down several mouthfuls.

'If the trolley was going too fast and Ben lost control,' he says, 'there's nothing Jordan could've done.'

'The police'll see that from his phone, won't they?' says Cheryl.

Xan frowns. 'What? You let the police take Jordan's phone?'

'She asked me if I minded. In the circumstances, I could hardly refuse.'

Xan huffs. 'Oh for Chrissake, Cheryl! Yes, you could.'

'But I don't see… I think we need to be as helpful as we can.'

'Helpful?' Xan shakes his head in disbelief. 'He's a witness. To a tragic accident. That's all.'

'What d'you mean?'

He folds his arms in exasperation. 'For a clever woman, you can be dense at times. They'll take his phone apart. And who knows what else they might find? He's a teenage boy. They'll be all sorts of dick pics and who knows what.'

'I'm sure the police are used to that.'

'Yes, but what if it's worse than that? Boys of his age circulate all kinds of stuff. Pictures of girls. Girls in his class. Underage girls that they get to do things. It can get pretty hard-core.'

'I'm sure Jordie wouldn't do anything like that.'

'He's fourteen. Peer pressure? He wants to impress his mates. Why do you think he sneaked out tonight to do this bloody stupid thing? He wants to prove he's cool, that he's a big dog.'

Cheryl listens. This is not her son he's talking about. It can't be. He's not that sort of boy. She refuses to believe it.

Xan shakes his head. He's annoyed. 'Well, what's done is done,' he says.

He's making this her fault.

Her chin quivers. 'You weren't here. I thought I was doing the right thing.'

He sighs. 'We'll just have to keep our fingers crossed.'

Another thing she's got wrong.

She feels as if her knees might buckle. The tears erupt. She can't stop them; her head dips, her hands fly to her face. Xan exhales. Turning on the waterworks, as he calls it, annoys him. But he steps forward and puts his arms around her. It's what she's been waiting for. It's what she needs.

She lets him rock her. She sobs.

He leans forward, rubs his face in her hair. 'It's okay,' he whispers. 'It's going to be okay.'

But his shirt stinks!

It's a perfume she doesn't recognise. Heavy and acrid.

Or does she? The VC woman?

She pulls away. 'How?' she splutters. 'How is it going to be okay? Our son could've been killed this evening. You think he has pictures of girls on his phone? Did you have any idea him and Ben were doing stuff like this too?'

'Of course I didn't.'

'But we should've known, shouldn't we? He's only fourteen. And we were just too busy to see what was under our noses.'

'Cheryl, come on, you can't—'

'Can't what? Take responsibility? No, that's you Xan. You're the one that can't take responsibility. For your actions. For this family.'

He shrugs. 'You can blame me if it makes you feel any better.'

'But you blame me for giving the police his phone.'

He raises his eyebrows. 'It was ill-advised. That's all I'm saying.'

'You are such a shit!'

'I'm sorry,' he says. But there's no conviction in his voice. He doesn't think he's done anything wrong. He's just saying it to shut her up. To close her down.

Stupid crying woman, that's what he thinks.

'Go back to your whore,' she says. 'I don't want you here.'

He grabs her by the arm. 'Cheryl, stop it. You're being silly. You're over-wrought. And you're talking nonsense.'

He pulls her towards him. She resists. But not much. He drags her into his arms.

He gazes down at her. Those blue eyes. Like a kind but disappointed father. 'Don't do this,' he says. 'We don't need to do this. Not now. We'll get through this together. For our son. That's what matters. Isn't it?'

He's so much bigger than her, and he's holding her tight. She can't escape.

Does she even want to?

Her head spins. Stroking her hair back, he kisses her forehead.

'Ssh,' he says. 'It'll be alright. I promise. You just need to calm down. If not for me, then for Jordan.'

10

Tuesday, 7.45am

Hannah Blakeney orders breakfast in her room. When she's on expenses, she likes to make the most of it. Eggs Benedict. And the Hollandaise isn't bad for a four-star hotel.

On reflection, it's not the best sex she's ever had; he was a bit too drunk. But he was witty and self-deprecating, which made up for the mediocre performance. He slunk away about two thirty, having discovered a barrage of missed calls from his little wife. Hannah was in the bathroom, so he thought she hadn't seen him checking his phone.

As she pours herself a coffee, she wonders if she's miscalculated. She acted impulsively and maybe that wasn't the smartest move. But, before he left, using the excuse of some problem with his kid, he kissed the fingers of her right-hand one at a time and said, 'Sorry. To be continued.'

She liked his old school shtick. And less tanked up, he might make a half decent lover.

She eats her breakfast in a leisurely fashion and contemplates her next move. She needs to be judicious. But if she's to turn this into a connection she can exploit, she must assure him of her discretion. No problem with that. She's not a marriage wrecker. This is a business liaison.

Her boss, Nat, is another question. He's made it clear that he expects her to hand over to Freddie.

Freddie!

Negotiating her way out of that will be a delicate process.

Although it's not yet eight, she jumps out of bed, takes a shower, and blow dries her hair. It's her secret weapon and well worth the effort with the straighteners to create the perfect look. The make-up she keeps simple. Her complexion is good, so it doesn't need much. Plus, she doesn't want to come over like some reality TV bimbo. The daily ritual of getting herself suited and booted gives her confidence. She psyches herself up in the mirror.

Nat is always first in the office and last to leave. This is the best time to ensure she has his full attention.

A few deep breaths, she picks up her phone and Face-Times him.

He answers immediately. He's at his desk, consuming a pastry. For a thin man, he seems to spend an inordinate amount of time eating. But he's so hyper, he burns it all off. He's a workaholic, which is the key to his success.

'Morning,' he says. 'I didn't expect to hear from you this early.'

'Early bird, Nat,' she says with her best smile.

'How did the rest of the evening go?'

'Well,' she replies.

'When's Dr Woodward going to give us her pitch?'

'I'm hoping to set something up today. She's super-keen. I had a good talk with her at the party.'

Slight exaggeration. She has to remedy that.

'What do you make of her? Has she got the drive we're looking for?'

Hannah shrugs her shoulders. 'She's quite an introvert. I think it's the husband who's the driving force.'

'Umm,' says Nat, as he digests this. 'Not ideal. Anyway, I spoke to Freddie first thing. He's sent a list of questions. Unfortunately, he's going to be in Germany until the end of the week. So you need to keep the ball in play. Can you do that?'

Thank you, Germany!

'Of course.'

'Freddie gave me a name. Kayleigh Burrows?'

Who the hell's she?

'She's his contact. Works for Dr Woodward in the lab. One of the post-docs.'

'Oh yes,' says Hannah. 'I met her at the party. Lovely girl.'

There was a whole gaggle of female student types. M&S dresses and bad haircuts. Which one was she?

'Good,' says Nat. 'Because we're going to need to do some digging. Proper background on Woodward's team and how it works. I don't want to back a loser here.'

'Yeah, I'm already on that.'

He blinks at her. His eyes are sharp and feral, like a small rodent. They miss nothing. 'Really?' he says 'Just listen to me, Hannah. And don't bullshit a bullshitter.'

'Sorry, boss,' she says. 'I'm listening.'

'Good.' he replies. 'Grab your laptop. Take notes.'

She reaches across, pulls her laptop from her bag and extracts it from its sleeve.

As she gets set up, she can see Nat talking to someone else in the office. His hand is over the mic. He turns back to the screen.

'You ready, Hannah?'

She has the phone propped up and her fingers on the keyboard.

'Absolutely,' she says.

'Now this is what we need to know,' says Nat. 'What kind of leader is Woodward? Is she driving the research forward? How good is she at managing the team? Who generates the breakthrough ideas? Is it her? Or is it her post-docs? In the end, that doesn't matter. What matters is whether she's a good leader and has the drive to get this done. You got all that?'

Hannah's a fast typist. 'Yes,' she says.

'Freddie's checklist is a bit more technical. But I'll send that to you. Your priority is to get inside the lab and see what makes it tick. Or rather, who makes it tick? Does Woodward have the dynamism we're looking for?'

Seems unlikely.

'I'm on it,' says Hannah.

'And what about the husband? He's the CEO?'

'Yes.'

'I get the impression he thinks he's slick. Is that going to be a problem?'

'No, I don't think so,' says Hannah. 'I think he and I have already reached an understanding.'

Those ferrety eyes are boring into her.

Does he know?

'Concentrate on Dr Woodward,' he says.

'Okay.'

'Keep me posted.'

'Of course.'

The screen goes black. He's gone.

Hannah sighs, gets up, and takes a turn round the room.

Shit! Shit! Shit!

She's done this all wrong. Xan is the CEO. She'd

assumed he was the key to driving this forward. Apparently not. That's how it works in other start-ups. How was she supposed to know? She's never done biotech before.

She stares at her laptop. But this could still be her big opportunity. Nat knows she's a rookie. Now she has a chance to demonstrate to him how fast she can learn.

Slight problem.

How do you make friends with a woman when you've just slept with her husband?

11

Tuesday, 8.30am

Cheryl wakes with a start. A car door slamming in the street? For a moment she's disorientated. She reaches out to the bedside table for her phone to check the time. Eight thirty? How can it be? Her brain is sluggish. But then she remembers. Jordan! The events of the night tumble into place.

She struggles out of bed and makes her way into the bathroom. Her sleeping tablets are beside the basin with an empty glass. This breaks another memory. Xan persuaded her to take a sleeping tablet and put her to bed. That's why her head feels like cotton wool. She splashes her face with water, dabs it with a towel.

Putting her dressing gown on, she goes out into the hallway. The doors to both of the kids' bedrooms stand open and the murmur of voices drifts up the stairs from the kitchen below. She makes her way downstairs willing her jangling thoughts into some sort of order.

It was after three when her husband came home. The

conversation they had about Jordan was fractious. She got upset. She cried.

But he comforted her, didn't he? He took her in his arms. In the end, he was there for her.

She hates taking sleeping tablets. They slow everything down. Her brain ends up in a kind of suspended animation. Memories become hard to retrieve. Even if they're recent.

She walks into the kitchen to find Xan standing at the hob with a frying pan. Her two children sit on stools at the counter.

'Daddy's making us pancakes,' says Sasha brightly.

A bit too brightly?

Only eight, but already she's a placater. She reads the anxiety in other people and tries to make things better. It pains Cheryl to think that unwittingly she has trained her little girl to do this.

'I thought we could all do with a bit of cheering up,' says Xan, turning to smile at her.

Cheering up?

'I've arranged for Sasha to get a lift to school with Alicia's mum,' he adds.

'I don't want to go to school today,' says Sasha. 'Do I have to?'

'Of course you do,' says Xan.

'Why can't I stay here with Jordan?' says Sasha.

'Because you're not suspended, duh brain,' says her brother with a grim little chuckle.

Cheryl stares at her son. He avoids her gaze. There's a bowl of cereal in front of him. He shovels another spoonful into his mouth.

'Who says you're suspended?' says Cheryl.

'Dad spoke to Henderson first thing,' mumbles Jordan.

'It's Mrs Henderson, Jordan.'

Oh no! She didn't mean to sound so prissy.

He reacts. 'Whatever. She made it clear. Two weeks apparently. Stupid cow.'

Why is he being like this? Surly and aggressive? His best friend just died.

She's about to challenge him, but Xan turns around, frying pan in hand.

'Right,' he says. 'Who wants this one?' He gives his wife a sidelong glance. He's trying to shut her down. But she won't be silenced.

'Jordan,' she says. 'This is a serious situation.'

'He already knows that,' says Xan.

Jordan stares down at his bowl.

Xan slides the pancake onto a plate. No one speaks. Sasha's gaze is darting anxiously back and forth between her parents.

This is awful. Not in front of Sasha. Wait until she's gone.

'Well,' says Cheryl. 'I wonder if we've got any maple syrup? Has anyone looked?'

'Try the fridge,' says her husband. 'Come on Sash, I'm sure you can fit another one of these in.' He pushes the plate in his daughter's direction.

Cheryl opens the fridge and takes out the maple syrup.

'Ah, here we go,' she says.

She also gets a carton of orange juice. She places the maple syrup on the counter in front of her daughter.

'I'm full,' says Sasha.

'Cheryl, how about you?' says Xan.

She shakes her head. Goes to the cupboard, takes down a glass and pours herself an orange juice.

'I'll just have to eat it myself,' he says with a shrug.

Cheryl scans the back of her son. He's perched on the stool, shoulders hunched over the counter. Eating on autopilot. He finishes. The spoon clatters into the empty bowl. He shoves it away.

'This is so fucking lame,' he says. 'Why are you all fucking pretending? Making out like everything is alright. Cause I know what you're thinking.'

'Hey, come on mate,' says Xan.

Jordan ignores him and turns to glare at his mother. 'And I know what you're thinking,' he snaps.

Cheryl looks at him. There's anger on the surface, but beneath that fear. He's using it to fight the tears.

Now she gets it. Why has she been so slow? Blame the sleeping tablets.

'I doubt you do,' she says.

Her baby. Her little boy. He's hurting.

'You think it's all my fault, don't you?' he says. 'I killed Ben. Because it was my idea.'

'Your idea?' says Cheryl calmly.

'To do the dare,' says Jordan. 'And they're gonna find this out. And everyone's gonna blame me. And hate me.'

His distress rips into her. He can't blame himself. She can't allow it.

Now the tears are rolling down his cheeks. He swipes the cereal bowl off the counter; it hits the floor and cracks in two. His shoulders crumple and he puts his face in his hands.

If only he was still little enough to scoop him up in her arms and rescue him.

Cheryl moves towards him. She places her palm on his back.

'Oh Jordie,' she says. 'No one is blaming you. This was a terrible accident.'

'We saw this video on YouTube. It was spectacular.'

He turns to face her. The desperation and panic floods out of him.

'But I persuaded him to do it, Mum. I did it first, showed him how. And I told him it would be alright.'

He's sobbing now. Cheryl draws him into a hug. He rests his head on her shoulder. She lets him cry.

He whispers. 'I'm sorry, Mum. I'm so sorry. I never meant this to happen.'

She strokes his hair. 'Of course you didn't,' she says.

Over his head, she and Xan exchange looks. At least they agree on one thing. This is their boy and they'll do whatever's necessary to protect him.

12

Tuesday, 8.55am

DS Jo Boden stands on the doorstep. It's been a long shift and she just wants to get this thing done and dusted. Get home, take a shower and sleep. Once she's written up her report, the matter will be passed on to the coroner. Two teenage boys had engaged in a stupid prank, driven by a desire to look cool and collect followers on social media. Not such an unusual story, but with a disastrous outcome.

In the early hours, she stood on a similar doorstep when she went to the other boy's parents to break the news of their son's death. She told them simply and in the way she'd been trained. The mother went from disbelief to collapse. But the father escalated from shock straight to anger. He demanded to know what the police were going to do about it. Boden explained the matter was being investigated, but it looked like a tragic accident. There may not be any criminal culpability on anybody's part.

Mr Whiston wasn't buying that. He needed someone to

blame. It had to be someone's fault. Ignoring his sobbing wife, he demanded details. And he wanted to know who had forced his son to do such a stupid thing. Boden assured them that the matter would be looked into thoroughly. She couldn't wait to get out of there.

Social media? Extreme sports? Stunt-based reality TV?

The Coroner would point the finger at all those. Reports would be written and ignored. If her years in the Met had taught her anything, it was that reports get ignored. Sensible, common sense reforms hit the political interests and the pocket of some powerful group, and that's that. Dead in the water.

She's exhausted, but needs to wrap this up. As she reaches up to press the fancy brass bell again, the door opens.

It must be the father. He looks at her in surprise. He's probably had enough surprises for one night.

'Oh,' he says. 'Can I… '

He stops as she holds out her ID. 'DS Boden,' she says.

He covers his confusion with a beaming smile. 'I'm so sorry,' he says. 'You brought Jordie home. Sorry. Sorry. My wife told me. I was expecting my daughter's lift to school. Come in. Please.'

'I hope it's not too early,' says Boden. She steps into the house. 'I thought it was best for all concerned to deal with this matter quickly.'

'Of course. Absolutely. I'm Xan Woodward by the way. We're just finishing breakfast.'

She follows him down the spacious hall to the kitchen, which is enormous. Huge windows at the back. A glass skylight in the centre.

Boden scans the large, tasteful prints and the pristine bank of high-tech appliances. It all gleams with money and privilege.

Two upper middle-class boys, who attend the same posh private school and who live in similar houses. One of those houses is now full of grief. And here, in the other one, there's what? A guilty sense of relief and the smell of pancakes?

The boy is sitting at the marble breakfast bar. He looks at her with trepidation, as if she's come to arrest him. She feels sorry for him. Whoever egged the other on, that's not her problem. Jordan Woodward is the one who'll have to live with it. As he grows up, he'll have to come to terms with his own moral culpability for his friend's death. The criminal law can't help him.

'Hello Jordan,' she says. 'How are you doing?'

He shrugs.

'Good morning, Dr Woodward,' she says to the mother. 'I'm hoping this won't take long.' She notices a second child, a little girl.

'Coffee?' says the father.

'No, I'm fine,' says Boden. She's been drinking coffee all night. What she wants now is go home and get some sleep. But she has to do this first.

'Let's go into the sitting room,' says Dr Woodward, glancing at her daughter. 'That'll be more comfortable.'

A small woman, but formidable in her own way, Boden suspects. She puts a hand on her son's shoulder to shepherd him along.

A mother intent on protecting her son, thinks Boden. Nothing wrong with that.

13

Tuesday, 11.30am

Cheryl arrives at the coffee shop first. It's a regular haunt of theirs, and close to her sister's office. She orders a double espresso and finds a table at the back.

After such a stressful morning so far, she's relieved to just sit. She stares down at her drink, imagining the molecules jostling each other in the hot liquid, as she tries to collect her scattered thoughts.

The police officer who talked to Jordan was kind. She simply asked for his account of what happened, and, as her son spoke, she recorded it. She mentioned that they'd recovered CCTV from the car park. Jordan had calmed down. His chin trembled, but he got through it.

No mention of the phone.

As Cheryl escorted the police officer to the door, she said, 'Will there be any… further action?'

'That's a matter for the coroner.'

'But you're not taking it any further?'

The police officer smiled. 'Dr Woodward,' she said. 'I looked at the CCTV clip before coming here. It shows Ben Whiston pushed the trolley and jumped into it of his own volition. Jordan was waiting at the bottom of the slope to film it, as he said in his statement. There's no evidence of criminality. Two young teenagers agreed to do an extremely stupid and dangerous thing. That's what my report to the coroner will say.'

Cheryl was relieved.

Then she'd phoned Ben's parents to offer her condolences. Xan was against it, but she felt it was the proper thing to do.

She'd never spoken to Tony Whiston before. Some kind of businessman who went abroad a lot; that's all she knew.

'Well,' he said. 'At least you've had the decency to call. But I'm going to get to the bottom of this. My son would never have done such a stupid thing, unless he was pressured into it. Someone's going to pay.'

He'd hung up on her. His aggressive tone was upsetting. This is when Cheryl decided she needed to talk to her sister. What was he threatening? Legal action? Could he harm Jordan? Lorna'll know.

She gazes round the coffee shop. There's the usual smattering of students peering at their laptops, mothers with toddlers in strollers, women loaded with shopping bags meeting for a chat. She's been in this place many times. The ordinariness and predictability is soothing. The call to Tony Whiston has unnerved her.

'I told you not to,' said Xan. 'The poor bloke's distraught. He's going to lash out. He'll get over it, eventually.'

Cheryl wasn't so sure. But it was a relief to escape from the house and get some breathing space and time to think. Xan was taking care of their son.

The least he could bloody well do after last night.

Her phone pings with an incoming text from Lorna.

Sorry. Bit mad this morning. Be there ASAP xx

Cheryl doesn't mind waiting. She finishes her coffee and lets her thoughts coast. Her gaze drifts across the room, scans the queue waiting to order. Should she get herself another espresso? She's jangly enough. Probably not a good idea. She checks her phone. It's only been ten minutes. Lorna's law practice is small, not enough staff because legal aid work is poorly funded. As a result, she has many demands on her time.

Cheryl notices that a young woman in the queue is staring right at her. She looks familiar. An old student? She gives the girl a tepid smile.

Oh no, she's coming over.

This is not what she needs this morning. An exchange of pleasantries with someone she can't remember. The girl is beaming; cropped leather jacket, jeans, woolly scarf, bobble hat. She looks like a student.

But then recognition hits Cheryl like a thunderclap. The venture capital woman from the party? Hannah something-or-other? No! She looks completely different; her mane of hair tucked away and no make-up.

It bloody well is.

A tumult of thoughts tumble through Cheryl's brain. None of them good.

The awful woman approaches the table, all smiles.

'Good morning, Dr Woodward,' she says. 'This is a great place. How's the coffee?'

Did she sleep with Xan?

When he came home last night, his shirt stank of expensive perfume. And Cheryl's pretty sure it was the same perfume this woman was wearing at the party.

'It's fine,' she replies with as much frostiness as she can muster.

Hannah, yes, that is her name, points at a chair. 'Mind if I sit?'

But no perfume this morning.

Cheryl gives her a stony stare. 'Actually, I'm waiting for my sister.'

Hannah raises her palms. 'Of course, I'm sorry. I don't want to intrude.' She gives a little shrug. Is she trying to look cute? She adds, 'But I should 'fess up.'

My God! Is she serious? And embarrass them both?

Cheryl cringes. Hasn't she had enough bad news? This is the last thing she needs.

'I called in at your lab,' Hannah says brightly. 'I wanted to touch base with you this morning. They told me you might be here. I tracked you down. So there, now you know my guilty secret.'

Not her only secret.

'I can't think why,' says Cheryl. 'Surely you prefer to deal with my husband?'

Hannah tilts her head and gives Cheryl a quizzical look. 'Am I missing something here, Dr Woodward?'

Cheryl glares straight back. She won't be intimidated. 'I don't know,' she says. 'Maybe you think I'm missing something.'

Hannah frowns. 'Oh dear,' she says, plonking her back-pack on a chair and sitting down on another. 'If there's been some kind of misunderstanding here, I think we should clear it up. Have I done something to upset you, Dr Woodward?'

For a moment, her earnestness floors Cheryl.

Could she have got this all wrong?

But images of Xan with this woman flit through her brain, fuelling her anger. She can't stop herself. She blurts it out.

'What happened at the end of the party last night?' she says. 'I left early.'

Hannah is gazing straight at her with a concerned frown.

'Yes, I saw you go,' she says. 'I didn't stay much longer myself. Things were getting quite drunken and rowdy. And I'd promised to call my girlfriend.'

What does she mean? Her girlfriend?

The confusion must show on her face. Hannah is watching her. Cool, grey eyes that give nothing away.

Is she saying she's gay?

Hannah chuckles, as if the penny's dropped. 'Oh now, I get it,' she says. 'You think something happened between me and your husband?'

'Did it?' says Cheryl.

Hannah leans back in her chair and laces her fingers. 'Well, we had several conversations. Mainly about you and your work.' Her expression is earnest and dignified, tinged with disappointment. She tilts her head wistfully and says, 'Ask yourself this, Dr Woodward. Do I look like a stupid woman? This is an important gig for my firm. Do you think I'd put that in jeopardy? I take my job, and the ethical responsibilities that go with it, very seriously.'

Cheryl is confounded. She has a terrible sinking feeling. Has she got this wrong? Xan slept with someone, no question of that. But there were plenty of attractive twenty-somethings—his usual type—at the party. She just assumed it was Hannah because of the way he was looking at her. And the perfume.

But what does she know about perfume? She rarely uses it.

Hannah seems to read her mind. 'Okay,' she says. 'I know how I appear. The heels, the make-up, the hair. My boss expects me to get on with people. Let's face it, I think we both know that it's still a man's world. Men come on to me all the time. That's not what I want.'

'Then why dress like that? You invite it.' Cheryl knows she sounds snippy. She can't help it.

Hannah smiles. 'I see it as a uniform. It protects me. I don't know about your field, but finance is awful. If anyone at my firm had the slightest inkling about me, they'd make my life a misery. Gay blokes, fine. Women have a hard enough time. It's a toxic environment. I pretend in order to survive.' She dips her head and says nervously. 'I hope my sexuality isn't a problem for you?'

This throws Cheryl on to the back foot. Now she's embarrassed.

How could she get this so stupidly wrong?

'Oh my god, no,' she says. 'I don't want you to… my sister is gay.'

Hannah is still smiling. She looks very young without the make-up and vulnerable. A kid in a bobble hat.

Cheryl shakes her head. 'You must hear that excuse all the time. I'm so sorry.'

'Don't be. And you've got a point about the clothes. My girlfriend—her name's Kate—she calls me a lipstick lesbian.' She grins. 'Actually, I reckon she quite likes it.'

'I feel a complete fool,' says Cheryl. 'I should apologise.'

'What for? You only just met me. People jump to conclusions all the time. But I'm so looking forward to working with you. To have a woman founder of a tech company is so exciting. I just want us to be honest with each other. I'm sure you'll agree, that's the basis of all good relationships.'

Their eyes meet.

'It is,' says Cheryl.

Unless you're married to Xan Woodward.

It feels awkward. Cheryl doesn't know what to say. Lorna is going to laugh about this.

But Hannah smiles, pulls out her phone and holds it up in front of Cheryl to show her a picture. A girl in football kit, part of a team photo.

'This is Kate,' she says. 'She plays for West Ham's second team. But she's really good. Do you like football, Dr Woodward?'

'No, not really. My husband and son watch.'

Cheryl feels so bad. She's insulted this poor girl. But now it's Hannah who's trying to gloss things over.

Hannah giggles. It's warm and infectious. 'To tell you the truth, I've never been a fan. But she's educating me. And women's football is becoming such a big thing.' She hesitates, then says, 'Can I ask you a favour, Dr Woodward?'

'Oh please, call me Cheryl.'

Hannah dips her head and smiles. 'Well, Cheryl. When you meet my boss, Nat Harrington. And he's dying to meet you, by the way. Say nothing about me and Kate.'

'Why would I? It's nobody's business.'

'Thank you. I always felt we'd get along.'

With some relief, Cheryl notices her sister has just come bustling through the door. She looks frazzled, glancing around. Cheryl raises her hand and waves.

'Here's my sister,' she says.

Hannah gets up. 'I'll leave you in peace,' she says, slinging her backpack across one shoulder. 'And I'm sorry for turning up out of the blue.'

'I think it's good that you did,' says Cheryl sheepishly.

Lorna joins them. 'Sorry!' she says. 'Had to get an emergency injunction for a client. Her old man keeps threatening her.'

'Not a problem,' says Cheryl. 'This is Hannah.'

'Hannah Blakeney,' says Hannah. 'From HDZ Venture Partners. But, I must dash. I'll catch up with you later, Cheryl. I'm looking forward to working with you.'

She turns on her heel and scurries away.

Lorna plonks down her bag and frowns. 'Wasn't she at the party? All teeth and tits?'

'She's just come out to me.'

Lorna raises her eyebrows. 'Really? Well, my gaydar's not what it was. Nowadays, all these new categories, non-binary or Cis, it's confusing.' She gazes at Cheryl. 'I have to say, kiddo, you look like shit. What's up?'

Cheryl's lip trembles. 'I don't know where to begin. My marriage, my family. Everything's coming apart at the seams. Jordan's…'

She can't go on. The tears flood out. She buries her face in her hands.

Lorna sits down next to her and puts a comforting hand on her shoulder.

'Hey,' she says. 'I'm sure it's not that bad.'

'Believe me, it is.'

14

Tuesday, 12.15pm

He wanders through the busy streets like a zombie. Must be lunchtime. People scurry by him. The smell of food wafts from everywhere. Sweet smells. Curry. Beer. Chips. Last night's soup feels like a long time ago. He's become used to the lightheadedness. Sometimes it's just about water. Hydration. If he can get into one of the public toilets, he can drink from the tap. But in the town centre, they have turnstiles. Thirty pence. And you can pay with a card. People wonder why the homeless piss in doorways.

He's heading towards the town centre. He has one thought in his mind. This time of day, the bins outside McDonald's are likely to be full. There may be some good pickings, unless someone has got there first. Hunger drives him on. Passersby give him a wide birth. It's the smell. The last shower he had was a distant memory. He used to go into launderettes and wash his clothes. But in winter, that's impossible. Take off your clothes in a laundrette and you'll get arrested.

There are two bins outside McDonald's and he's a regular visitor. He finds them overflowing. A flock of pigeons is already picking over the spillage from the bags and cartons. He claps his hands to shoo them away. But they're persistent. It becomes a battle between him and the birds. They seem to know he's not important. Not a real person.

Just a ghost.

They sweep in and scoop up the chips.

As he leans over to grab a Styrofoam carton, someone shoves him from behind. The pigeons rise up squawking, and he hears laughter. The kids are on skateboards; they're circling around and jeering at him.

One of them has a half-eaten burger in his hand, which smells delicious. The kid holds it out.

'Here doggie doggie!' he says. 'Fetch!'

He throws the burger down on the pavement. They all laugh, cruising round him on their boards.

'C'mon, doggie! Nice juicy burger. Fetch!'

One boy, balancing on his board, films him on a phone.

The others circle him, woofing.

But the burger is fresh. Still warm.

As he reaches out to pick it up, one skateboarder glides past him, missing him by a whisker. 'Look at this!' the kid shouts. 'Trying to nick my burger! Bad doggie!'

He tries to ignore them. It's easy. Things that happen to him often feel odd, as if they're outside of time, or in another dimension. He's on his knees, crawling. The burger is almost within reach. He can smell it. Soon he'll taste it. He reaches out. The skateboarder makes another pass and rams right into him. He's knocked sideways. His head cracks into the metal edge of the bin. The pain. Sudden. Blinding. Real. As he rolls on the ground, his hand goes up to his forehead. It's damp.

Blood?

His eyebrow is throbbing.

Some people stop. A curious crowd is gathering around him. The pain is intense. His vision blurs. Everything's spinning. He holds his head; the blood oozes through his fingers.

Voices echo around him. Laughter. The grinding roll of the skateboarders wheels inches from his face. He cowers, rolling into a ball to protect himself.

Then he hears a booming female voice. 'Oi!'

A woman leans over him. Dark suit. She looks professional.

She shouts at the skateboarder filming him. 'Fuck off, you little bastard! Now! If you know what's good for you!'

With her, is another woman, smaller. She's holding a phone.

'I'll call an ambulance,' she says.

His head is exploding with pain. He clutches it with his hand. Is he going to be sick? Or pass out?

Then someone speaks his name. The little woman?

His name?

No one knows his name. He never gives it. When he talks to the social workers, he always lies. He keeps his eyes tight shut. The pain is confusing him. He's imagining this.

No one knows his name. That's important.

But the woman is talking to him. She says his name again. He hasn't heard it spoken for months. He opens his eyes and looks up at her. She looks familiar. But without his glasses, all faces are a blur. The pain in his head is blinding him.

'Don't you remember me, Arran?' she says. 'I'm Dr Woodward.'

15

Tuesday, 12.20pm

Hannah Blakeney walks. She has to keep moving, and fast, to burn off some of the adrenaline. This is a buzz like no other. Her performance was pitch perfect. It was a risky strategy, but she cracked it.

Fortunately, she'd stuffed jeans and trainers in her hastily packed overnight bag, planning to wear them for the return train journey; heels were a pain when travelling. So creating the right look wasn't that hard. On her way to the coffee shop, she'd passed a quirky little boutique. The scarf and bobble hat were hanging on a rack near the door; each one only a tenner.

As soon as she approached Dr Woodward, she knew she was making the right move. The poor little woman was spitting with jealousy. Clearly, she was all too aware of what her old man got up to. Xan Woodward had form; no surprise. He might think he fooled his little wife, or maybe he just didn't care.

Hannah knew she had to go for it. A curve ball was the

only thing that was going to turn this around. And it worked like a dream. Dr Woodward went from resentment to embarrassment and apologies in a matter of minutes.

Wow! Winning is so addictive.

As the only girl surrounded by brothers, Hannah's childhood had been one long battle. She survived on tactics and learning to create the perfect story. All kids lie; psychologists say it's a mark of intelligence. But Hannah saw it more as tailoring circumstances to her point of view. She was the innocent girl; her brothers were the bullies. Over time, her parents agreed. They accepted she needed special treatment.

At Oxford she got into acting, which came naturally. She realised she'd been doing it her whole life. She toyed with it as a career until she concluded it'd be a dog of a job and she'd make no money. Her acting skills were better deployed in a different arena. Finance was a no brainer. The rich have a better life, everyone knows that.

Slowing down, she finds herself in the water meadows near the river. She sits on a bench. It's a grey morning, quite cold. As she exhales, her breath condenses into vapour. But the vigorous walk has warmed her up. She's missed her morning meditation and yoga, so before proceeding any further, she needs to review and refocus.

Relaxing and loosening her gaze, she let it drift along the river. A couple of moorhens are squabbling. A solitary swan glides by.

Failure only matters if you don't learn from it. This is her mantra, one of several. She read it in a business book. Sleeping with Xan Woodward was a mistake in that it put her relationship with Cheryl in jeopardy, but that's been dealt with. She miscalculated because she was too desperate for the deal, and as a result, had put too much focus on him. She reminds herself that her target at HDZ is to become a full partner before she's twenty-eight. Four years to go, which should be loads of time. If she was a bloke, it wouldn't be so much of a problem.

Hannah pulls her laptop out of her backpack. She finds the document that Freddie has sent. It seems sensible at this point to do a reality check. No more mistakes. She can't bypass him completely. She needs his input. But making herself the go-between with the Woodwards will make her indispensable to him. And indeed to Nat. Scanning through the list of questions Freddie's made for her, there's some homework to do.

At the bottom of the document is the name and number of Freddie's contact. She gets out her phone, taps the number in and calls it.

'Yeah?' says a surprisingly high-pitched female voice.

'Hey, Kayleigh,' says Hannah. 'I'm Hannah Blakeney from HDZ. Freddie suggested I call you.'

'I noticed you at the party,' comes the cool reply. 'I was expecting Freddie to be there.'

'He's in Germany,' says Hannah. 'But he tells me you're a pretty crucial part of Cheryl's team.'

'Really?'

There's a reticence here. Sarcasm even. Why?

'Well,' says Hannah. 'Perhaps you and I should meet and talk about this?'

An audible sigh of hesitation.

'I'm not sure. This is a difficult situation for me.'

Intriguing. Difficult why?

'I get that,' says Hannah. 'Absolutely. You don't know me. But let me assure you, Freddie and I work together closely.'

'Yeah, but the problem is, I've been thinking. And I don't want people to get the wrong idea. I am loyal to Cheryl.'

Okay! More intriguing.

Well, Nat told her to dig.

'Of course you are,' says Hannah. 'I was just having coffee with her. We spoke about how important it is for me to understand how the lab operates. I'm not a biologist. I'm just trying to get my head round this.'

'Oh, well, if you've spoken to her.'

That worked.

'If you could help me, that would be great. I'm sure she'd appreciate that. Because we all want the same thing here, don't we?'

'Yes, I suppose so.' More hesitation. 'But… it's just… oh, I dunno.'

'Kayleigh, you can trust me. Whatever you'd say to Freddie, you can say to me. Use me as a sounding board.'

Silence on the end of the line.

Softly softly.

'A totally private conversation?' says Kayleigh.

'No question. You just say where and when.'

16

Tuesday, 12.25pm

Cheryl and Lorna wait for the ambulance to arrive. He lies on the pavement with Lorna crouched beside him, trying to reassure him. She isn't put off by the state of him, by the dirt and the smell. But this is her sister; she's always been a good person. Cheryl doesn't seem to have that gene. She'd rather ignore the people who live on the streets. There's nothing she can do.

'You know him?' says Lorna.

Cheryl nods. Even admitting it fills her with shame.

'He was a student. I was supervising his PhD.'

'How the hell did he end up like this?'

'I don't know,' says Cheryl.

Which is true.

He's sprawled on the pavement, his eyes shut. But Cheryl suspects he's not unconscious. He's shutting the world out. And who can blame him? There are curious glances of disgust from passersby. They must assume he's drunk or high. Someone tries to video the scene, but her sister sees them off.

'Have you not got any empathy?' she shouts.

Lorna is a crusader, a campaigner for the underdog; always has been. And it makes Cheryl proud.

And guilty.

At least one of them has the guts to stand up to the world. She envies her sister's determination and fortitude. Always has. Cheryl is more dogged; she can stare through a microscope for hours.

The ambulance finally arrives and the paramedics jump out. Two young men, jovial and kind. They treat Arran with respect and consideration. This too seems like a reproach.

'Well,' says Lorna. 'I reckon we can leave them to it.'

Cheryl nods. Lorna is smiling at her, but it seems to Cheryl that she's being judged. She turns impulsively to the paramedic.

'Look,' she says. 'I'd like to help him. I work at the university, and I think he was once a student.' She pulls out a business card. 'Can you see he gets this? So he can contact me.'

The paramedic takes the card and nods.

Her sister smiles with approval and says, 'Sorry, I have to run. I've got a client at 12.45.'

'No problem,' says Cheryl.

The paramedics are lifting Arran onto a stretcher. He opens his eyes for a moment. They're full of panic.

'Alright, mate,' says the paramedic. 'Just gonna put you in the ambulance now.'

That frightened gaze meets Cheryl's, and he looks away.

Lorna takes her arm. 'There's nothing more to be done now,' says her sister. 'Go home and talk to Jordan. It'll all be okay.'

Reassuring words. She doesn't know the half of it.

Cheryl takes the bus home. As it meanders through the town, past the august colleges, and then out to the more residential areas, she contemplates the mess that her life has become.

Her encounter with Arran Patel is a painful reminder of her failures as an academic. She's now heading home, where she will be reminded of her failures as a parent. Her unfaithful husband, who continues to lie to her, will remind her of her failures as a wife.

She stares out of the window, mired in self pity. And Xan's behaviour niggles away at her.

He definitely slept with someone. If not Hannah, then who?

She casts her mind around for candidates. There's a PR girl, who works in admin for the university. She liaises with the media. Cheryl met her a while ago, a leggy blonde. Xan's mentioned her a couple of times. But was she even at the party? It's possible. And if it is her, this could've been going on for months.

It's a desolate thought. She wonders if he'd even stay with her if it wasn't for the kids. Or the prospect of making millions.

She gets off the bus at the top of her treelined road. This walk home used to please her. The elegant houses full of good, successful families, whose hard work had earned them the right to live in this lovely street.

Hard work and discipline will be rewarded.

This was the philosophy she grew up with. Where did she get it? From her school? From her parents? She couldn't remember. She suspects it's rubbish. As a biologist, she sees no inherent morality in the material world. Homo sapiens is just another species competing for survival.

Letting herself into the house with her key, she's greeted with a pale shaft of wintery sunshine flowing down the hall from the velux windows in the kitchen's roof extension at the back. The house is quiet. But her husband and son are here somewhere.

She calls out. 'Xan?' There's a tremor in her voice. She sounds on the edge of panic.

Her husband appears in the study doorway, reading glasses perched on the end of his nose.

'What's up?' he says, scanning her.

'Nothing,' says Cheryl. 'I wondered where you were.'

'Well, I'm working,' he says. 'We're going to need office and laboratory space. So I've been talking to agents, and I might've found something suitable in the business park.'

'Aren't we jumping the gun a bit?'

'Cheryl, the idea of securing investment is that we can get the infrastructure in place to move this thing on.'

Move things on.

How can he talk like this?

'Where the hell's Jordan?' she blurts. 'I thought you were spending time with him while I went to talk to Lorna.'

'Oh for Crissake, Cheryl. He's in his room. He doesn't need a babysitter.'

That's exactly what he needed last night.

But she bites back a retort. All this resentment and self-pity is no good. She needs to pull herself together.

She has a sudden memory flash from her childhood. On the day of her mother's funeral, her father sat her and Lorna down on the old leather sofa in his study. She remembers him towering over them in his black suit. 'Now girls,' he said. 'You've got to pull yourselves together and get on. It's what your mother would've wanted.' Three days later, Lorna was shipped off to boarding school. Cheryl followed a year later; she was only nine. It was a horrible year without Lorna.

She's vowed never to treat her children like that.

'Is he alright?' she says. 'Have you talked to him?'

'What he needs is time to process what's happened. Come to terms with it.'

'He's fourteen, Xan. How's he supposed to do that on his own?

Xan sighs. He's trying to suppress his irritation. She wants to scream at him. He has no right to be irritated with her.

He changes the subject. Typical Xan.

'What did Lorna say?'

'She said if the police were satisfied it was an accident, it would be hard for Ben's parents to accuse Jordan of wrongdoing. Depending on how hard they pushed it, it could be slander.'

'There you are,' says Xan. 'I told you it would be okay.'

He has a smug expression on his face. He likes to be right.

'Do you want to see the new offices I've found for us?'

Too ridiculous.

'No,' snaps Cheryl. Kicking off her shoes, she heads upstairs.

'Suit yourself,' says Xan. 'But listen to me, Cheryl, be careful what you say to him. Don't upset him.'

She's close to exploding. But ignores him.

As she walks along the upstairs hallway, she sees that the door to her son's bedroom is ajar. He's sprawled on the bed, playing a computer game on his laptop. For a moment, it looks as if he's home from school convalescing from some illness.

If only.

She taps on the door. 'Hey,' she says. 'Can I come in?'

He shoots her a hostile glance and nods.

She walks across and perches on the end of the bed.

'How are you doing?' she says.

He shrugs and exhales. 'Bored.'

'Perhaps, while you're suspended, you should do some schoolwork. So you don't fall behind.'

'What's the point?'

'As I said, so you can keep up.'

Jordan glares at her. 'They're going to boot me out. So it'd just be a waste of time.'

'Who's told you that?'

'I've been talking to people.' Cheryl knows he means texting. 'Henderson's gone ballistic. Wants to make an example of me.'

'Jordan, whatever gossip is circulating online, that's not necessarily the truth. Mrs Henderson does not have the power to expel you arbitrarily. There are processes that must be followed.'

'Whatever. I'll still be out.'

'I've been to talking to your aunt. She doesn't think anyone can blame you for what happened to Ben. The important thing is you shouldn't feel guilty.'

'I don't.'

Cheryl hesitates.

This is the complete opposite of what he was saying this morning.

'I talked to Dad about it,' he adds. 'We agreed. Ben was a twat. When I did it, it worked fine. He misjudged it. Absolute twat.'

'Jordie, you shouldn't use that kind of language about him.'

Jordan gives her a scathing look. 'You mean 'cause he's

dead? I'm not stupid. I wouldn't go around saying it to anyone else. All the girls in my class, especially all the ones who ignored us and treated us like shit, are going online and saying what a great person Ben was, how they all loved him. They've created a tribute page.'

'If they're upset, which I'm sure many of them are, that's a nice thing to do.'

'It's crap. He'll end up getting loads more likes now he's dead.'

Cheryl sighs. Her son's understanding of the hypocrisies of the world is far more sophisticated than she thought.

'Sounds to me you're quite angry with Ben,' she says. 'And it's natural.'

'Course I'm angry. He was a twat, but I'm gonna pay for it. I'll have to go to a crap school. All my videos'll get taken down. And his father's going to tell everyone I should go to jail.'

'I think you're exaggerating, Jordie.'

'Am I? Why did you go running off this morning to talk to Auntie Lorna? Cause she's a lawyer. And you're worried. Right?'

He is right.

'What worries me is that you were engaging in these kinds of stunts. It was a crazy thing to do. What if you'd been the one to get killed? How do you think I'd feel about that?'

'Relieved probably.'

'Oh, come on, Jordie. Now you're being stupid. I'd've been devastated. And so would your dad. And Sasha.'

He hunches his shoulders. 'Whatever.'

'You will not get expelled from school.'

He shrugs and exhales. But he has tears welling in his eyes. She takes a chance and ruffles his hair.

'It'll be okay.'

He nods and says, ‘I’m starving. Have we got any pizza in the freezer?’

‘I’ll check.’

He goes back to his laptop. ‘Cheers. And can I get a coke too?’

‘I’ll see what I can do.’

She goes down to the kitchen. As she passes the study door, she can see Xan on the phone.

She’s wrung out. She should be glad that Xan has talked him out of his guilt, shouldn’t she? And that Jordan has reverted to stroppy teenager mode. But it leaves her with a nagging feeling. Is he just putting on a brave face? Trying to be tough. And if so, why does he think he has to be? Is this what she’s taught him?

Or maybe he doesn’t care his friend’s dead? All he cares about is himself. Have they taught him that too, her and Xan?

17

Tuesday, 3.30pm

For several hours, he lies waiting on a trolley in A&E. It feels as if an enormous lump of molten lead has been welded to his left eyebrow. It throbs. He can't see out of the eye. A red mist. That whole side of his face feels weird. A loose dressing has been placed over it. His beard is caked in blood. He's drowsy and tries to sleep, but the pain gnaws away like a hungry rat.

Still hungry.

Finally, a nurse appears. She's fat with a weary but kind face.

'Got yourself in quite a mess, haven't you, lovey?' she says. 'Doctor'll be along in a minute.' She has an iPad in her hand. 'Just need to take a few details. What's your name, lovey?'

Who does he want to be today?

Listen to the voice. Keep them guessing. Stay off grid.

'Mohammed,' he says. 'Like the prophet.' He uses this often. Plenty of them about.

She taps away. 'Second name?'

'Rafiq,' he says. It's the first thing that pops into his mind. His college roommate, in his first year, was called Ali Rafiq.

'Date of birth?' says the nurse.

'Ninety-four,' he says. That bit is true. Pick a date. 'February 15th.'

'Oh, your birthday next week,' says the nurse with a smile.

He has no idea of the date. Winter. January. February. Somewhere thereabouts.

Maybe ten minutes later, a doctor appears. She's young and pretty. Her hand shakes as she points a light in his one good eye.

'Did you lose consciousness?' she says.

He shrugs.

'Feel dizzy?'

He can see her wrinkling her nose. She's battling her disgust. Junior doctors get the crap jobs. The down and outs. The dregs.

'Sick?' she says.

He's not sure.

Be smart. Don't give them any ammunition.

He closes his one good eye. When he looks again, she's gone. The nurse is dragging a drip stand into the cubicle.

'Just going to pop a little needle in your arm. Get some fluids into you. Okay, lovey?'

As she puts the cannula in his arm and connects it to a saline drip, she says, 'You're going to have a CT scan. But we found you a bed for the night. Get you cleaned up a bit, get some food inside you. How does that sound?'

He nods. It hurts.

He knows enough about medical procedures to have worked out what they're doing. But he doesn't let on. The saline drip is to rehydrate him. They need to check whether his skull is fractured and if there's any bleeding in the brain which could create pressure. Hence the scan and the overnight observation. It's not an act of kindness. They'd boot him out if they could.

The drip is doing its work. His mind drifts and he loses track of time. The painkillers have kicked in. They bring him some respite. He's still hungry. They promised him a sandwich. They must've forgotten.

He thinks of his mother, in the kitchen, cooking. The rich aromas of his childhood. So long since he's tasted good food like that. He hopes she understands. His father never would. Not in a million years. That's why he had to walk away and disappear. He could never face them. The shame of it. See that look in their eyes.

Coward. Dirty, stinking coward.

He knows that's what he is. Are they still looking for him? Sometimes he wonders. He threw his phone in the river, ages ago now, so he'll never know.

The swish of the curtain on the rail. Another nurse appears. Young, male, with a toothy grin. Vinyl gloves, plastic apron.

'Alright, mate,' he says. 'Need to get you out of these clothes, put you in a hospital gown.You okay with that?'

He doesn't answer. But he lets the nurse pull him up into a sitting position and ease him out of his jacket. That jacket is still good, but it's filthy. He wonders if they'll bin it. As the nurse folds it to stuff it into a plastic sack, something falls from the pocket and lands on the floor. Rectangular, white. The nurse picks it up.

'This yours?'

He takes it, turns it over in his fingers. He has to peer at it to read it:

Dr Cheryl Woodward. Fancy lettering, website address, phone number.

So it was her. He didn't imagine it. And she gave him her card?

Why?

This is the woman who ruined his life. Now he remembers. She said, *I want to help you*, and gave him her card.

Fuck her! They won't use him again. Suck him dry and throw him away.

He hands the card back to the nurse. 'Nah,' he says. 'Chuck it away.'

18

Tuesday, 6.30pm

Hannah takes a taxi. The pub is several miles out of town, in a small hamlet on the banks of the river. On a wintery evening, its riverside terrace is damp and deserted. The interior is rustic and low-ceilinged, with a roaring log fire.

At other times of the year, this would be a popular tourist trap. But tonight, there are only a few locals gathered round the fire. A couple playing darts, and a nervous young woman sitting in a wood-panelled alcove in the furthest corner.

Hannah concludes this is Dr Kayleigh Burrows to use her full title. She heads straight over, wreathed in smiles.

Kayleigh looks up. A large girl with a square chin, who looks like she could be lethal on a rugby field. She's cradling a half pint of beer, which is almost empty.

'Kayleigh?'

The girl blinks at her, then gives a curt nod.

Hannah holds out her hand and beams. 'I'm so glad you agreed to this. Believe me, you won't regret it.'

They shake hands. A damp fleshy palm.

'I hope not.' There it is again, the high-pitched voice which doesn't match the body.

'Let me get you another?' says Hannah.

'Just a half of lager,' says Kayleigh.

Hannah orders from a cute barman, who offers to bring the drinks over. Although she'd much prefer a gin and tonic, Hannah opts for lager too. Making Kayleigh Burrows believe they could be best friends is her priority.

She sits on the bench seat opposite Kayleigh.

'I'm in awe,' she says. 'According to Freddie, you are one smart lady.'

Kayleigh shrugs. 'That was back when we were undergrads. It's a different ballgame now. My thesis was ignored.'

'Oh dear,' says Hannah with a sympathetic smile.

When the barman delivers their drinks, Kayleigh gives him an awkward adolescent glance.

Ugly woman in need of a shag?

Hannah decides to sit back and listen.

Kayleigh scans her. She's jittery. But she's also assessing Hannah. For her, this meeting is a strategic move.

She sighs and says, 'Okay, the reason I feel bad is I'm lucky Dr Woodward took me on.'

Dr Woodward, not Cheryl.

Hannah says nothing. She lets the silence expand, putting pressure on Kayleigh to say more.

'She could've picked someone better, but she knew I'd had a rough time. The supervisor for my PhD was a sexist pig. I think she knew that.'

'Female solidarity is important,' says Hannah.

Kayleigh takes a sip of her beer; she's relaxing.

'When I got in touch with Freddie, I suppose I was

boasting a bit. We were undergrads together. It was very competitive.'

'I get that. Freddie's a bright guy, but I find myself trying to compete with him all the time.'

Mostly because he's an arrogant shit.

'I didn't expect HDZ to react this quickly. I assumed Freddie and I would have a meeting first. It was a bit of a surprise.'

'Is that a problem?' says Hannah.

'I think it could be. For Dr Woodward.'

'Why?'

'Because of her husband.' Kayleigh is gazing at her earnestly.

Now they're getting to the nitty gritty.

'Okay,' says Hannah. 'He's an outsider, a businessman who's keen to see his wife's work receive the investment it needs to succeed.'

'I think he's pushing her too hard. She's very meticulous. Checks all the data. Double checks it.'

'Which is good, surely?'

'In some ways.'

Ambiguity. Why?

Hannah tilts her head and gives a self-deprecating smile. 'Thing is, Kayleigh,' she says. 'I need to come clean with you. I'm not a scientist. I'm filling in for Freddie. So you need to explain this to me as if I'm an idiot.'

Kayleigh sighs. Her eyes are hard and shiny, like a judgemental cyborg in a sci-fi movie.

'Okay,' she says. 'All this talk of setting up a business has changed the vibe in the lab. People want to be included, of course they do. But it's all got a bit chaotic, because everyone's trying to prove how good they are.'

'What are we saying here? Individual ambition is trumping team work?'

Kayleigh frowns. 'I never thought of it like that, but yes, I guess everyone's jockeying for position. And, well, it's affecting the data.'

She's squirming.

'What d'you mean?' says Hannah. 'People are faking results?'

'It's more that everyone wants to be seen to meet expectations.'

'And do you think Dr Woodward knows?'

Kayleigh is fiddling with her glass, turning it obsessively. She wants to evade the question. 'I don't know,' she says. 'Maybe.'

Hannah frowns and takes a swallow of beer. Fizzy and disgusting. She remembers why she never drinks it.

'I'm confused,' she says. 'If you knew all this, and you think Xan is putting too much pressure on his wife, why get in touch with Freddie and say your lab was close to a breakthrough?'

Kayleigh stares into her glass and sighs. 'I dunno… I suppose I... one night, I was pissed. I sent him a text.'

She raises her eyes and gives Hannah a pleading look.

Now it makes sense.

This is nothing about biotech and the research that's going on in Cheryl Woodward's lab. It's about this stupid woman and Freddie. She did it to impress Freddie.

Hannah gives her a quizzical smile. 'Kayleigh,' she says. 'Have you got a thing for Freddie?'

Kayleigh Burrows blushes from her neck to the roots of her hair.

Bingo!

'No, of course not,' she says. 'I realise he's gay.'

Hannah shrugs.

'Yeah, but he's very attractive. And a terrible flirt.'

'I shouldn't have got involved in any of this. I feel I've let Dr Woodward down.'

'No,' says Hannah. 'You haven't. But let's keep this conversation between the two of us.'

'You won't tell Freddie?'

That depends.

'Of course not. Don't worry, you can trust me.'

Hannah says goodbye to Kayleigh Burrows in the freezing pub car park. Kayleigh has a pathetic 125 cc motor bike. She climbs on it and putters off. An Uber picks Hannah up.

As she settles in the back of the cab, she has some serious thinking to do. This is Freddie's fuck up, not hers. She could just tell Nat the truth. Cheryl Woodward is not as near to a breakthrough as her ambitious husband is claiming. He's obsessed. She isn't. As founders of a start-up, they're completely mismatched. And Cheryl is a crap manager of her team. Withdraw the offer, and cut their losses.

But is that the smart move?

19

Tuesday, 7.05pm

It was never Cheryl's intention to stay this late. But having spent the morning away from the university—a rare occurrence, she's always at work—she wanted to make it clear to everyone, or maybe just herself, that her mind is on the job.

She arrived at lunchtime to face another faculty meeting that she'd forgotten about until she checked her diary. Her colleagues were full of congratulations and compliments. News that her work is attracting serious investment from a venture capital firm had spread fast. But behind the smiles, she could smell the envy round the table, and it made her uncomfortable.

Since the meeting ended, she's been holed up in her office, staring at her laptop. Solitary work is her escape. It's a relief to retreat into the world of concepts and numbers and formulae that live only in her head. The awkwardness of dealing with other people's complicated needs and emotions slides away. Her mind becomes fluid. Analysing the data, interpreting, planning, taking incremental steps forward. This is the one time she's free. She knows that most people don't think in this way; it's a gift. And sometimes a curse.

Only when the numbers and symbols begin to dance off the screen, does she realise it's time to stop. She has a stiff neck and eyestrain, but she's calmed down. The anxious chatter in her brain is gone.

Temporarily.

She walks across the deserted car park. A hazy drizzle is falling, causing the light from the street lamps to refract. She pulls up the hood on her jacket.

Unlocking her car with the key fob, she wonders if she should call Xan? She gets out her phone and looks at it. Nothing from him. No friendly text asking what time she'll be home.

Does he even worry about her?

She drives home in a resentful funk. She can practically guarantee that he'll be in his study with a glass of scotch, staring at some flashy website on his laptop and making amorphous plans for the future. Sasha will be on her own in front of the telly, and Jordan'll be upstairs on his PlayStation. But she can't be in two places at once, can she? The fact their family has deteriorated into this dysfunctional mess, kids neglected and unfed, is not her sole responsibility. The prospect of cooking depresses her; they'll have to order a takeaway.

She opens the front door to the pungent aroma of sizzling sausages. As she enters the kitchen, she sees Sasha skipping round the dining table, laying out the cutlery, and Jordan perched on a bar stool with a can of Coke.

How many has he had? She dreads to think.

'We were beginning to think you'd done a bunk,' says her husband, as he stirs a saucepan of baked beans. 'I decided we'd have a fry-up. Sausages, chips, eggs and beans. How does that sound?'

Sounds like he's trying to prove a point.

'Great,' she says, pulling off her jacket.

'Feel like opening a bottle of wine?'

She shrugs. So now they're playing happy families. Her brain is squirrelly with annoyance and her body aching from too long at a desk. She goes to the fridge and takes out a bottle of white wine. He's cracking eggs into the frying pan.

Glancing in her direction, he frowns and says, 'With sausages? Perhaps something a bit more robust, darling? How about Shiraz?'

He reckons he's a wine buff.

She replaces the white and goes over to the wine rack. 'After what you drank last night at the party, I'd've thought you'd want a night off,' she says.

He gives her a shifty look, then chuckles. He knows she's needling him. This is his story: he didn't come home until three and wasn't answering his phone because he was boozing. Where and who with? That question he's evaded. Too drunk to remember, apparently.

'Well, y'know,' he says. 'Hair of the dog.' Then he pauses and pretends to ponder. 'Actually, perhaps that's why I got a yen for a fry-up?'

She pours him a glass of red wine and places it on the counter beside him.

'Aren't you joining me?' he says.

She glances at the bottle. A couple of glasses of that and all her anger and resentment is likely to explode.

She hesitates.

What the hell!

Returning to the cupboard, she takes down another wine glass and pours herself a hefty measure.

She takes a sip. The wine is tangy. Raising her glass, she says, ‘Cheers. Here’s to… I don’t know, happy families?’

He chinks her glass with his own. ‘Absolutely,’ he says.

Sasha is watching them. She giggles nervously. Jordan is staring at his iPad, but gives them a side-eyed glance.

Even the kids aren’t fooled, thinks Cheryl, as she takes another slug of wine.

‘And here’s to clever mummy, who’s about to make us rich,’ adds Xan, with a flourish of his glass.

Cheryl stares at him. His eyes are as bright as bullets, the edges crinkled with laughter lines.

‘What will we do when we’re rich?’ says Sasha, jumping up and down.

‘We’ll have a big swimming pool in our garden,’ says Xan. ‘And you’ll invite all your friends round for pool parties. Like they do in the States.’

‘Yippee!’ says Sasha, clapping her hands.

Cheryl has a sudden cramp, like a fist in the middle of her chest. She can’t tell if it’s tension and she’s about to burst into tears, or else puke. She looks at her husband.

Now the company is set up, everyone’s expectations will skyrocket. Her husband, her colleagues, the money people, they’ve all decided she’s the magician who can deliver.

It’s too much, too soon.

And Xan is beaming; that beguiling smile of his. He’s so charming. He thinks he’s got the better of her.

Lying bastard.

She takes another mouthful of wine.

20

Tuesday, 8.25pm

Back in her hotel room, Hannah pours herself a large G and T. She watches the tonic bubbles effervescing in the glass. She needs to give her next move some careful consideration.

There are two options: phone her boss and tell him what she knows. Freddie's "contact" is a love-struck lump who's fed him duff information. The advantage of this is she looks smarter than Freddie. Gold star to her. However, Freddie'll weasel his way round Nat; he hasn't made it to blue-eyed boy status for no reason. Plus, where does that leave her? Back to trawling through half-baked ideas for apps.

Second option. Find a way to salvage the deal. In the last twenty-four hours, she's read enough about the biotech industry to know that the development phase for emerging technologies can go on for years. VC firms regularly pour money into bottomless pits and don't see a result. The key concept is "potential". Companies have gone public on less and still seen their share price soar.

And there's obviously potential here. Buckets of it. More investment can be leveraged using the proper presentation of the work's potential. The 3D printing of human organs for transplant. What's not to like? Throw enough money at it, eventually some smart lab rat will make it work. Cheryl? Someone else they bring in? It doesn't matter. Managing these people, finessing the narrative, and looking out for the money, that's the crucial job. She's absolutely suited to do it. And if she can engineer herself a seat on the Board, who knows where it could take her?

Carpe diem, as the public school toffs she works with would say.

If she can pull this off, then perhaps her father will drop his sexist assumptions and give her the credit she deserves.

She sips her gin and picks up her phone. Nat Harrington answers on the fourth ring. He's wearing a startlingly white towelling bathrobe and looks rather flushed. There are disadvantages to FaceTiming.

'Sorry if it's a bit late, boss,' she says.

'Just having a massage,' he replies.

Yeah, and the rest.

'A quick update. I won't keep you.'

'Okay.'

'I think there's huge potential here,' she says. 'A young and ambitious team. A really driven CEO in Xan Woodward. Cheryl is undoubtedly brilliant.' She sighs theatrically. 'But…'

'Oh fuck,' says Nat. 'But what?'

'She lacks confidence.'

'In the work?'

'No, in herself, I think.'

Nat sighs. 'A neurotic female founder? That's not gonna work.'

'Depends if she's got the right support. Can I make a suggestion?'

'Go on.'

'Give me three months up here, and I'll make it work.'

Nat chuckles. 'I know you're ambitious, Hannah.'

'And that's why you hired me. But here's the pitch. Someone is going to make this technology work, and soon. Freddie's right about that. The issue here is management of the team and of the relationship between the two founders.'

'But they're married.'

'Maybe that's the problem. You're always saying, this is a people business.'

'Okay, but if Cheryl Woodward is not the right tech lead for the project, then you need to do some lateral thinking. Is there someone in that lab who's younger and smarter, and who can drive it through?'

'Yeah, probably,' says Hannah. 'And I'll find them. But that's why I need three months, not three days.'

He's considering it.

Hannah crosses her fingers.

'Okay,' says Nat. 'Show me what you can do.'

Yes!

As soon as he's hung up, Hannah fist pumps the air.

21

Tuesday, 8.55pm

Cheryl sits at the end of the dining table staring out of the window at the dark silhouette of trees and shrubs that fringe the garden. It's pleasant to just drift. The wine has softened everything. Her thoughts have slowed.

Xan is clearing away the plates and loading the dishwasher. The children have retreated into the sitting room to watch a movie on Netflix. Jordan seems surprisingly relaxed. He ate two chocolate desserts and is back to tormenting his little sister. Cheryl gave her sausages to Xan. She hates sausages. After nine years of marriage, you'd think he'd know that.

Cheryl has never been a drinker; she's a small woman with no capacity for alcohol. He knows that too, and now he's opening another bottle of wine.

Who cares?

A brief image of her old student, Arran Patel, bleeding on the pavement, flickers through her mind. She wills it away.

A burden she doesn't need. She followed the rules, didn't she?

Xan strolls over to the table and tops up her glass. Watching him pour, she knows she should refuse. She watches him, her gorgeous, charming husband.

'Oh, Xan,' she says. 'How did we get to this?' She sounds pathetic. And tipsy.

'Get to what?' he says. 'You just need to chill out.'

'But it's our responsibility to keep him safe,' she says. 'He could've been killed.'

'I know. And if you want my opinion, for all his bravado, he's scared himself shitless. He won't be doing this again anytime soon.'

'I'm all for reassuring him. But we can't just let him off the hook. His friend died, and he doesn't seem to have absorbed the enormity of that. He's just concerned about himself.'

'You need to give him time.'

'He's as good as admitted that he talked Ben into it.'

'Cheryl, you need to let this go.'

'Maybe he needs some counselling?'

Xan laughs out loud. 'I presume that's your bloody sister's idea.'

Lorna once suggested couple counselling for her and Xan; he'd laughed at that too.

'No,' she says. 'It's my idea. I think he needs… I don't know. He needs something.'

'Don't worry. I've dealt with it.'

'By telling him Ben was a twat? That's hardly—'

'No,' he snaps. 'I've persuaded him to agree to a tracking app on his phone.'

'What?'

What's he talking about? Her head is spinning from the alcohol.

'That's the deal I made with him.'

'The deal?'

'Yeah. I got him a new phone. To replace the one the police took.'

'That's like rewarding him for what he's done, surely?'

'He's a teenager. How can he live without a phone? But the tracker I've installed gives us his location, which is the bit he knows about. Plus a few added extras, which he doesn't. We can activate the microphone remotely and monitor his texts.'

Cheryl stares at him in disbelief.

'You've put him under surveillance?'

'Basically.' He grins. 'Pretty smart, eh? Now you can stop worrying about him.'

She looks at her husband, standing there, sipping his wine with a smug look on his face.

It's ridiculous.

'How is that going to teach him responsibility?' she says.

'Isn't the priority to keep him safe?'

'Yes, of course.' She takes another slug of wine. 'But it's a bit extreme.'

'I think the situation calls for it.'

'I know, but… I wished we'd discussed this.'

'Why? What's to discuss?'

'Well, I suppose, the ethics of it.'

'Really, Cheryl? Ethics? Don't be so bloody wet. He's a fourteen-year-old boy. Our son. And he needs reining in. I also thought it'd give us leverage with the school.'

'What do you mean?'

'Demonstrate to Mrs Henderson that we take this seriously. It won't happen again, or anything like it. Because we'll always know what he's up to. Problem solved.'

'He's not stupid, Xan. He'll figure it out. Then what? He'll never trust us. Ever.'

'We'll cross that bridge when we come to it.'

'I don't know that I want to bring up my son like this.'

He looks at her, tilts his head and huffs. 'Oh what? So now he's your son?'

'I didn't mean—'

She didn't.

'Yes, you did. It's the card you always play when we disagree.' He sighs and puts his glass down with an irritable snap. His chest swells with righteous indignation.

'I meant our son. Of course I did.'

'Well, the situation's handled. I've handled it,' he says crisply.

'I'm sorry.'

She's wretched. The wine has made her feel worse. Why couldn't they have discussed this? Made a proper decision together, as parents, as a couple.

'Listen,' he says. 'We've got other things we need to focus on. I want to get back to HDZ. Firm up the deal. And you'll have to prepare a proper pitch for them. Doesn't need to be detailed. But we must keep their excitement going.'

She sighs. Her brain is fuddled. She can't think about this as well.

'I don't know. Let's talk about it later. Tomorrow.'

He drums his knuckles on the counter. 'Cheryl, we needed to talk about it this afternoon. But where were you?'

'I was working.'

'So was I. And babysitting *your* son.' He has a spiteful glint in his eye. She knows her husband. When he doesn't get what he wants, he goes for the jugular. 'I mean, am I wasting my time here? I've worked my arse off for this deal. For you. For us. For the life we deserve.'

'I can't discuss this now. I'm too tired. I need to go to bed.' She stands up; he towers over her.

For an instant, she senses a wave of frustration and rage rolling towards her. She rocks back on her heels.

Does he want to hit her?

He glares at her, folds his arms and turns away.

She's never felt that with him before, that there's a volcano of molten fury inside him about to erupt. It's a shock. She doesn't know what to say. But she is drunk, probably very drunk. Is she reading this all wrong, getting everything out of proportion?

He turns back towards her again. His face is tight and closed. He gives her a chilly look. 'Okay, you go and hide under the duvet,' he says. 'I've got some calls to make. And I may need to go out.'

He stalks out of the room.

Cheryl sits back down and finishes her glass of wine in two mouthfuls.

She feels guilty. And stupid. What's the matter with her? Why didn't she just say, yes, I'll think about a pitch. He's right. He is doing this for her and he's sacrificed so much. She wanted to tell him about Arran Patel, as well. They should do something to help him.

Apologise. Smooth it over.

Standing up, she's unsteady. Her head swims; definitely too much booze. Just go and tell him she's sorry and that she knows, even if she disagrees, that he's trying to do his best for Jordan.

She gets as far as the kitchen doorway, then she hears the front door slam. He's gone.

22

Tuesday, 9.45pm

The tapping on the door is getting insistent. Hannah is taking a long, celebratory soak in the bath and has been trying to ignore it. It must be obvious to whoever that she's not answering.

Tap Tap Tap!

Then she hears a muffled voice. 'Hannah, you asleep? It's me, Xan.'

Oh fuck!

'Hannah?'

Through the open bathroom door, she can see the bedside table. Her phone is vibrating. Now he's trying to call her. What does the dickhead want?

Three guesses.

Pretending to be asleep and not hear is the sensible option here. She'll meet him tomorrow, when she can shift everything on to a proper professional footing.

Tap Tap Tap!

‘I know you’re in there,’ he says. ‘They told me downstairs at the desk that you ordered room service.’

Cheap hotels, what can you do? If this was a five-star establishment, he wouldn’t have got past the concierge.

Using her arms, she levers herself up from the warm, scented suds and climbs out of the tub. There’s a towelling robe on the back of the bathroom door.

Do they launder these things between guests? Probably not.

Reluctantly, she pulls it on and pads out into the bedroom, trailing water drips behind her. She opens the door on the chain and peers out.

Xan Woodward holds up a bottle of bubbly that he must’ve bought at a garage. ‘Thought we should have a drink.’

‘Really?’ she says. ‘You look pissed already.’

‘Not pissed enough,’ he says. ‘C’mon, take pity on me. Just one drink. And I promise to behave.’

She doesn’t believe him. Of course, she doesn’t. She can tell from his hangdog expression. This is a man in search of a sympathy shag, but it might be useful to know why.

Closing the door, she unhooks the chain and lets him in.

‘I was having a bath,’ she says.

He’s grinning from ear to ear. ‘I can see that,’ he says. ‘And I must say, you smell delicious.’

‘Don’t get any ideas,’ she says. ‘I’m tired. I just want to get some sleep.’

‘Why is everyone tired?’ he says. ‘A girl your age should have loads of stamina. Got some glasses?’

‘Xan,’ she says. ‘Let’s get a few things straight here.’

He extracts the plastic cork from the bottle with dull pop. She hands him a tumbler.

‘Straight as you like,’ he says, pouring and spilling a

quantity of fizz on the floor. It foams on the carpet. He rubs it in with his foot.

'HDZ's investment doesn't come with a complimentary shag every time you fall out with your wife.'

'No? Can't we put that in the contract?'

She gives him a disapproving glare. But that seems to encourage him.

'Just kidding,' he says, offering her the tumbler. She takes it and walks across the room, deliberately putting some distance between them, and places it beside the kettle.

'Right,' she says. 'You can drink this disgusting stuff and tell me your troubles. Then you can bugger off home. Because I do not want Cheryl to think anything is going on between us.'

'Cheryl won't suspect a thing.'

'What planet are you living on? She most certainly did know what happened last night.'

He's shaking his head. 'Listen, I know my wife. She prefers to ignore these things.'

'You think so?'

He raises his glass. 'I do.' Then he ponders. 'Why do you think she knows?'

Hannah exhales wearily. 'Yeah, well, when I tracked her down to a coffee shop in town this morning, she gave me the evil eye.'

'Yes, she was very upset this morning. A problem with our son. He got into some trouble last night.'

'Who was he off shagging?'

He doesn't even smile. His expression flips to mournful and self-righteous. 'He's fourteen. Actually, there was a terrible accident. He and his best friend were trying to film a crazy stunt. The other boy was killed. Police involved.'

He dips his head and frowns.

‘Shit.’ she says. ‘That sounds awful.’

‘Yes, it is. And Cheryl’s been extremely upset all day. So that’s what you were getting. If it was that coffee shop in the centre of town, she went to meet her sister, who’s a lawyer.’

‘Are the police blaming your son?’

‘No. They accept it was a tragic accident. But he’s been suspended from school and Cheryl’s worried.’

‘Understandably.’

He sits down on the end of the bed and sips his fizz. ‘I’ve put a tracking app on his phone, so we can keep tabs on the little bugger. That’s what Cheryl and I had a row about, if you want to know.’

He gives her a sorrowful look, like a puppy hoping to be fussed. Hannah hates stuff like this. Tragedies and their messy fallout. What are you supposed to say?

She shrugs. ‘I’m really sorry. The whole thing sounds like a nightmare.’

He nods.

‘I had to get out of the house. Just needed someone sympathetic to talk to. Teenage boys, eh? What do you do with them?’

Horny middle-aged men, what do you do with them?

He wipes his face with his hand. There are tears in his eyes. ‘It could so easily have been him. I’d never have forgiven myself.’

He hangs his head forward. His shoulders shake.

He’s crying!

And that makes him rather boyish and cute.

Hannah moves across the room and sits down beside him.

‘All I want is to be the best dad I can, to both my kids,’ he says.

She puts her hand on his back. ‘I’m sure you do.’

He snivels, shakes his head ruefully and then chuckles. 'Take my advice. Don't ever have any!'

Doesn't intend to. She's already made up her mind about that one.

They'll be no snivelling brats to mess up Hannah Blakeney's life and cause her tits to sag. She has three sisters-in-law, all of whom hate their lives, regret their choices, and once they've drunk enough gin will say so. Loudly.

Xan Woodward gazes at her with those baby blue eyes. 'Can I stay for a bit? Chill out. No hanky-panky, I promise.'

Hanky-panky? Sounds like a Regency romance.

The trouble is she can imagine him in a pair of knee breeches and Hessian boots. They'd suit him.

'Okay,' she says. 'But I'm not drinking that shite you brought.' She goes to the fridge and opens it. 'Gin or vodka.'

'G and T, if you can manage it,' he says. He's immediately more cheery. She cracks open four miniatures, loads two more tumblers with ice from the ice bucket, and fills them.

He watches, a little cheeky grin hovering round his lips. Most men, with a few drinks inside them, think they're charming. But he does have something compelling about him. For a bloke over forty, he is eminently fuckable.

'We're going to need some ground rules,' says Hannah.

'A bit of discipline never hurt anyone,' he says with a roguish wink.

'Oh, shut up!' she replies, handing him a drink. 'I've talked to my boss. If we go ahead, then we need a very open and honest dialogue with Cheryl about what she and her team hope to achieve, and the possible timeframe.'

'She wants that too.'

'Good.'

'I'll be the CEO and I'll deliver.'

'Surely that depends on Cheryl.'

He sighs, takes a swallow of his drink. 'What you have to understand is my wife doesn't see the world the way most people do. Intellectually, it's like playing chess with someone who's always ten moves ahead of you. It's like she sees too much, and often what she knows, what she calculates, frightens her. She can probably tell you the odds of me keeling over with a heart attack before I'm sixty down to two decimal places. Or the chances of keeping climate change to 1.5 degrees C. She's always anxious, but at the same time brilliant and intimidating. I can tell you, it's hard to live with that.'

Hannah listens. She has no idea if any of this is true. Sounds like a bullshit story he's repeated more than once. But he's a bloody good salesman. And this is about cementing his role in the business.

'The thing is,' he says. 'I understand how to look after her. How to create an environment for her to do her best work.'

Not what Kayleigh Burrows said. She thinks the opposite.

'Fair enough,' says Hannah. 'No one's trying to exclude you. Plus, you understand the business. What it takes to make a start-up work.'

'I do,' he replies.

'But we still need direct access to Cheryl.'

'I get that.'

Those blue eyes with the dark lashes. He's so good at this.

'And to that end,' she says. 'You should know that she thinks I'm a lesbian.'

He laughs out loud. 'What? How?'

'I told her. It seems to me that in spite of what you say, she would mind if she thought I'd screwed you. I need her to feel comfortable with me, not threatened.'

'And she believed you?'

'Oh yes.'

He chortles. 'Well, you're quite a slick operator, aren't you, Ms Blakeney?'

If only he knew.

'How did you convince her?' he adds.

'Showed her a picture of my girlfriend. She's a footballer.'

Now he's gazing at her like a hungry dog. 'Is she really your girlfriend?'

'We're acquainted.'

He giggles. 'Does that mean you're a bit… ambidextrous?'

So predictable.

'I have been.'

'Well,' he says. 'If you've convinced Cheryl, seems a shame to waste such a good lie.'

His hand slides across her bare knee and slowly up and under the flap of her bathrobe.

And the sensation is pleasant, well, more than pleasant. It sends an electric tingle to all the right places. She allows him to ease her back down on to the bed. Should she give him what he wants?

Why not? Blame it on the gin.

23

Wednesday, 12.05am

Cheryl is still awake, and the hangover is already kicking in when Xan returns. Whoever she is, she must've booted him out. He perches on the end of the bed.

'You asleep?' he whispers.

'Not any more,' she says, sourly.

'I'm sorry,' he says. 'I'm as worried about Jordan as you are. But if you think the app's the wrong response. Heavy-handed.'

She rolls towards him, leaning on her elbow. 'I don't know.'

It's been churning in her brain for hours. Part of her wants to wrap her son up in a cosy blanket, as she did when he was little, and keep him safe forever.

Be realistic.

She looks at her husband. 'Oh Xan, it could so easily have been him. And I can't seem to get beyond that.' Her hand flies to her mouth to suppress a sob. 'If we'd lost him—'

Xan moves up the bed and takes her in his arms. 'Hey,' he says. 'C'mon, we didn't. We dodged a bullet.'

She buries her face in his neck. He smells clean, freshly showered.

Ignore it. He's here. He's back.

'And,' he says. 'The app is a temporary measure. Just to keep tabs on him now. I'll take it off before he ever figures it out. He'll never know. I promise.'

'I just want him to be safe.'

'Of course you do,' he replies. 'And I'm sorry for what I said earlier.'

'It's been a difficult day.'

He strokes her hair. 'I know.'

'You only know part of it. After I had coffee with Lorna, we were walking back through town and we saw some yobs tormenting a homeless man. Lorna stepped in.'

He chuckles. 'Well, yeah, she would.'

'But the thing is Xan, I recognised him. You remember all that trouble we had with that post-grad at the beginning of last year?'

'The one accused of falsifying his results?'

'He was clearly mentally ill. I said that to the Dean at the time, but they insisted on expelling him.'

'You did your best for him.'

Did she?

It was complicated. Xan doesn't know the details. And it's been niggling away at her.

Did she do the right thing?

'It's on my conscience,' she says. 'He's ended up on the streets, which is terrible. And I feel responsible. I should've handled it better. Supported him. I was his supervisor.'

'How is it your fault he forged the data?'

'No, but he wasn't coping with the pressure. And I should've seen that. I'd like to help him.'

'Sounds like he needs a social worker and a therapist, not you. What can you do?'

'Give him another chance. If we're setting up a business—'

He stares at her in disbelief. 'Seriously, Cheryl? You want me to employ some mentally ill down and out to salve your conscience? Don't be ridiculous.'

'Lorna thinks—'

He pulls away from her. 'I might've guessed she'd have her oar in this somewhere. This is a business. Not a fucking charity.'

Pulling off his trainers, he flings them across the room.

'I don't understand why this makes you so angry?' she says.

He stands up. 'I'll tell you why. Because this is just another one of your distractions. A diversionary tactic. We've got a chance here, a window of opportunity—'

'Yes, b—'

'Don't give me any buts.'

'You don't understand.'

'Oh, but I do. You've dragged me half the way across the world on a promise. If you came back here to Cambridge, you could do the work you wanted. You had a vision. You could see it all, how it would play out. And I bought into that, Cheryl. I gave up my dream for yours.'

'I know and—'

'Then don't let me down. Don't let yourself down.'

'I'm just not sure we're ready yet.'

'Will you ever be ready? You've got the patents. Now's the time to move ahead.'

'Yes, but I'm not going to lie to them, Xan.'

He shrugs his shoulders and opens his palms. 'Where's the lie? I'm not asking you to lie. How does any start-up break through, get serious money on board? You big up the potential. You hook them on the dream. You fake it until you make it. That's how they do it in the Valley. That's how Jobs did it. That's how they all do it.'

Fake it until you make it. She hates that expression.

'You're not in the Valley anymore, Xan. This is serious science.'

He laughs. But there's a bitter edge to it. 'You know how naïve that sounds? What do you think other biotech outfits are doing? Not hiding away in their bloody labs until the results are perfect. This is a billion dollar industry. They'd grab what HDZ is offering with both hands.'

She can feel the tears. They're about to erupt.

He folds his arms. 'Oh, don't bloody cry.'

She swallows hard. 'I'm not.'

He sighs. He's changing tack, softening his approach.

'Cheryl, I'm not trying to make you do something you don't want to do,' he says.

He is.

He shakes his head, boyish and earnest. 'I want you to believe in yourself, the way I believe in you.'

He is a genius at this.

'Okay,' she says. 'You win. I'll prepare a pitch for HDZ. Present the patents to them. And we'll take their offer.'

He looks at her, tilts his head and smiles. 'See, it's not that hard, is it?'

'No.' Her lip trembles. She's determined not to cry. She forces herself to smile.

Why does he do this to her? Get a grip!

'You're right,' she says. 'We don't want to miss the boat.'

He's gazing at her now. His face is so familiar, and yet, in an odd way, he's inscrutable.

What's he thinking?'

She's always found the mystery of him enticing. There's a compelling quality to his charm and his confidence. How does he do this? Where does it come from? He's like a problem she can never solve. He always remains tantalisingly out of reach, even when they make love.

For a second, he just stands there, doesn't move a muscle. Then he unfolds his arms and claps his hands, like an overexcited game show host. 'Okay then!' he exclaims. 'Let's do this! You and me against the world, Cheryl. Let's show the bastards, eh?'

24

Wednesday, 9.30am

Hannah stares up at the plate glass facade of the building. Swanky. It's in the newest part of the business park and aimed squarely at ambitious start-ups or medium-sized businesses, who want to impress.

She's arranged to meet Xan Woodward in the car park. She gazes at the careful line of silver birches planted round the perimeter and the banks of evergreen shrubs. It's obvious why this is his choice. It's all about creating a confident image; one that says we've made it already. He seems to understand this, which is a bonus; many founders of start-ups miss this vital point.

Their second night of passion was short, but more intense than the first. And, Hannah realised, they do have something in common. They both like to take risks. It's the buzz of the forbidden. A secret tryst in an anonymous hotel room and knowing you're getting away with it. It gave them both an extra rush.

She still insisted he left once they were done. She'd watched him from the bathroom doorway as he took a quick shower. He knew how to play this game so well. No telltale smells. No evidence to contradict whatever lies he served up to his wife. But that was to the good.

It's a chilly morning, but Hannah is enjoying the hint of frost in the air. She's got a full agenda, and she finds the cold energising, like going for an early morning run.

The estate agent arrives first in a bright yellow mini with a startling black logo on the side. He gets out, wreathed in smiles. Young and hot, tight suit jacket, firm handshake, wide toothy grin.

Been watching too much Selling Sunset.

'Hi, I'm Rafi Khan,' he says. 'You are going to love this place. I mean, a full-sized orange tree in the main atrium? What's not to like?'

'It's my colleague you need to convince,' says Hannah. 'I'd save the patter for him.'

Xan is five minutes late. He sweeps into the car park in the kind of boxy, boring four-by-four that you need if you've got too many kids and a dog.

He jumps out, but he's not alone. Next to him, in the passenger seat, is a teenage boy.

Must be the son.

Xan shoots her wink and a quick greeting, then focuses his attention on Rafi Khan. They seem to be acquainted already and enter into an elaborate, blokey greeting ritual as if they're two mates meeting at the pub.

Hannah glances at the boy as he climbs out of the four-by-four, giving her a sheepish smile.

'Hey,' she says. 'You must be Jordan. I'm Hannah.'

He nods, struggling with eye contact. He's lanky and angular; his clothes look too small, as if he's grown overnight, taking everyone, including himself, by surprise. But his trainers are like boats; they must be at least a size eleven. His hair is bordering on ginger and shaved up the sides, and he looks nothing like his father.

Hannah smiles. 'Hear you've been having a rough time,' she says.

'Yeah, it is what it is,' he replies with an indifferent shrug.

Xan and Rafi are heading towards the building.

'Shall we?' says Hannah. She and Jordan follow. The boy walks with his head down and loping strides.

Rafi accesses the alarm system from his phone. He's giving Xan the full spiel about the high-tech security. Hannah ignores them. She's seen enough office buildings, all basically the same. Woodward junior is far more intriguing.

And possibly useful.

The electronic sliding doors open with a whisper and they all step into a vast echoey space. The floor is shiny and marble-like in appearance, although Hannah suspects it's a cheaper material. There is indeed a small, sad tree in a large tub in the middle. She gazes up the sweeping staircase to the mezzanine level.

Turning to Jordan, she says, 'Pretty cool, huh?'

His shoulders are hunched, his hands deep in his pockets. 'Yeah, it's okay,' he says.

He's big for fourteen and reminds her of one of her nephews. His body is ambushing him in so many ways. Limbs are suddenly out of control. He wears a trademark teenage scowl, but he seems a sweet kid.

'So you're out of school for the time being?' she says.

He nods, looks away.

'I was expelled from school twice,' she says. 'Once for drugs. The other time for some online stuff they didn't like. Nude pics basically.'

He shoots her a startled look. Eyes grey, not blue.

That's got his attention.

It also has the benefit of being largely true. The drugs were no big deal. She was caught with a couple of spliffs. But that school was a small independent girl's grammar in London, with a stellar reputation, but an extremely stuffy head. After that, her parents were forced to go upmarket. This meant classier skiing trips and some great parties at country estates or on the yachts of school friends whose parents had serious money. Hannah preferred it. She didn't feel guilty. Her parents could afford it.

'I think they'll probably expel me,' says Jordan.

'It's no big deal,' says Hannah. 'What matters is your attitude to it.'

He is looking at her now. Shy and boyish, but listening.

'I feel bad,' he says. 'Obviously.'

'No no no,' says Hannah, wagging a finger. 'You can feel bad about your friend. That's personal. And private. But on the outside, it's fuck them. They expel you, it's their loss. Public contrition gets you nowhere, gets you bullied. Just keep thinking, fuck all of them. It's your life.'

Now Jordan Woodward is smiling.

She goes on. 'All you need to do, and you do this for yourself, no one else, is you turn up for the exams and you get A grades. My last school, I was excluded for most of Year 13. I had a tutor at home, and it was a breeze. Four A stars. I got into Oxford, and no one gave a toss about what I did at school.'

'Awesome,' he says with a grin.

'Exactly,' says Hannah. 'Fuck them. No one respects you unless you demand it.'

They spend the next fifteen minutes trailing round the rest of the building. But now he's watching her. Surreptitiously. Admiringly. He's hooked and his hormones'll do the rest.

On the two upper floors, they wander past the glass box offices and into the shell laboratories. Xan has adopted a neutral expression, but it seems to her he's pleased. He takes snaps on his phone to show his wife. He opens the negotiations with a diffident shrug. Hannah leaves him to it.

She joins Jordan, staring out of the window.

'Where's your mum today?' she says.

'Dunno. She leaves all this to dad.'

She leaves too much to dad, which could be the problem.

'I hated my mum for the best part of ten years,' she says. 'Then I realised she was far smarter than I thought. Now we get on really well.'

Jordan sighs. 'My mum's always just… I dunno. Everything's a problem.'

'It's a mother's job to worry. You should cut her some slack.'

'She's impossible to talk to.' She watches his eyes, nervously scanning her.

Not like you, that's what he's thinking. Good.

'Well,' says Hannah. 'She's been taking care of you since you were born, protecting you. And now she can't any more. You're your own man now. Remember that. But it's mega tough on her.'

His shoulders relax; he stands up straighter.

'Yeah, I suppose,' he says in a more manly voice.

Xan comes over.

'What d'you think? They're offering a six-month lease initially, at a competitive rate.'

'What d'you think?' says Hannah.

She knows nothing can happen until HDZ releases the funds.

He shrugs. 'I've knocked him down as far as he can go.'

Rafi is hovering. She strolls over to him.

'Well, Rafi,' she says. 'You've got our interest. But there is something else I need from you.'

'Okay,' he says. 'If I can—'

'Oh, you can. I'll need a one-bed apartment. High spec, centre of the city.'

'No problem,' he says. 'We've got quite a few—'

'Thrown in,' she says. 'By that I mean the cost will be covered in the proposed price of this deal.'

'Oh,' says Rafi, face falling. 'I don't know if my boss'll—'

'He will,' says Hannah. 'Because that's the sweetener we require. Call him, or we move on.'

Rafi looks flustered, but he nods, gets out his phone and scurries off into a corner.

Both Xan and Jordan Woodward are watching her, eyes shining with admiration.

Father and son. Not a combo she's ever tried.

She turns to them and shrugs. 'If I'm spending time up here, I'll need somewhere to stay.'

25

Wednesday, 9.45am

DS Boden strolls through the office. It's the base for the Cambridge unit of the tri-force Major Investigations Team, covering the counties of Bedfordshire, Cambridgeshire and Hertfordshire. But with a shortage of trained detectives and vacancies that can't be filled, many experienced officers like Boden pick up the slack for the local CID. The unit has its own corner, separated off from the rest of CID. It's housed in a dismal sixties block in need of refurbishment.

The radiators are wheezing in a desperate attempt to pump out enough heat. It's quiet for a weekday morning. As Boden settles at her desk, DC Prisha Chakravorty appears, carrying a mug of coffee.

'Morning,' says Chakravorty. 'Thought you were off for a couple of days.'

'Can't afford to be,' Boden replies. 'I need the overtime. I'm never going to get a mortgage unless I up my savings. The rental on my current place is killing me.'

'Weren't you doing duty cover for CID on Monday too?'

'Yep, but Hepburn called me yesterday, asked if I'd come in because he's got three off.'

Chakravorty sips her coffee. 'Tom Roscoe's sprained his ankle, apparently.'

In MIT, Roscoe is the DI with most experience. Several others have come and gone on temporary secondments, but none have met the exacting standards of the boss, DCI Alistair Hepburn. He's a stickler. But he appreciates a solid and capable DS like Boden. She's often asked to step up but keeps resisting the pressure to take the Inspectors exam.

Being promoted to DI would mean a more managerial, office-bound role; it would definitely irk her. Boden likes to get out there, doing the legwork, asking the questions, interacting with people. This is what makes being a cop enjoyable for her. Although the extra money would certainly come in handy.

Boden chuckles. 'Sprained his ankle doing what?'

'Went skiing. With his new girlfriend.' Chakravorty gives her a quizzical smile. 'Aren't you jealous? Just a tiny bit?'

'No!' says Boden. 'We had one date. It was awful. And we both agreed it was a mistake. In the same team. It never works.'

'I think it's 'cause he knows you're a far better detective than him.'

Boden ignores this comment. 'On the subject of annoying men,' she says, 'where's Mackie?'

'On a course.'

'Let hope nothing kicks off. Because frankly, I'm knackered. I could do with a slow day.'

Right on cue, the DCI comes barrelling through the swing doors with a frown on his face. Boden glances at Chakravorty.

Never tempt the fates!

'Jo,' he says, 'Teenage boy died in the multi-storey car park on Monday night? You handled the call out?'

'Yes, sir,' says Boden. 'Accidental death. Report's gone to the coroner.'

Hepburn puffs out his cheeks. 'Dead boy's father plays golf with the Chief Constable and the Police Commissioner.'

Of course he does.

'Alleges his son was put under undue pressure.'

Boden sighs. 'Two fourteen-year-olds, boss. Trying to film a stupid stunt to put on social media. We've got CCTV. I've sent both kid's phones to digital forensics. I doubt they'll find anything untoward, beyond a few dick pics. I've got footage of the dead boy. It's clear he was a willing participant.'

The DCI shakes his head. 'Okay,' he says. 'Call them and tell them to expedite the phones. A full breakdown too. Copy me your report to the coroner. And make sure we've dug under all the rocks.'

WTF?

'If you don't mind me saying so, sir. If this was some kid off an estate, we wouldn't be doing this, would we? It's hardly the best use of resources.'

'No,' says Hepburn, putting his hands on his hips. 'You're right. But his father is a rich businessman with a network of influential connections and levers he knows how to pull. So let's not kid ourselves we live in a classless society with equal justice for all. Just make sure our conclusions are absolutely watertight. I don't want any comebacks or claims of negligence. Got it?'

'Sir.'

He glances at Chakravorty. 'Prisha can help you.' Then he

sighs. ‘Believe me, this pisses me off as much as you. Keep me in the loop.’

He turns on his heel and walks out.

Boden glances at the young DC and sighs.

‘Get yourself a coffee,’ says Chakravorty. ‘I’ll call digital forensics for you and give them the good news.’

Boden smiles. ‘Thanks, Prish.’

26

Wednesday, 10.15am

Cheryl is holed up in her neat and compact office next to the lab. Her neck is stiff, shoulders tense. She glances at her coffee mug. Still full, but stone cold. She must've been sitting here for over an hour. Some of her best ideas have come from periods of intense concentration like this. But today she isn't in the zone, quite the opposite. She has an oppressive headache from too much wine, and her mind is jittery and full of foreboding.

Xan is babysitting their son. He's a fourteen-year-old boy; it shouldn't be necessary. But this is just one aspect of the mess their life is in right now.

How has this happened?

This is what she can't seem to grasp. She married a man she loved, and he loved her. It felt as if her life was finally blossoming; she was becoming the person she always wanted to be. So what happened? How did they get from there to here? It's all too difficult and painful to fathom.

She has to stop this pointless ruminating. Put it aside and focus.

She's staring at her laptop. Displayed on screen are her registered patents, and she's been scrolling between them.

There are five in all, each one in her sole name. These are her inventions turned into concrete assets and protected by the law. Her intellectual property. This is how the system works. She can claim ownership of these things because they're based on her theories and created in her lab. But she's not a one-woman band. She's in charge, but it's a team effort. Ideas are tried, they fail, they're modified, and then you try again. Science is a conversation, as well as a competition. Few things happen in isolation.

Is this fair?

Arran Patel is there in the back of her mind, creating a queasy guilt. The fact he's ended up a down and out, living on the street, feels like a terrible rebuke.

Her failure. She let him down.

There's a polite tap on the door. It opens and Kayleigh Burrows is peering at her.

'You said in your text you wanted a word.'

'Yes,' says Cheryl, smiling. 'Come in and sit down.'

Creating the right relationship with the graduate students and post-doc researchers who work in the lab has always been a problem for Cheryl. She's awkward in company, doesn't waste time on idle chat. Her ideal situation is to work alone. As a small woman, she finds it hard to project herself and act with authority. She prefers to fade into the background, which means she comes over as brusque. She's well aware of this, but can't seem to change it.

Kayleigh takes the chair opposite the desk. There's a gawkiness to her and a tendency to blush for no apparent reason.

'Did you make it to the party?' says Cheryl brightly.

Kayleigh nods. 'Yes. Thank you. It was great.'

They stare at each other.

Too similar, is that the problem?

'Good,' says Cheryl. 'I'm glad you enjoyed yourself. But I just wanted a quick word.'

'Oh, okay,' says Kayleigh, looking even more uncomfortable.

Cheryl has been brooding all night. She still wonders if what she's about to do is a good idea.

Probably not.

She knows what Xan would say. But if an injustice has occurred, she has no choice but to put it right. It's her responsibility. She must act.

'What I wanted to ask,' says Cheryl, 'is, didn't you used to be a close friend of Arran? Arran Patel.'

Kayleigh bristles. 'I wouldn't say close. I had no idea he was faking the data.'

'I know that,' says Cheryl, raising her palm. 'I'm not accusing you of anything. Just wondered if you know what happened to him? If you're still in touch.'

'No,' says Kayleigh emphatically.

'Well,' says Cheryl. 'I saw him yesterday in town. And I hardly recognised him. He appears to be homeless, living on the streets. In fact, my sister and I intervened. Some hooligans were attacking him. He was injured. Had to be taken to hospital.'

Kayleigh blinks a couple of times and leans back in her chair.

Shock?

'Oh,' she says. 'That's… horrible.'

'Have you any idea how he ended up like that?'

Kayleigh seems wary, weighing up what to say next.

'Last time I saw him, he was very depressed,' she says.

'When he left the university, why didn't he go home to his family?'

Kayleigh fidgets in her chair. Again she hesitates. Then she says sourly, 'Dr Woodward. He was chucked out and disgraced. He was so ashamed, he couldn't face his family. His parents sacrificed a lot to pay for his education. He thought he'd let them down.'

Kayleigh is clenching her left fist. Cheryl gets a whiff of anger simmering below the surface.

Were they more than friends?

She tries to remember. Relationships in the lab tend to pass her by. A bunch of twenty somethings; they always seem to be getting in emotional and sexual tangles with each other. She ignores it.

'I didn't know any of this,' she says.

'Why would you? He broke the rules. But he got caught.'

Meaning what? He wasn't the only one?

'You think we treated him badly?' says Cheryl.

Kayleigh shrugs and looks away. 'It's not up to me to say.'

'Except I'm asking you. The university has strict protocols. They were followed. But…well, perhaps his state of mind wasn't sufficiently considered. Maybe he should've been offered proper professional support for his mental health.'

Kayleigh is glaring at her. She folds her arms defensively. It looks like she's struggling to contain her feelings. She takes a breath.

Then it all tumbles out. 'For months he was working eighteen hours a day,' she says, 'because he wanted to prove his theory was right. He was exhausted. And stressed. I guess the temptation was too much. Everyone knows the money that can be made nowadays. You come up with one brilliant idea in your twenties, you're set for life. No more worrying about your student loan or paying the rent.'

Cheryl can see the belligerence in the young woman's eyes. And the naivety.

Do they really think it's that simple?

'It's not quite that easy,' says Cheryl.

'Isn't it?' says Kayleigh. The tone is challenging.

Cheryl decides to ignore it. She's well aware that since the expulsion of Arran Patel nearly a year ago, the work hasn't been progressing as well as she expected. There are underlying tensions and rivalries in any lab. In a competitive field, it's bound to happen. But she's failed to address the situation. Her response has been to ignore it and work long hours checking every bit of data herself.

She sighs. 'I'd like to contact Arran and try to help him get back on his feet,' she says. 'I think it's the least we can do.'

'Why do you think I know where he is?' says Kayleigh. 'You just said he's in hospital.' More belligerence.

'They've probably discharged him. All I'm saying is, if I find him, will you help me?'

Kayleigh frowns. It looks as if another outburst is coming. Then she seems to change her mind. 'Yeah, of course,' she says.

But what's she not saying?

'Good,' says Cheryl.

They exchange nods. Does that mean there's some measure of understanding between them? Impossible to tell. Kayleigh scrapes her chair as she gets up to leave.

Cheryl tries to stretch and ease the tension in her shoulders. She looks out of the window. A dingy car park and beyond belching traffic crawling along the road into town. Xan is not the only one to miss California.

There are eighteen clever and ambitious people working in the lab. Mostly in their twenties. And Kayleigh Burrows may not be the only one to resent her. She's a leader who's failing to lead.

You can't run away all the time and hide in the library. She has a fleeting memory of her schooldays. That grim boarding school. And her big sister shaking her and saying that. And Cheryl crying.

This is a mess. On the outside, Xan has been pushing hard. He has a business plan. And a dream. But she's hesitant because she knows they're not ready. She needs to get the work back on track and the team motivated again. There are no excuses; it's her fault. And she needs time.

What will she tell him? She's no idea.

He'll be mad.

Her phone buzzes. She glances at it. An unknown caller, so she ignores it. But then it occurs to her she gave Arran her card, and it could be him.

She picks up the phone from the desk and answers.

'Dr Woodward,' says a female voice. 'It's Detective Sergeant Boden here. I need to arrange a time to come and speak to your son.'

The police, again?

'Why?' she says.

'Just a few points of clarification. Would later on today be convenient? I know your son's not in school.'

'I don't understand why this is necessary. He's told you what happened.'

'I know. We need to make sure we've got the complete picture. That nothing's been left out.'

Have they found something on his phone?

Cheryl can feel her heart pounding.

This is not good, not good at all.

'I need to speak to my husband. Find a convenient time. Can I call you back on this number?'

'Of course, Dr Woodward. Thank you.'

Cheryl hangs up. Her hand is shaking. She's close to panic. When a mother neglects her children, this is the result. When a wife ignores her husband's needs, he's unfaithful. But it's not about sex with her and Xan. It's about power. The imbalance between them. Ever since she took the job in Cambridge, his ambitions have depended on her and his ego can't cope. She's always known this, sensed the danger, but she hoped that if she loved him enough…

The thoughts swirl in her head.

Blame. Jordan, Xan, Arran Patel.

It feels as though, however hard she tries, she keeps coming up with the wrong answer.

27

Wednesday, 4.28pm

The light is fading. As Cheryl gazes out at the fine drizzle falling in the garden, her nerves are in shreds. Lorna puts a gentle hand on her shoulder.

'It'll be okay,' she says.

How? The police are after Jordan.

It's been an afternoon of panic and frantic calls. Lorna has rearranged meetings to be there.

Jordan is perched on a kitchen stool, head down, texting on his new phone. Sasha has gone for a hastily arranged sleepover at a friend's house.

Since the call from the police, Cheryl has been in a spin. Why does no one see the danger here in the way she does? Her child's life could be ruined.

Xan agreed with her that Lorna's presence would be reassuring.

'Make the cops realise that they're not going to dump the blame for this on our son. Not without a fight,' he said.

And for once her sister and her husband seem to be on the same page.

The meeting is set for four thirty. And the doorbell rings on the dot. Xan goes to answer it.

While he's out of the room, it seems to Cheryl that time is ballooning. She stares at her hands; her knuckles are white. She opens her hand and examines her stubby fingers; eczema from always wearing vinyl gloves in the lab, and the nails are looking ragged

Why is it taking so long?

Finally, he escorts two police officers into the room. The woman who brought Jordan home on Monday evening, plus a young Asian girl, who looks like she should still be at school.

Keep it polite and formal, was Lorna's advice.

'This is DS Boden,' says Xan. 'And…?'

'DC Chakravorty,' says Boden. 'Thank you for agreeing to see us.'

Jordan shoots them a sullen glance and returns to his phone.

'I hope you don't mind,' says Cheryl. 'My sister is here in case we need any legal advice.'

'This is just an informal chat,' says Boden.

'Shall we all sit round the table?' says Xan.

The long dining table has six chairs. There's a certain amount of shifting and shuffling as the adults take their places.

'Come on, Jordie, come and sit next to me,' says Lorna.

He slides into a chair next to his aunt, putting his phone on the table in front of him.

Xan does the same with his phone, but he clicks it to record. 'Hope you don't mind,' he says, smiling at the cop.

The DC does the same with her phone.

'Not at all,' says Boden. 'They're so much a feature of our lives, aren't they? I see you've got a new one, Jordan.'

Another mistake. They'll think he's an over-privileged brat.

Jordan shrugs. Cheryl wishes his expression wasn't quite so petulant. It gives the police totally the wrong impression of the kind of boy he is.

'What we'd like to understand,' says the cop, 'is whose idea was it to go to the car park on Monday night, and what were you hoping to do?'

All eyes turn to Jordan. But he sits up straight and says in a clear voice, 'My idea, because I knew the parents would be out. Ben just told his he was coming over to my house. We wanted to make a video to post online.'

The parents would be out?

Jordan was supposed to be babysitting his sister, but he's making the duplicity sound normal teenage behaviour. And both boys lied.

'Have you done this before?' says the cop.

'Yeah. We've done it loads. Different stunts. Different locations.'

Cheryl feels sick.

'How did you decide who would carry out the stunt and who would film it?'

'We'd take it in turns. But I was better at doing a quick edit and posting.'

'So you did more of the filming?' The cop smiles. 'I've seen some of the footage from your phone. You're a very good cameraman.'

Jordan juts his chin. 'I'm planning to become a director.'

Cheryl glances at him. It's news to her.

'How did Ben feel about doing the stunts?'

'He loved it, cause it made him look great. Meant he got

all the likes. But if you lot have taken my old phone apart, you know that.'

An edge of defiance is creeping into her son's voice. Cheryl tries to catch his eye. But he stares at the cop.

'Your phone will be returned to you,' says Boden.

'Great,' says Jordan. 'Then I'll have two.'

Why is he being sarcastic?

There's an uncomfortable pause. She looks at her hands.

Stay calm.

'I realise this is difficult and upsetting for you, Jordan,' says the cop.

'Do you?' says her son. 'So when are you lot going to sod off and let me get on with my life?'

What!

There's a stunned silence around the table. Xan splutters and almost laughs. Cheryl can't believe what she's just heard. Why on earth would he speak to a police officer like that?

Lorna jumps straight in. 'I think my nephew has been under considerable stress since the death of his best friend.'

Jordan picks up his new phone and checks it.

Why is he behaving like this?

DS Boden raises her eyebrows and says, 'I get that.'

But Cheryl can't keep silent. 'Jordan,' she says. 'I think you should apologise. I know you're upset about Ben. But that sort of language is not acceptable. Nor is your attitude.'

Jordan glares at his mother, shoves back his chair and stands up. 'Like I give a flying fuck about what they think, or the school, or anybody. I've done nothing wrong. Just leave me alone.'

Taking his phone, he stomps out of the room.

Cheryl looks at the two police officers. 'I'm so sorry,' she says. 'This is completely out of character.'

'He's obviously upset,' says Boden.

Cheryl is shaking like a leaf. The police officers' eyes are on her, judging her, concluding she's a terrible mother.

She is a terrible mother.

28

Wednesday, 4.35pm

Hannah has spent a pleasant enough afternoon viewing apartments with Rafi Khan. Once he got over having his arm twisted, they've been getting on well. He's driven her around town, bought her coffee and tried to entertain her with his attempts at banter. His favourite word is epic.

The first apartment Hannah dismissed before they even went inside. Too much traffic pollution at the location. The second she judged too small. They're now on the fifth, and Rafi is looking anxious.

But now she's manoeuvred him into a higher price bracket, Hannah is all smiles.

'Yeah, this is a maybe,' she says, as he holds open the door for her to enter. It's a compact one-bed, on the top floor of a prestigious development, a retro-fit of a beautiful old building in town. Plenty of glass, nice views from the balcony, high spec kitchen.

'Gym in the basement,' he says with a flourish of his hand.

It's furnished as a show flat, in an array of inoffensive neutral shades with the odd splash of colour.

'Furniture included?' she says.

'I'm sure.' He replies with confidence. She suspects he's lying, but she doesn't care. He'll make it work if he hopes to earn his commission.

Hannah wanders around. It smells of paint and cleaning fluid. The engineered wooden flooring flows through the entire apartment like warm honey. The early winter darkness is already closing in. Still, she opens the door onto the balcony and is greeted with a bracing blast of cold, drizzle-laden air.

He's watching her.

'Five floors up,' he says. 'I guarantee you, in daylight, one of the best views in the city.'

She gazes across the rooftops and nods. Twinkling lights, glittering in the rain. Not bad. On a fine day, it's probably spectacular.

'Okay,' she says, nodding.

He grins from ear to ear.

As if she's just offered him a blow job.

He's amusing, but not her type. Too young and eager.

Her phone buzzes in her bag. She gets it out.

'I need to take this,' she says.

He dips his head. 'Take your time. Get the feel of the place. I'll wait outside.'

As he disappears out of the door, she glances at her phone. This is the call she's been waiting for most of the day: Freddie.

'Hey, Fred,' she says. 'How's Germany?'

'German,' he replies. 'But they're being extremely thorough with the vaccine trials, which is why I'm still here. Nat says you've got some questions.'

'Yeah. Tell me about Kayleigh Burrows.'

It sounds like he's in a public place. A murmur of voices; the chinking of cups and cutlery.

She can hear his voice, away from the mic. 'Ein stück Schokoladentorte, bitte.'

Freddie runs on sugar, yet he's tall and willowy without an ounce of fat. His metabolism must be turbo-charged.

'Sorry,' he says. 'Just ordering. I've known her since uni. Very bright. Emotionally, a bit of a train wreck. She had a bad supervisor for her thesis, mucked things up a bit.'

'You think she's got something to prove?'

'Darling, everyone's got something to prove.'

Hannah hesitates. She needs Freddie's advice. But how honest can she afford to be?

'There's huge potential here,' she says. 'But things are a bit chaotic.'

'Chaotic how?'

'Lack of effective leadership. I've talked it over with Nat, and we both think that Cheryl Woodward may need some coaching. Or even someone else at the helm.'

'And you're looking at Kayleigh?'

'She's the one who got in touch.'

He sighs. 'Once I'm back, I'll assess the situation. Advise Nat accordingly.'

Little shit!

'Obviously. But in the meantime, do you think Kayleigh is the kind of person we could be looking for?'

'Well,' he sighs again. 'That depends. Hang fire would be my advice.'

Miserable, conniving bastard! He's doesn't want to be cut out of the loop.

'Okay,' says Hannah. 'You're the boss.'

'Whatever you find out, call me. We'll discuss it.'

In your dreams.

'Absolutely,' she says. 'I think you're right. There's no need to rush.'

'Exactly. Now can I eat my cake?'

'Of course. Enjoy!'

She hangs up. With any luck, he'll choke on it. But that's not something she can rely on. So she has to move fast. Dig in and make sure everyone agrees she's indispensable. This is her deal. No way Freddie Turner is going to swan in and take it over.

29

Wednesday, 4.45pm

He dozes fitfully. He's been in hospital since yesterday. When he woke this morning, they gave him a meal. Then, it can only have been a few hours later, they gave him another.

One day. Two lots of food!

He fingers the dressing on his forehead. The pain is a background ache, dull and constant. He's cleaner than he's been for a long while. People in blue theatre scrubs have paused at the bottom of his bed a couple of times. He ignores them. Eventually they disappear. The cannula is gone from his arm.

He allows his thoughts to skate over what happened. But most of it is already gone. He knows he has to let it fade.

No kids on skateboards.

When he first became homeless, he developed his *special technique.* He divided his brain into discrete compartments. Whatever happened to him, the bad things he kept on the outside. If you don't think about them, refuse to accept them, they're not real. You can teach your brain to believe this. His body may bear the scars, but his mind keeps the damage at bay. It doesn't exist.

But since then, his thoughts have become more random. His mind has wandered into a strange place. He sees things. Hears things. They warn him.

If it was her, she probably set the skateboarders on him. Paid them to do it.

A tubby little woman pushing a trolley stops at the end of his bed. He watches her through half-closed lids.

She smiles. 'You want tea?'

He nods. She pours from a massive teapot and places the mug on his bedside table.

She smiles again. 'You want biscuit?'

Suddenly, her kindness overwhelms him. He can't reply. There are kind people in the world, honest people.

Don't cry!

His head hurts. His vision is swimming with tears. She watches him for a moment. Then takes two chocolate chip cookies and places them beside the mug. The trolley moves on.

He reaches over for the mug and picks it up. Warm sweet tea. He rolls it round his mouth. The biscuit has a rough, crumbly surface. He takes a bite.

Actual chocolate.

He nibbles the biscuits as slowly as he can, like a small mouse.

Mindful. He went on a course once, where they taught you to eat a raisin. But that was in another life. Another man. Another place in time.

Forget about that.

The ward is busy with people coming and going. Blue scrubs, mauve scrubs, visitors with flowers. Living on the street has taught him to become oblivious to the constant stream of bodies passing by. So he doesn't notice her at first. It seeps into his consciousness. Someone's standing at the end of his bed staring at him. How long has she been there? Their eyes meet.

Kayleigh?

She gives him a sad little smile. 'Hey, Arran.'

Sounds like Kayleigh.

'How d'you find me?'

'Someone told me.'

This is confusing and unexpected. He points to his forehead. 'I got beat up.'

'So I hear.'

He scans her. He's got to be careful. The mind can play tricks. And he has had a bang on the head.

'You real?' he says. 'Only sometimes I see things. People talk to me, but they're not there.'

She moves forward along the side of the bed, gliding almost, stretches out her arm and gently touches his hand.

'Feel that?' she says.

Fingers, actual flesh brushing the back of his hand. Not vinyl gloves. Skin.

'Yeah,' he says. He looks up at her. It's definitely Kayleigh.

'I must stink,' he says.

She smiles. 'Not too bad. I quite like the beard.'

He rubs his face. He's forgotten about the beard. It's part of who he is now.

'I've been talking to the nurse,' she says.

'They want to boot me out, don't they?'

'They want you to have a proper place to go. I said you can come and stay with me.'

No! It's a trap.

He turns away, shakes his head, even though it hurts.

'Can't,' he says. 'I'll stay here until they boot me out.'

They sent her.

'Arran, listen to me. You need proper help.' She keeps touching his hand.

'No, I don't. I'm better on my own.'

'Please, Arran. I'm begging you. Come home with me.' Her fingers clasp his hand; he pulls away.

An idea drops into his mind, like a pebble in a well.

'Did we… get married?' he says.

She's standing quite close. Too close. 'No,' she says. 'But we were engaged. We had a lovely party in that country pub near the river. In fact, I was there yesterday. But it was too cold to go out onto the terrace. Do you remember it?'

Is she crying? She's silent. But her cheeks are wet. Why?

'No,' he says.

Long time since he's been near a pub. The bouncers chase him off.

'I can help you.' She wipes her face with the back of her hand. 'Let me help you, please.'

This is making him nervous. He's panicking. Stuck in this bed, flat on his back. He's trapped.

'Everyone thinks I'm crazy,' he says. 'I'm not crazy. I know what they did to me.'

'I talked to your mum on the phone.'

'You didn't tell them where I am? It'll kill my father if he finds out.'

'Arran—'

This is getting desperate. 'Promise me you won't tell them. You have to promise me.'

'Arran, he died. Your dad died. You know that. It's nine months ago now. Your mum really needs to see you.'

He died? She's lying. She must be.

'I can't risk it.'

'You can. You have to trust me. It'll be alright.'

She's a smart woman. How can she be so naïve?

Just tell her the truth.

'You know they did this, don't you?' he says. 'She was there. Stood over me. I saw her. I always told you what they were capable of. But no one believed me.'

'Who do you mean?'

'She gave me her card. But I knew. So I threw it away.'

'Arran, let's take one step at a time. First, you need to come home with me. Rest up. Get well again.'

'You think I don't know her name? I know her name. Dr Cheryl Woodward. That's her name.'

'I know.'

'Then why do you make out you don't? She did this. They want to shut me up. I knew it would come. I've been expecting it.'

'Don't get upset.'

He's not upset. Not at all. Why doesn't she understand? Speaking about it is a relief. The danger he lives with every day. The fear.

'If she knew you were talking to me,' he says, 'you'd be in danger too. I'm just trying to protect you. Stay off the grid. Stay safe. It's the only way.'

'Well, let's think about this, Arran. If they did this, then they know where to find you. You're not off the grid, are you? But if you're with me, or around other people, like now, then you're protected. They can't do anything, can they? Think about it, it's logical.'

He thinks about it. It is logical. She could be right.

'You saying you can hide me?'

'Let me help you.'

He's so weary. His head hurts.

Kayleigh. Is it really her?

How do you know who to trust?

30

Wednesday, 9.35pm

Jordan has shut himself in his room. Since the police left, Cheryl has made three attempts to communicate with her son. They've all floundered.

'Leave him be. Let him simmer down,' said Xan.

She didn't. She stormed into his room, demanding an explanation.

Her son had shrugged. 'Like you give a shit what happens to me?'

Attack to defend. He's learnt that from Xan.

'Don't use that language to me, Jordan,' she said. 'I won't have it. And I won't be manipulated by my own son. Now if there's something here, something that's happened, you'd better come clean and tell me now.'

'Like what?'

'I don't know,' said Cheryl. 'But the police must be suspicious about something. What?'

He was staring at his PlayStation. Outside it was black

and raining. Cheryl could only see his profile from the light on the screen. His lip was trembling. She only got a glimpse. It was momentary. But it broke her heart.

This is her boy!

She put her hand on his shoulder. 'Jordie,' she said. 'I just—'

'Mum, I don't know what they want. What they expect me to say.' He'd morphed back into a child, his voice timid and pleading. The bad language and aggression were gone. His eyes were full of tears.

Her little boy.

Her anger evaporated. She stroked his hair. 'Okay,' she said. 'It's going to be alright.'

An hour later, when he failed to come down for the beans on toast his father had cooked, Cheryl took a plate up to him. They didn't speak. She rubbed the back of his head. He let her.

When she looked in again, he'd fallen asleep. Or he was pretending. But the beans had been eaten. She cleared the plate away and turned on the small Buzz Lightyear lamp, a relic of his childhood that had been dumped in a corner.

The police had seemed less bothered by Jordan's outburst than Cheryl. The sergeant left another card. And that was that. Lorna assured her they were used to people swearing at them.

'He's a teenager. He's scared and upset and therefore reactive,' said Lorna. 'They'll get that.'

'Will they?'

Lorna had left for a special dinner date. It was her wife's birthday. Cheryl used to worry about her sister's unconventional lifestyle. Now she envied her happiness. Lorna didn't much care what other people thought of her; what mattered, she once said, was what she thought of herself.

Cheryl is pondering this as she returns to the kitchen with her son's dirty plate. Xan takes it from her and puts it in the dishwasher. They're left facing each other. Sasha is away at her sleepover, Jordan is upstairs, leaving them alone together. This rarely happens nowadays. She looks at him. His expression is detached, neutral, but also indifferent.

How did they turn into these people?

'Glass of wine?' says Xan.

Cheryl nods. Not because she wants wine, she probably doesn't. But knowing what you want all the time takes so much effort. Allowing her husband to take the lead, and acquiescing, is easier. It's a habit. Like letting him drive when they go out.

'White or red?' he says.

'You choose.'

He takes a bottle of Sauvignon Blanc from the fridge and pours two glasses.

'What do you think will happen?' says Cheryl.

'Not a lot,' says her husband. 'I agree with Lorna. It's a box ticking exercise. The report will go to the coroner. Eventually there'll be a hearing. Accidental death. Jordan'll get on with his life.'

'You're very sanguine.'

Xan shrugs. 'I see no reason not to be.'

Cheryl sips her drink. 'I couldn't believe it when he swore at them.'

Xan chuckles and raises his glass. 'Balls of steel,' he says. 'That boy'll go far.'

'Don't admire him for this, Xan.'

'Why not? I'm pleased he can stand up for himself.'

She considers this. Her husband has always been so good with Jordan. From the moment they met, when her son was five, Jordan has adored Xan. Preferred Xan.

Is she jealous? Probably.

'He told me I didn't care about him,' she says.

'Oh, come on,' says Xan. 'He's trying to wind you up. Teenage boys have to separate from their mothers. Much easier for girls.'

Cheryl sighs. 'I've made such a mess of things.'

He pats her shoulder in a comradely way. 'Don't be daft.'

'Crap mother. And crap wife. That sums it up, doesn't it?' She meets his gaze, then takes a long swallow of wine.

He tilts his head and sighs. 'Don't do this to yourself, Cheryl. It's been a tough couple of days. Just let it go.'

She shakes her head. 'Why can't we just be honest? I must be a crap wife. If I wasn't, you'd want to come home to me, wouldn't you?'

He looks at her. Impossible to know what he's thinking. The eyes are supposed to be the window of the soul. But Xan's have always seemed more like a barrier, a dazzling blue facade to keep everyone at bay. He huffs and takes a mouthful of wine.

'I always come home to you,' he says.

It's not enough. Can't he see that?

'Yeah. Afterwards. After you've screwed someone else. Someone you prefer. Someone better. Is it that PR girl? I don't know her name.'

He sighs. 'Don't do this,' he says. 'Not tonight. We don't need this nonsense tonight.'

Nonsense. The curt dismissal cuts. He turns away and checks his phone.

She watches him from behind. His broad shoulders. Solid and reliable. When she married him, it felt as if those broad shoulders would protect her from the world. In many ways, they have. What she never imagined, is that she'd need protecting from him too.

There's never been physical violence. She can't accuse him of that. But he's so much bigger than her. And last night she sensed it; it was palpable. He had to hold himself back. But she felt the threat. The possibility of what might happen if this time she doesn't comply. He has a look he gives her from time to time. Diamond hard. As if he's saying: *don't even try it.*

But she won't be shut down and dismissed. Not tonight.

'I don't understand why you don't just divorce me,' she says. 'Wouldn't that be easier for both of us?'

He exhales and gives her an exasperated look. 'I love you. Why would I divorce you? You overthink these things, Cheryl. And it makes you paranoid.'

He goes back to his phone, thumbing a text. Who to? He doesn't say.

Her? The PR girl.

This is how it always goes. He makes her seem the unreasonable one. The nagging wife. Jealous. Paranoid. She watches him, ignoring her. He thinks he's so good at this. And it riles her.

You know what'll get his attention.

'I went through the patents this morning,' she says. 'For the pitch to HDZ.'

He glances at her. 'Good.'

'I'm a bit worried one of them could be challenged.'

He frowns. 'What do you mean?'

His anxiety is weirdly gratifying.

Now who's paranoid?

She pours herself another glass of wine and adopts a matter-of-fact tone. 'It's just the way we started to work on the question of vasculature at the beginning of last year,' she says.

'Cheryl, if it was all done under your supervision—'

'Initially, I dismissed this idea. I reckon that's why Arran got impatient and started faking data. It was only later, when he'd left, that I saw how we could make it work.'

Partly true.

'Arran? Not that fucking researcher you had to sack?'

'Xan, I told you. He's living on the streets. I feel guilty because he sowed the seed.'

Xan is scowling. His phone, his text, abandoned. His attention is firmly on her.

'I told you at the time you need to be tough. Getting rid of him was the right thing. You can't have people faking data.'

'Yes, but don't we have an obligation?'

'Bullshit,' he says. 'Why are you caving in now? Because you feel sorry for him? Sowing the bloody seed? Who else have you said that to?'

'I'm not sure.'

Let him squirm. He deserves it.

Xan huffs. 'Why didn't you tell me this before about the patents?'

'I don't think we've done anything wrong. Plenty of people have vague ideas. Applying them and making them work—'

'There's a great deal of money at stake here, Cheryl.'

'I think it's more that we have a moral obligation.'

He stares at her in disbelief. 'A what? Listen, we can't say this to HDZ. Not any of this.'

'Why not?' She manages a disingenuous smile.

Xan erupts. He slams his palm on the kitchen counter. 'Oh yeah, and while we're at it, maybe pay a few mil to someone whose paper you read last year that made you think a bit.' He rakes his hand through his hair in exasperation. He does this when he's mad. 'Jesus wept, Cheryl! The patents must be watertight. Fuck this damned researcher. He was working for you.'

She watches. There's an odd satisfaction in rattling his cage. She knows she's being spiteful, but she can't help herself.

Don't go too far.

'Well,' she says. 'You know I don't get all the legal stuff in the way you do. So I'll leave it up to you to decide what's best. I don't want to make waves.'

He's scanning her. His jaw is set, and with that chilly look in his eyes. As if he hates her. Perhaps he does?

'Yeah,' he says curtly. 'You're right. You'd best leave it to me.'

Don't cry or let him see the pain.

'No problem,' she says. 'I'm going to bed.'

She walks out of the kitchen towards the stairs. It's a tiny victory, pathetic really. But she's more than entitled to it, surely? All she's doing is playing him at his own game.

But is it worth it? She swallows down the tears.

31

Thursday, 9.15am

The outside door to the flat is accessed down a narrow alley, which is full of bins. Hannah wrinkles her nose at the stench of urine.

She was in the gym, doing her early morning workout and considering her next move, when she received a text from Kayleigh Burrows asking if they could meet again. And if this is where she lives, then it's no surprise. Who wouldn't be looking for a way out of here?

There are three doorbells. Hannah presses the top one, marked Burrows, as she balances the two takeaway coffees she's brought.

Seconds pass, then a muffled sound within, which turns out to be someone clumping down the stairs. This place is pretty basic, not even an entry phone.

The door opens and Kayleigh peers at her, bleary-eyed.

'Oh,' says Hannah. 'Hope I'm not too early.'

'It's fine. Come in.'

The communal hall and stairs are covered in a dull grey vinyl. Grit has accumulated in the corners. There's a smell of stale air laced with rancid bacon fat, though it's hard to tell where it's coming from.

Kayleigh leads the way back up to the top floor. The last flight of stairs is much cleaner; she must regard this as her territory. There's a dusty skylight high above and a surprisingly healthy looking rubber plant outside the door to the flat.

Kayleigh pauses before entering and says, 'Can you keep your voice down?'

Hannah nods.

Intriguing.

Boyfriend? Flat mate? Girlfriend? No one's been mentioned.

Hannah follows Kayleigh into a narrow hallway, which smells of lavender air freshener. The contrast with the rest of the building is stark. A neat hall runner in a stylish geometric pattern. They turn to the right and into the sitting room. The walls are lined with bookshelves, loaded with neat rows of alphabetised books. In between, there are some tasteful prints and a poster for a classical concert at one of the colleges. Everything is symmetrical; evidence of Dr Burrows' tidy scientific mind.

A small IKEA sofa and a Scandi style rocking chair with a bendy wooden frame sit on either side of a metal framed coffee table. A singleton's bolt hole? Kayleigh herself may be a bit of a lump who lacks style, but her flat is tasteful.

'I brought coffee,' whispers Hannah.

'Oh, thanks,' says Kayleigh, accepting the proffered cup. She looks nervous, as if she's having second thoughts about whatever she was planning to say.

Without waiting to be invited, Hannah sits on the chair.

'I love your place,' she says with a big smile. 'So many books.'

Kayleigh puts her coffee on the table and closes the door.

'Oh no, don't want to wake your flatmate,' says Hannah.

Kayleigh sighs. She looks a complete wreck, as if she's been on an all night bender and the paracetamol hasn't kicked in yet.

'I don't want him to hear what we're saying,' she replies. 'It'll freak him out.'

'Okay,' says Hannah, removing the lid from her coffee.

Weird or what?

Kayleigh manages a ghostly smile. She perches on the lip of the sofa, hands tightly clasped. 'I've been awake all night,' she says, 'trying to decide what to do. What would be for the best. And, well, you seem like a decent person. So I'm going to appeal to your better nature. I need your help.'

Oh no, she's not going to beg. Gross.

'To do what?' says Hannah.

Cash? A dinner date with the awful Freddie? Could be anything.

'To get urgent private psychiatric treatment for Arran.'

Hannah gives her a puzzled frown. 'Who's Arran? Your flatmate?'

'He was my boyfriend. He worked in the lab. But he got used, and discarded. The whole process sucked him dry, and he had a breakdown.'

'I'm sorry to hear that.'

'He's been living on the streets.'

'How awful?' Hannah sips her coffee. She's wishing she'd opted for the mocha.

'It is awful. And do you know how long the waiting list is for mental health referrals on the NHS?'

Hannah has no idea; her father and now her firm have

always paid for private medical insurance. She's only ever been to A&E once, when she got drunk as a student.

Kayleigh is staring at her. 'He's completely fallen through the system. I just want to get him the help he needs.'

Hannah sighs. 'Have you talked to Cheryl about this? Because it's not really—'

'Yes, and I don't trust her. She means well. But she can't stand up to Xan.'

'Surely she runs the lab. And the university could do something.'

'Everyone's going to make a lot of money, aren't they?'

'We hope so.'

'Then make Xan do it. Pay for private treatment at a proper facility. I bet he'll listen to you. And if you want my help, I need you to do this.'

Hannah sighs again. 'Um, well, I don't know what to say.'

Kayleigh meets her gaze; the eyes are the colour of pewter. She has a steeliness about her she obviously prefers to keep under wraps. But it's on full display now.

She laces her fingers. 'I'm not going to make accusations,' she says. 'Not unless I have to. But Arran's ideas were crucial. Cheryl built on them. She wouldn't have got to where we are now without him.'

Oh shit.

'You saying she stole his ideas?'

'I'm saying get him the urgent help he needs. Then we won't need to go into any of that, will we?'

Kayleigh is staring right at her. She's underestimated this nerdy lab rat, and as attempts at blackmail go, it's both clever and subtle.

32

Thursday, 11.25am

Hannah stands on the balcony of her new flat. Of course, nothing is signed and sealed, and this whole deal could fall apart. But she's determined to keep a positive mindset.

It's a cold morning, but shafts of wintery sunshine are filtering through the cloud base. The effect is dramatic. Laid out before her is a drone's eye view of Cambridge. She can see many of the ancient colleges, the weathered stone and historic towers. Trees fringing the river. The place is surprisingly attractive.

Kayleigh Burrows' little early morning zinger has thrown a spanner in the works. But she's been considering the problem and realised, like all setbacks, it contains the kernel of an opportunity. One she plans to exploit.

Hannah agreed to help Kayleigh. Obviously, she did. There was little choice. She also expressed her horror at Arran's plight. Kayleigh seemed reassured. She'd grabbed

Hannah's hand, tears welling in her eyes, and thanked her. It was embarrassing.

And as they emerged from the sitting room, Hannah caught a glimpse of him. Kayleigh had just opened the front door for her to leave when a shambling figure emerged from the bedroom. The feral smell hit Hannah first. His hair and beard were one dark, matted mess. He was wearing flowery women's pyjamas, presumably Kayleigh's, and half his head was bandaged. He avoided her eye, and clutching his genitals, scurried into the bathroom and slammed the door.

Kayleigh had turned and given her a piteous look.

In sickness and in health had always struck Hannah as a stupid commitment for anyone to make. And this couple wasn't even married. If any of her ex's had turned into a batshit crazy tramp, she'd would've dumped them flat. No question.

Hannah checks her phone. Nearly half eleven. She's getting impatient. Whatever the arrangement, it seems Xan Woodward is always late. She steps off the chilly balcony and back into the warm interior just as the doorbell rings.

She takes her time answering. His turn to wait. Xan has brought his son with him again, which is annoying. He does a circuit of the open-plan living area with a huge grin on his face.

'This is so nice,' he says.

He's probably imagining it's going to become his little shag pad, his home from home, where he comes for illicit sex. He can think again.

'Well,' says Hannah coldly. 'Nothing's finalised. At present, we're just making an offer. Contracts need to be signed before we can release our investment.'

He scans her face. 'Yeah, and Cheryl needs to make a

formal presentation to your bosses. But she's really fired up. The sooner the better.'

'Great.'

Jordan is watching them surreptitiously, as his eyes flick back and forth to his phone.

Hannah smiles at him. 'How's it going?' she says.

'Yeah, y'know,' he replies.

'Little devil swore at the police' says Xan, although he doesn't sound annoyed.

'Did you?' says Hannah, chuckling. 'That was bad.' She gives him a mock frown. He grins. The tops of his ears are turning pink.

She pulls out a credit card. 'Don't suppose you fancy going down to the coffee shop?'

'Yeah, no worries,' Jordan replies. He's eager to please her, which is nice. Testosterone is a wonderful thing; it makes teenage boys so pliable.

Xan pulls out his card. 'Nah, this is on me.'

A couple more minutes of shilly-shalling, discussing their orders, and she finally gets Jordan out of the door.

Xan folds his arms and looks her up and down. 'Your text said it was urgent.' He gives her a rakish grin.

This is getting tedious. A shag is a shag. Move on.

'It is.' She takes a couple of steps away. 'We have a problem. You know who Arran Patel is?'

That wipes the smile off his face. Xan exhales. 'Has Cheryl called you?'

'No.'

'Then how do you know about him?'

'So there is something to know?'

Xan rubs his chin and shakes his head. 'Listen, it's complicated—'

'No, Xan, it's very simple. If this guy who worked in your

wife's lab can claim he's entitled to be named in her patents, then our whole investment could be called into question.'

He stares at her, raising his palm. 'Hang on—'

'But that's only part of the problem. Kayleigh Burrows is an old friend of my colleague, Freddie Turner. They went to uni together. Her connection with Freddie is the reason we're here. And, I've just discovered, she's the former girlfriend of Arran Patel.'

He frowns, playing catch up. 'I didn't know that.'

'You can see that poses a problem. Now, I know Freddie and how he operates. It's clear he sees Kayleigh taking over the lab. That's the hidden agenda here.'

'What?' A look of horror spreads across his face.

Gotcha.

'And once he learns Cheryl's claim to be the sole originator of this work is compromised—'

'It isn't. That's rubbish. Arran Patel was sacked for faking his data.'

'Let me paint a picture for you, Xan. Freddie will come in all smiles. He's a charming guy, and very clever. And my boss really respects him. Everything will move ahead, you'll receive the seed capital, you'll become CEO. But Freddie will pack the board, then he'll use the question of Arran to undermine Cheryl's position. She'll end up side-lined in her own lab. You'll object and that'll put you at loggerheads with Freddie.'

'This is bloody ridiculous. This is my company, mine and Cheryl's.'

'Within three months, the board'll vote you out.'

His jaw is slack. He puts his hands on his hips and glares at her. When his blood is up, he's menacing.

Quite a turn-on.

'Fine,' he says. 'You can fuck right off. We don't want

your bloody money. There are plenty of other VC firms into biotech. Some of them came to the party. We'll go elsewhere.'

'Will you?'

'Too fucking right.'

'But you've still got the Arran Patel problem.'

'Who's going to listen to him? He's nuts, and he's been living on the streets.'

'Come on Xan. You know how this works. One toxic rumour can poison the whole well.'

He laughs in disbelief. 'Are you threatening me?'

'No. I'd call this more of a reality check.'

'What?'

Her ploy is working. He's been thrown onto the back foot, so he's not questioning Freddie's supposed motives.

'So, let's break this problem down and sort it out,' she says. 'Kayleigh wants proper psychiatric help for Arran. That buys her silence and co-operation and, you're right, I've seen him. Once he's in the rubber room, he's out of the equation. Freddie's currently in Germany. You and I need to take Cheryl to London asap to deliver a dynamite pitch to Nat. Nat signs off. Then I will come up with a list of board members, and I will cover your back.'

He's scanning her face; calculating.

'You think that'll work?'

'Yes.'

'And why would you do this for me?'

His anger's abating. The hook is in.

'Because it's obvious you're the real deal,' she says. 'And it's in my interests to back you. This is a business, and someone's got to take a firm hand and run it.'

He juts his chin. He agrees with that, or rather his ego does.

She tilts her head and gives him the girly smile. 'I think you're the best person to manage your wife. I believe she can turn this work into a major scientific breakthrough. But while she's doing that, we have to control expectations and the narrative. And I can do that. That's how I do my job and get the best return on investment for my firm. You just have to trust me.'

He inhales and rubs his chin. He's buying it.

'It's true we have to manage expectations,' he says. 'But what will Freddie do?'

'Fred's pragmatic. He'll move on, find another deal.'

Once she's in the driving seat and has Nat's backing, he'll have no choice.

He folds his arms and takes a turn around the room.

'Okay,' he says. 'And what do I do now?'

'Go and see Kayleigh. Get her onside. We'll find a way to cover this idiot's treatment. C'mon, it's small change.'

He nods; then he slowly smiles.

Yes! He's going for it.

'And in the middle of this, do I still get to sleep with you?'

She responds with a coy smile. 'I'll have to think about that.'

Men are so easy.

He steps forward and runs his fingertips up her arm.

Fortunately, Jordan arrives on cue with the coffees. Hannah makes a big fuss of the boy. Joking around and joshing him. She's coming to the conclusion his presence could prove a useful way of keeping his old man's libido in check.

But, for the time being, job done.

33

Thursday, 5.25pm

The bedroom in Kayleigh's flat is small and cosy. He remembers it from before. The soft white duvet and the two original watercolours on the wall facing the bed. Isn't her cousin a painter? He's not sure. He's not sure of anything.

But being in the warm, in a soft bed, and clean pyjamas is soothing. His head still throbs, but Kayleigh brings him painkillers, and toast, and milky coffee.

She doesn't say much. Her smile is so sad. She seems to be waiting.

He's been here maybe a night and a day? In the night, he slept alone. Now he's drifting. There's noise from the street; traffic, sirens. But it's outside. He's inside, in this cocoon. It feels as if he could rest here. Let go a bit. Really sleep. Not the fitful catnaps, where he wakes in a panic. But proper deep sleep. If only he could turn off his brain. Switch off. Reset. Reboot. That's what he needs.

Earlier, when he heard voices, he wondered if they were real. Soft whisperings seeping through the walls.

The mind plays tricks.

He was desperate for a piss, so he got up and went to the bathroom. And he saw this woman. She was real.

Kayleigh said it was just a neighbour. And Kayleigh doesn't lie. She's one of the few people he's ever met who doesn't. Besides his mother. But he can't think about her.

She must be so ashamed.

The shame tears at him, ripping his flesh like a ravenous monster. He's let her down. Let everyone down. He punches his bandaged forehead with his fist. That pain is better. Stops him thinking.

Don't think!

Kayleigh comes and goes. She doesn't talk. A mug of tea with milk and sugar.

For ages he watches the light wandering across the wall, shadows gathering in the corners of the room, as the day fades. But he's never minded the dark; even as a kid. It can make you invisible. But winter nights are long and cold. He's lucky to be inside.

Kayleigh brings him soup. She turns on the bedside lamp.

'Minestrone,' she says. 'Wasn't that your favourite?'

He nods. He can't remember, but he wants to please her.

She's a good person. Unlike him.

She perches on the end of the bed and watches him eat.

The soup is tasty. Kayleigh smiles. Everything has slowed right down, which helps. He's emptied his bowl.

The doorbell rings.

'Oh,' she says, frowning. 'I don't know who that could be.'

She gets up and leaves the room. And something changes. It's imperceptible. At first, he can't quite grasp it. An odd, visceral sensation. It comes from nowhere; beginning in his gut, it shoots up through his belly and explodes into his chest.

This is not good. Not good!

He shoves the tray aside, but his hand is shaking. He gets out of bed.

There's a voice in his head; he's heard it before, low and wretched.

Run! Before it's too late. Run!

The trackie bottoms and the old sweatshirt they gave him at the hospital are folded on the back of a chair. He grabs them and pulls them on over his pyjamas.

Shoes? Where are his shoes?

He wrenches open the cupboard. At the bottom, there are some trainers. He grabs them and rams his feet into them. They're too small. He flings them aside.

Voices!

He can hear them in the hall, close, too close, just the other side of the thin door.

'Cheryl insisted I come. She believes we owe it to Arran to help…'

Cheryl? A man's voice?

His pulse is thudding. He struggles to breathe. Is this a panic attack?

He sits on the bed. There's a drill. Remember the drill. He dips his head between his knees and it helps. Then back up. Deep breaths.

They've gone into the sitting room. And Kayleigh has closed the door. He must get out now. This will be his only chance.

Run!

Fear gives him the adrenaline he needs. Forget the shoes. He opens the bedroom door, lumbers down the hall, and pulls open the front door.

He's running down the stairs. Tumbles, then picks himself up.

A voice shouts after him. 'Arran!'

Is it Kayleigh? He can't be sure.

Get out! Run!

The cold hits him. It's raining. But he's out in the street. His bare feet lost their tenderness months ago. He's used to them being blistered and raw. Broken glass in the alley; none of it matters.

Which way?

The street looks familiar. And now he remembers, this place is close to the river. His old haunts. If he can get down there among the trees, he'll find a place to hide. No one goes there after dark in the winter.

He stumbles along, but he's making progress. It's pouring with rain, so not many people about. They pass him with umbrellas dipped forward, faces down. No one's interested.

He heads for Sheep's Green Bridge; there's cover there. Places to hide.

Then he hears it. Heavy footsteps behind him. Someone is running, splashing. Getting closer.

They're after him! Course they are!

He's always known this is how it would end.

'Arran! Stop! I want to help you.' Man's voice.

They're near the bridge. His pursuer is closing on him, sploshing through the puddles.

'Oh, for fuck's sake, Arran!' Same voice. A looming figure behind him, breathing hard.

As they hit the bridge, a hand grabs his shoulder and spins him round. The man is bigger. His grip is powerful. He shoves him against the metal railings. The steel bites into his back, knocking the wind out of him.

'You know how much trouble you've caused me, you

mad sod!' The man stands there, hands on hips, panting. 'You know who I am?'

He knows. And he knows what he must do. Taking a breath, he launches himself forward, fists flying, taking his pursuer by surprise. He can't see what he's hitting but something connects. One good punch. The man grunts and falls back.

Run!

But as Arran turns to escape, it comes at him from nowhere, the iron blow smashing into his face. His head ricochets backwards, his nose cracks and the pain explodes in a dizzying kaleidoscope of lights before the darkness comes screaming towards him. He's tumbling and falling into it; there's nothing he can do. But then the pain melts away, and the fall becomes rapturous. A silky soft pillow of blackness is enfolding him, cradling him and carrying him away.

34

Thursday, 7.25pm

Outside, it's a wet and windy night. Cheryl is curled up on one of the large squidgy sofas with her daughter snuggled beside her. They're watching something on the Disney channel. It washes over her; the dancing animals, the jaunty music. She let Sasha choose. Jordan is on the opposite sofa, feet up, scrolling and texting on his phone. But at least she has both her children there, in the same room.

She gave them pizza for dinner; always a popular choice. Jordan ignored the salad that went with it. But she didn't chastise him. Earlier in the day, she talked the situation over on the phone with her sister.

Lorna may be childless herself, but her understanding, as with most things, seems far deeper than Cheryl's.

'You can't manage him all the time,' she said. 'He has to find his own way through this.'

'I just want to protect him. He could've been killed.'

'Problem is,' said her sister, 'he has to learn how to

protect himself. How's he going to develop his own judgement if you're trying to control his every move? That just makes him react to you.'

Cheryl listened; she didn't mention Xan's tracker. She knew what her sister would say about that.

She also knew the arguments Lorna was making, the liberal point of view. Ever since he was little, it's been let him roll in the dirt, scrape his knees, fall off his bike. She couldn't be that sort of laissez-faire parent; it wasn't in her.

She strokes her daughter's hair. At least Sasha seems grateful for the care being bestowed upon her. But how long will that last? Apart from maternity leave, Cheryl's always worked full time; a combination of desire and necessity. And their childhoods have flashed by. Only moments ago, it seems, her daughter was a boisterous toddler. But by then, they employed a nanny; Xan had insisted.

She lets her mind drift to her husband. After last night's argument, he appears to have had a complete change of heart. When she got home from work, he informed her she was right about Arran Patel, and he was going to do something about it.

She apologised and said she'd handled the thing badly. He didn't really respond. He was in a hurry to go out. A game of squash, he said. But he wanted her to think about the pitch to HDZ; it needed to happen as soon as possible. She didn't argue. It left her with that miserable feeling of letting her husband down again.

As the end credits on the movie roll, Cheryl looks at her two beautiful children. She loves her work, but now, in this moment, with the two of them, she feels a rush of love and happiness. They give her life the most meaning.

'Okay,' she says, clapping her hands. 'Who wants hot chocolate?'

'Me!' Sasha replies.

Jordan gives her a speculative glance. 'With marsh-mallows?'

'Have we got any?' she says.

Her son gets up and heads for the kitchen. She and her daughter follow.

'I'm going to need some help,' she says.

As Jordan unearths the marshmallows, Sasha brings a carton of milk from the fridge.

'He's eating them!' squeals Sasha. 'That's not fair.'

Jordan pulls a marshmallow from the bag, tosses it up in the air and catches it in his mouth. His sister laughs.

'My turn! My turn!' she says.

He tosses it, but then shoves her out of the way so he can get it.

Cheryl wants to tell him to be careful. Not to be rough. But she stops herself.

Sasha grabs the bag and a brief marshmallow fight ensues. The pink and white puffs end up scattered across the floor. Jordan gets down on his hands and knees and eats them like a dog. Sasha laughs and follows suit. Cheryl watches them. She tries not to think about the mess. How dirty the floor might be. Her sister's advice echoes in her head.

Stop trying to control them. They're having fun.

'C'mon,' she says. 'They'll be none left for the hot chocolate.'

Out in the hall, the front door slams. Sasha jumps to her feet.

'Daddy's home,' she says, running to meet him.

Cheryl gets a saucepan down from the hook and pours milk into it.

Xan appears in the doorway from the hall, holding his daughter's hand.

'He's hurt,' says Sasha in a tremulous voice.

What?

Cheryl looks round at him. He's soaking wet and holding a bloody wedge of tissues to his nose.

'It's nothing,' he says.

As he moves into the room, Cheryl rushes forward.

'My God, Xan,' she says. 'What on earth has happened?'

Sasha shepherds him to a stool. Cheryl grasps his arm to support him.

He's pale. His hair is plastered flat to his head and his clothes are sodden. He must've walked home in the pouring rain.

But he's hurt!

Jordan and Sasha watch him as Cheryl gently removes the tissues from his hand and inspects his nose. It's bloody and swollen to twice its normal size. The sight of it makes her stomach lurch. He winces. She's rarely seen him in physical pain and it throws her into confusion.

Focus. Help him.

'That could be broken,' she says, trying to sound matter-of-fact. 'What happened?'

His shoulders slump and he sighs. 'I was mugged,' he says. 'Think they were after my phone?'

'Oh my God, Xan.' She clutches his arm.

'Did they get it?' says Jordan.

Xan shakes his head, touches the tip of his nose gingerly with the back of his hand. 'No,' he says. 'Fought the little bastards off.'

He's shaking.

This is terrible.

'I'm calling the police,' says Cheryl.

'No,' he replies. 'No need.'

'But—'

He looks up at her. 'It's a waste of time,' he says. 'What are they going to do? Kids. They ran off. I don't want the hassle.'

'I think we should go to A&E?'

'No. We'll be there all night. Stop fussing, woman. I just want a hot shower and a stiff drink.'

Cheryl meets her husband's eye. She sees the determination, and a look of what? Desolation? She's never seen him like this before and it's disturbing. It must be the pain.

'Okay,' she says. 'Whatever you want.'

35

Thursday, 9.05pm

Cheryl walks into the bedroom carrying a glass tumbler loaded with ice and a generous measure of scotch. It had taken some cajoling to calm her anxious daughter and persuade her to get ready for bed. However, Jordan had escorted his father upstairs, collected his wet clothes, and brought them down to the laundry room. This was her son being concerned and mature. He can do it, which is reassuring.

Xan is in the shower. She places the scotch on the bedside table. The door to the en suite is open and steam billows out. She stands in the doorway watching her husband.

He has his left hand on the wall to steady himself. His head is dipped forward as the hot water streams over him. His right arm is bent, the hand cupped.

First Jordan, now this.

For all his bravado, the attack has shaken him. Raising his head, he looks at her. His face looks gaunt. She gives him a reassuring smile. But the anxious knot in her stomach is twisting and tightening. Both the men in her life have faced real danger, and she wasn't there to help either of them. She feels powerless and angry at the yobs who did this.

Xan turns off the shower. She lifts a bath towel from the rack and hands it to him as he steps out. He wraps it round himself.

'Come and sit on the bed so I can examine your face,' she says.

He sighs. She notices his eyes are red, as if he's been crying.

He never cries. Must be the shower.

He follows her meekly across the room and sits as instructed.

The bridge of his nose is enlarged and inflamed; it's already starting to discolour. But the line of the nose remains straight. It's narrow and classic, one of his best features. She peers at it.

Maybe not as bad as she first thought.

'Not sure,' she says. 'You might've got away with it. But you're going to have quite a shiner.'

He doesn't reply. He's cradling his right hand in his left.

'Let me see your hand,' she says.

He holds it out. The knuckles are puffy and the skin grazed in several places.

'Can you move your fingers?' she says.

He flexes them and grimaces. 'Shit,' he says. 'That hurts.'

'Wiggle each of your fingers if you can.'

He does. They seem to work.

'You must've delivered quite a punch,' she says proudly.

He sighs. 'I suppose instinct kicked in. You just defend yourself, don't you?'

'So, where did this happen? Why weren't you in the car?'

'I parked in the multi-storey. And I get in, and the bloody thing wouldn't start.'

'Oh no,' she says. 'But why the multi-storey if you were playing squash?'

He huffs. 'This was after squash. I went into town.'

She can sense the tension in him and his annoyance at being questioned.

She says nothing and waits.

He exhales.

'Listen,' he says. 'I was going to talk to you about this. Did you know that Kayleigh from your lab was involved with Arran Patel?'

'No. But when I talked to her, she was a bit odd. I did wonder.'

'Well, it's gets complicated. I decided to do what you wanted.'

'Yeah, you said.'

'So I went to see her.'

'You went to see Kayleigh?'

'Yes, Kayleigh!' He snaps.

Don't push.

He struggles to contain his exasperation.

Back off. Wait.

'Okay,' he says. 'I thought the best way to find Arran and help him was through her. I get back to the car. Bloody thing wouldn't start. It's pouring with rain. I was fed up. Tried to get an Uber. Long wait. I decided to walk home.'

She watches him. He's agitated. He shakes his head in disbelief.

None of this makes sense.

She has a string of questions. How did he find all this out? Why didn't he discuss it with her? And what did Kayleigh say? She has to bite her tongue.

'Anyway,' he says. 'They must've followed me from the car park. It was dark and wet. Three of them, I reckon. They jumped me on the Fen Causeway. Wanted my phone and wallet. I just fought back.'

Cheryl sighs. 'Might've been smarter to hand them over. Phones, cards, can all be replaced. It's not worth getting hurt for, is it?'

'Yeah, I know that,' he says in an irritated tone.

She reaches out, strokes his arm. 'Hey, I'm not criticising. I'm just upset you're hurt.' She picks up the glass of whiskey and hands it to him.

He takes a mouthful, rolls it round his tongue and says, 'I suppose I'm annoyed at my own stupidity. I just reacted.'

He sounds more than annoyed. Something else. But what?

'Well, it's understandable,' she says.

He looks up at her. His gaze is mournful. Wounded.

'I'm sorry,' he says.

'For what? It's not your fault you got mugged.'

He shrugs, looks away, and takes another drink.

'I know I'm not the best husband. Sometimes I let you down. But I believe in you. In us.'

She sits down beside him, taking hold of his good hand. 'Oh, Xan…'

He gazes at her. 'We're so close to making it, y'know. I can taste it. I don't want anything to go wrong.'

'I know.'

And she knows she's letting him down; it's her vacillation and indecision.

'Do you Cheryl? Do you even trust me?'

'Of course I do. You're a good businessman. And if we'd stayed in California, I know you'd—'

'I don't care about any of that. This deal with HDZ is perfect for us. We have to make it work. And I don't want you to worry. Once the business is up and running, you won't be under pressure. I'll protect you. You'll have the time and the space to do the work the way you want to do it. Not in some under funded university lab. You'll have better equipment. You can build a better research team. Have the money to attract the best people.'

She watches him. His face may be swollen and bruised, but his zeal is still mesmerising.

He lifts her hand and kisses the back of it.

'It's make or break,' he says. 'Simple as.'

He's right. Of course he is.

'You think I'm being a coward, don't you?' she says.

'No. I understand. You're a perfectionist. And you worry. We're completely different. But that's what makes us a brilliant team. Cheryl, together we're invincible.'

She smiles. 'Are we?'

'Yes! But you have to believe it.'

He's gazing straight at her. A pleading look in his eyes. But also the fervour. This is the man she fell in love with. Gorgeous and smart.

But he's hurt and he needs her.

'I do believe it,' she says. 'And we will make it work.'

36

Friday, 7.55am

It's a bright morning. Heavy overnight rain has cleared the air. But it still feels freezing to DS Jo Boden as she walks across the wet grass towards the river.

The scene is already taped off. Uniforms are standing about, deterring curious onlookers. An early morning rower was the first to spot the body; it was caught in reeds and overhanging branches in a sluggish bend in the river.

A specialist team with a diver has been called in to recover it, and they're already at work.

DC Mackie is on the scene. He's standing, arms folded, watching. He's large and tough, often mistaken for a thug.

'Morning, Skip,' he says. 'Where's the coffee?'

He calls her Skip to be annoying. Boden knows this and has given up rising to the bait.

'Prish's getting it,' she says. 'What have we got?'

'Male. Looks like he hasn't been in the water long. Still floating.'

'Drunk who fell in?'

'Could be. But it was bloody awful weather last night. Not exactly an evening for a few bevies by the river.'

Boden surveys the landscape. Many of the trees and shrubs following the course of the river are skeletal and bare. The winter wood offers little cover. But the river is swollen with storm water and fast flowing. He could've gone in anywhere. She looks upriver; in the distance there's a footbridge.

'What's that bridge called?' she says.

Mackie smirks. He likes to be the local copper in the know; she's the outsider from the Met. 'Sheep's Green Bridge,' he replies.

She looks across towards the road. There's a footpath cutting across the grass towards the bridge.

'Someone taking a shortcut in the rain?' she says.

'Yep. Possible,' says Mackie.

They stand side by side, waiting for the recovery team to do their work. The first responders thought the situation suspicious. This is why they've been called. The CSI vehicles are already parked up nearby and the Crime Scene Manager has taken charge of the scene.

But Boden knows it's likely this will turn out to be a stupid accident. Any city with a river running through it will have its share of accidental drownings. Idiots thinking they'll go for a swim; that's more of a summer problem. Lost individuals under the influence of alcohol or drugs. But a fresh corpse, properly recovered, will provide the evidence they need to determine the cause of death.

Boden is tired; working too many extra shifts. She pretends the overtime is to fill her bank balance. But it's also to fill her time. She's still a stranger in this place, an exile from London, here for the job and missing her old life.

She shivers and wraps her scarf round her neck. Mackie is wearing a thin suit jacket and no coat.

'Aren't you cold?' she says.

He shakes his head. 'Sun's out. Practically shorts weather,' he says.

Boden glances up at the pale winter sun. It was too wet for frost overnight, but the pervasive dampness seeps into her bones. She wishes she hadn't left her gloves in the car.

When a body is found, there's always loads of hanging around. Still, she prefers to do it in the fresh air. Corpses can turn up in some grim places. She notices a figure heading towards them across the grass. It's Prisha, finally, with hot coffee.

As DC Chakravorty approaches, Mackie grins. 'Hand roasted the beans yourself, did you?' he says.

'Bog off, Mackie,' Chakravorty replies. 'It's not even my turn.'

He glances at Boden. 'She loves me really.'

Boden just smiles. She has a sneaking suspicion this might be true. She has a front-row seat to this awkward courtship between her two young colleagues.

Opposites attract?

As Chakravorty hands them their coffees, the recovery team slowly winches the body from the river and it's transferred to the waiting gurney.

'Right, let's take a look,' says Boden.

They walk over to where the suited and booted CSIs are carefully arranging it. The CSM is searching the sparse clothing.

'Any ID?' says Boden.

'No,' he replies. 'Beard and hair. Doesn't look that old. Might be a student. But look at the head, a couple of nasty wounds there, already attracted some feeders.'

Grounds for suspicion? Definitely.

Boden's day just got far more complicated.

Chakravorty grimaces and backs away. Mackie chuckles at her discomfort. But Boden leans forward for a closer inspection.

'Okay,' she says. 'So he might've been attacked?'

'Preliminary assessment? Yeah, a possibility,' says the CSM.

'A youngish person who's been attacked?' says Boden.

'Or just fell. Hard to say.'

Boden looks at the CSM, standing stiffly in his white suit; they always hedge their bets.

'There's been a spate of attacks on the homeless this winter,' says Chakravorty. 'No fatalities I know of, but I can check.'

'February,' says Mackie. 'Christmas is a distant memory and all the nasty little scrotes are miserable and looking for someone to pick on.'

Boden sighs. That's a possibility.

'Okay,' she says. 'Until we get the post mortem results, we're treating this as a suspicious death. So let's start with a trawl of all the CCTV covering any potential approaches to this area. Can we find where he went in? Because that could be the scene of the violence.'

'On it, Skip,' says Mackie with a mock salute.

Boden frowns. 'You're annoyingly cheerful this morning. Why?'

He beams. 'Thought you'd never ask. We won last night. Despite the bloody rain. Twelve eight. I scored the winning try.'

Boden shakes her head and smiles. She takes a last look at the body. The next time she sees it will be laid out on a mortuary slab.

Someone's son? Someone's brother? Someone's husband?

As they're bagging it up, the arm falls loose. The cuff of the top is pulled back, and she notices some kind of plastic bracelet on the wrist.

'Hang on,' she says. 'What's that on his wrist?'

The CSM looks. 'Well spotted. Looks like a patient ID band. He's been in hospital.'

'Can you cut it off for us?' says Boden.

Some scissors are found. Chakravorty gets an evidence bag out. Part of the label stuck to the band has peeled off. There's no name.

'I think the bar code's still intact,' says Chakravorty, peering at it.

'That might give us an ID,' says Boden.

A ray of hope in what otherwise could be a grinding process. She sips her coffee and prepares to head back to the office.

37

Friday, 8.05am

The London offices of HDZ are in a redbrick Victorian warehouse on the edge of Clerkenwell, close to Pentonville Road. The building is coolly anonymous; it could be a design studio, a media company, an upmarket private residence. The nameplate beside the door is small and discreet; visitors come by invitation only. Hannah taps her ID on the entry sensor, pushes open the plain black door and heads up the stairs into the main open-plan area above.

She returned to London late last night, having received a text from Xan Woodward confirming that he and Cheryl would be there for a nine-thirty pitch meeting with Nat Harrington.

Hannah feels energised and ahead of the game. Walking in here always gives her a buzz. The vast industrial space at the centre is divided into activity zones by the reclaimed, retro furniture. Round the edge, glass partitions separate off the meeting rooms plus the offices of the partners. Most people hot desk on the long, refectory style tables in the middle.

Nat salvaged the food bar from an old East End pub. It must be twenty-feet long, solid oak, but with a new marble top.

It's early; only a few of her colleagues are milling around, chatting and helping themselves to breakfast.

'Hey, Hannah,' says one of them. 'How's it going?'

He's new, but she's already got his number: younger than her, ambitious, super-pushy and fishing for information.

'Yeah, great,' she replies, without stopping.

There's a proper barista to dispense the coffee. The casual, serve-yourself approach had to be abandoned. Nat got annoyed that the technician was being called out three times a week because some idiot had wrecked the Italian state-of-the-art machine.

Hannah smiles at the nervous barista. 'Can I get a double espresso?' she says.

The girl looks so meek and eager to please; Hannah watches her grind the beans and tamp them down. She's pretty enough, but doomed. Attitude is everything. Followed closely by front. Hannah has both, but this poor girl doesn't. She's a doormat.

'D'you know if Nat's in yet?' says Hannah.

'Yeah, umm, oh, I'm not sure, actually…' whispers the girl.

Doomed.

Hannah peers across the room to the far corner and the boss's office. She can just glimpse his head bobbing up and down. Doing press-ups?

Nat Harrington is small and wiry and well over forty. If he resembles anything, it's a bald ferret. Collecting her coffee, Hannah saunters over.

He stands up, smiles at her through the glass and waves her in. He favours expensive sportswear; this morning it's a Castore zip tee with matching black joggers.

'Morning,' he says. 'So we're all set?'

'Absolutely.'

Be cool. Don't oversell.

He tilts his head. 'You still concerned about Cheryl's leadership skills?'

Hannah shrugs. 'She's a brilliant woman. She wants to save lives. But she wants to get it right. I think I prefer that.'

Nat checks his watch and says, 'Freddie texted me. He got an early flight from Munich. He should be here in time.'

It hits like a knife in the gut; shock followed by disbelief.

What the fuck! Freddie's coming!

Through a supreme effort of will, Hannah remains poker-faced. His bright little rodent eyes are dancing as he scans her for a reaction.

He enjoys this stuff. Playing the team off against each other.

She sips her espresso and says casually. 'I didn't know he was coming.'

'Don't feel threatened,' says Nat. 'I appreciate the work you've done on this.'

She shrugs. 'His input will be invaluable, obviously.'

'Yeah,' says Nat idly, 'it will.' But he's already scrolling on his phone and ignoring her. She's dismissed.

She smiles and retreats to one of the long tables. As she gets out her laptop, she fantasises about some form of divine intervention: an air traffic controllers' strike, a terrorist alert at the airport. She tries phoning Xan, but he doesn't pick up.

The minutes tick relentlessly on. She does a grounding meditation and some breath work. In the end, what will be will be. You can only play the hand you're dealt.

At nine-fifteen, she looks up to see the Woodwards being escorted to the sofa area by an intern.

She takes a deep breath, paints on a smile and heads over. Cheryl is fussing over her husband, then she sees why. He's wearing a black eye patch, which adds to his roguish appearance. But the bridge of his nose is visibly swollen and just below the patch on his left cheek there's a mauve half-moon.

'My God, what happened to you?' says Hannah.

'A stupid accident,' says Xan.

'He was mugged,' says Cheryl.

'When?'

'Last night.'

'But we didn't want to let you down,' says Xan. His one good eye is staring straight at her.

'How awful?' says Hannah.

He glances at his wife. 'Cheryl was up until midnight finishing the pitch.'

Cheryl smiles. 'As Xan said, we didn't want to let you down.'

'Well, we really appreciate it,' says Hannah. 'Particularly since my colleague Freddie Turner is flying back from Germany, especially to meet you.'

'Oh,' says Xan glumly. His shoulders sag.

At least he gets the implications of that.

But he does look rough. Hannah is rapidly calculating. This could provide the glimmer of hope she's been praying for; although obviously, she doesn't believe in prayer.

She focuses a concerned frown on Cheryl.

'Hey listen,' she says. 'This is ridiculous. We can't put you through this. Not today. We'll reschedule. I know Nat will understand.'

'No,' says Cheryl. 'We talked about it. And we're here

now. And it'll mostly be my presentation. Xan's tough. He'll survive. Won't you, darling?'

Xan nods and smiles weakly.

'If you're sure?'

Bollocks!

'Quite sure. Who's Freddie Turner?' says Cheryl.

'A colleague who specialises in biotech.' Hannah catches Xan's eye.

Will he still back her against Freddie? Who knows?

'I look forward to meeting him,' says Cheryl. 'I'm sure he'll find what we have to say exciting.'

All Hannah can do is smile like an idiot.

But she is puzzled. This is a side of Dr Woodward she hasn't seen before. Brisk, business-like and confident. The scientist's small body is wound up, like a spring. She's full of energy. Grey jeans, a smart jacket with a silk scarf, chalk white sneakers with red laces. Matched with red lipstick. Hannah expected her to turn up in a boring trouser suit, looking like a lawyer. But Dr Woodward seems to get how the game is played. She's exuding the founder vibe; three parts nerd, one part rock star. And the outfit makes her look ten years younger.

Hannah hopes Freddie's late. And Xan sticks to their deal. It's in the lap of the Gods.

'Okay,' she says with all the enthusiasm she can muster. 'Let me get you coffees. And pastries?'

38

Friday, 9.30am

As they walk into the meeting, Cheryl has one thought uppermost in her mind: she doesn't want to let her husband down.

This will prove it. Despite her reservations, she's backing him.

Once she's sold her ideas to HDZ, he'll see that, won't he? They'll go back to being the couple they were. He'll love her, won't get frustrated with her and look elsewhere. He'll stop lying about it.

Or is she fooling herself?

Nat Harrington is the man they've come to see. He runs the venture capital firm. He's small, with a firm handshake.

'Such a pleasure to meet you, Dr Woodward,' he says. And it sounds as if he means it.

Cheryl lifts her laptop from her bag for the PowerPoint presentation. Nat steps forward to connect it up to their projection system. He has a reassuring gentlemanly quality. The kind of man who opens doors for a lady.

There's an oval conference table. Xan and Hannah sit on the other side of it. Nat is at one end.

What they're buying is you. Her husband's words roll around her head.

During the train journey to London, they didn't speak much. She went over her presentation. He gazed out of the window. Since the mugging, he's been in a strange space. Uncommunicative. Snappy in response to questions. And she has loads of questions, about Kayleigh, about the kids who attacked him. But she's put them all on hold because she doesn't want to upset him. He could still be in shock. It's the most likely explanation.

She stands at the other end of the table, beside the screen, holds up her hands, opens her palms and smiles.

'Science is about data,' she says. 'Everyone knows that. It's one of the things we try to drum into our first year undergraduates. A theory is a theory until you prove it. Or disprove it. That's how the body of knowledge moves forward.'

She lets her gaze travel round the table, looking at each person. This is what she does in the lecture theatre or a seminar, focus on several individuals. Students are a fidgety lot. It helps them settle.

'But that's only half the story,' she says. 'It's also about imagination.'

Nat Harrington steeples his fingers and grins. 'The true sign of intelligence is not knowledge but imagination. Didn't Einstein say that?'

Cheryl dips her head. 'Yes, he did. So let me tell you what I'm imagining. It's simple. I think we can create, through a type of 3D bio-printing, replacement organs. A biocompatible plastic forms a scaffold that acts as a skeleton for the organ being printed. We cover it with the recipient's own cells before implantation to reduce the risk of rejection. It's been done successfully with a bladder. But with more complex organs, the problem is recreating the vasculature, all the blood vessels and tiny capillaries, needed to keep the organ alive. This is what we're researching. This is the problem we're trying to solve. And I believe we're ahead of the field. Our data shows that.'

'And you're happy to share that data?' says Harrington.

Cheryl looks down the table at him and meets his eye. 'Yes, because then you'll know that backing us is the right decision.'

Is it? Fake-it-until-you-make-it, that's Xan mantra.

She smiles confidently. He's tapping his index finger on the table.

'Okay,' he says. 'I think—'

Without warning, the glass panel door swings open. It makes her jump. A flustered young man in a wet trench coat erupts into the room. Everyone turns to stare at him.

Freddie Turner?

He makes a beeline for Cheryl, holding out his hand to shake. It's icy.

'Dr Woodward,' he says. 'It's a tremendous privilege to meet you. I've been following your work for some time.' He's out of breath; must've been running. But his presence dominates the room. He turns to Nat. 'Sorry,' he says with a tragic frown. 'Couldn't get a cab at the airport. Absolute nightmare. I was forced to take the tube.'

'You're here now,' says Harrington with a benign smile. 'This is my colleague, Freddie Turner. He specialises in biotech.'

Cheryl smiles. But the atmosphere in the room has changed. Freddie removes his wet coat and tosses it on the chair next to Hannah. He doesn't look at her or greet her. She smiles at him but seems uncomfortable.

In her career, Cheryl has encountered plenty of young men like Freddie. He expects to be the centre of attention in any room. The world revolves around him.

He settles in a chair next to Nat, folds his long bony hands and looks at her expectantly.

Is he assuming she'll start again for him?

She glances at her husband, who's scowling. He sits up in his chair and says, 'That's the vision. Cheryl'll talk you through the experimental data and then I'm happy to answer questions on how we see the business developing.'

Freddie raises his eyebrows. 'Oh,' he says. 'I feel I've missed out. I was looking forward to the vision.' He gives Cheryl a smug smile.

Spoilt brat.

Cheryl looks at Hannah, then back to him.

'Hannah will have our written presentation for you to go over,' she says with a chilly smile. She turns to Nat. 'And I have to say that I'm so glad you sent her to Cambridge to meet us. Working with a woman makes such a difference to me. And that's why we decided to talk to you first.'

Let them chew on that.

Hannah is giving her a look of stunned disbelief. Then she grins.

Nat settles for a wry smile. His small feral eyes are twinkling.

Freddie shrugs. 'Absolutely,' he says. 'Science can be such a male-dominated field.'

'Like finance, I should imagine,' says Cheryl. She turns back to the screen. 'Right, let me tell you about some of the experiments we've created to pursue these aims.'

39

Friday, 10.25am

Boden taps on DCI Hepburn's door and gets waved in. He's on the phone, tie loosened and a harassed expression. The DI's still off sick and they're down two analysts. It's already turning into a busy day.

He hangs up and looks at her. 'What have we got?' he says.

'Suspicious death. Male. Youngish. Just fished him out of the river. But his face is a mess. Looks like he was in a fight. We're on CCTV trying to establish where he went in.'

'Okay, let also see if we can get any hint of where the altercation took place. Did he know his attacker? Was it a random attack or a dispute?'

Boden listens. She's already thought of all this. Listed all the possibilities in her notebook. But Hepburn is SIO. She waits while he reels off more instructions.

Then she says, 'He was wearing a hospital wrist band. So Prisha's using it to try to get an ID.'

'Oh, okay,' he says. 'That's something.'

She smiles. Now he knows she's on it. Doing her job.

He meets her eye and gives her an approving nod. This is Hepburn's version of praise. He doesn't get much more effusive that this.

Boden returns to her desk.

Prisha is grinning. 'I love bar codes,' she says. 'I sent a picture to hospital records. His name's Mohammed Rafiq. He was in overnight. And they noted him down as a rough sleeper. Had a blow to the head. Discharged on Wednesday.'

Boden sighs. 'Why do people keep attacking the homeless?'

'Because they can,' says Chakravorty.

Boden shakes her head. 'I need another coffee. Okay, discharged two days ago. So was he injured again and pushed in the river? Or is it just that he had a pre-existing head injury, got off his nut on booze or drugs and fell in? We'll need the post mortem results to tell us that.'

'Are you going to ask Hepburn if we can park it up until we get them?' says Chakravorty.

Boden sighs. 'No,' she says. 'Because if we leave it, any scene will get contaminated and be useless. Let's tackle this from the other end. We've got a name. The hospital reckons he could be homeless. Let's see if any of the agencies who support the homeless know him. Where's Mackie?'

'On a hunt for CCTV.'

'That'll help too.'

The day shelter for the homeless is in a small boxy warehouse unit on an industrial estate on the edge of the city. It's run by a local faith charity and was forced to migrate from a church crypt in town when the numbers requiring help kept increasing.

The manager, Hazel, is a rotund, motherly figure in her fifties. Unflappable, unshockable and with a warm smile for everyone. Boden wonders at her compassion. People come at her with knives and threats; the police are frequently called. But her relaxed and kindly demeanour rarely slips. She's widely known amongst police officers and paramedics. No one uses her last name; she's just Hazel.

'Fancy a brew while you're here,' she says to Boden. In this place, the tea urn never sleeps.

'No thanks,' says Boden. 'We're trying to find out more about a man called Mohammed Rafiq.'

'Drugs or robbery?' says Hazel.

'He's dead,' says Boden. 'Recovered the body from the river this morning.'

Hazel shakes her head sadly, then gives Boden and Chakravorty a shrewd look. 'But you're detectives. So this is not an accident.'

'We're not sure yet.'

Hazel nods and sighs. 'Not a name I recall. But I've got a brain like a sieve nowadays. Hang on.'

She flaps her hand and calls out. 'Ferris! You got a minute?'

'In the far corner, a man sitting on a battered sofa looks up. He's reading a dog-eared newspaper and could be a stand-in for Gandalf. His silver beard reaches down to his belly. He struggles to his feet and ambles over.

'Don't fancy lending me a tenner, do you Haze? There's a dead cert in the two o'clock at Kempton Park.'

'No, Ferris. These ladies are police officers. They need some help.'

'Always on the side of the law,' says Ferris with a mock salute. He smells of some form of alcohol.

'Did we have a Mohammed Rafiq in our merry band?' says Hazel.

Ferris ponders the question. He mouths the name silently to himself. Boden suspects his memory is far worse than Hazel's.

'No but…' He frowns until his bushy brows join in the middle.

'Okay, thanks,' says Hazel. She turns back to Boden. 'Just a idea. I don't think we knew him.'

'Hang about,' says Ferris, raising a gnarled index finger. 'That Asian lad, the paranoid one. He's always using false names. That might be one of his. Yeah, I reckon I've heard him use that.'

'Who's he?' says Boden.

Hazel focuses on Ferris. 'You mean Arran? The lad that got beaten up outside McDonald's on Tuesday?'

Ferris nods enviously. 'I heard he got an overnight for that.'

Hazel interprets. 'He means a night in hospital.'

Boden and Chakravorty exchange looks. 'This might be our man,' says Boden.

'Oh dear,' says Hazel. 'His poor girlfriend still comes round from time to time.'

'His girlfriend?' says Chakravorty.

'It's a terribly sad situation,' says Hazel. 'She tries to look after him, been trying to get him off the streets. But he won't stay put.'

'Crazy as a coot,' says Ferris, twirling his finger. 'Thinks they're after him, the little green men.'

'She's not homeless herself then?' says Boden.

'On no. She works at the university,' says Hazel. 'I think

he did once, too. In his calmer moments, you could tell he was a bright bloke. But in need of proper psychiatric treatment. His girlfriend tries to keep tabs on him. But it's a struggle when they don't want to be helped.'

'You know her name and where we can contact her?' says Chakravorty.

'Her name's Kayleigh. Don't know her second name. But I've got her number on my phone. She rings up most weeks, asks if he's been in, if he's alright. She must still really love him.'

'Did you say his name's Arran?' says Boden.

Hazel nods. 'Too many like him falling through the net for lack of treatment,' she says, shaking her head.

'Could this be drink or drugs related?' says Boden.

'Didn't drink. Drugs?' She shrugs. 'I wouldn't have said he was a user. I'll get you the number.'

'Thanks,' says Boden. 'And thank you too, Ferris.'

He nods. 'Want a hot tip for the two o'clock at Kempton Park?'

'Nah, we're fine, thanks,' says Boden.

40

Friday, 12.10pm

The restaurant is bustling and busy, and on a wet and miserable Friday lunchtime, it's a popular destination. Even at midday, it's filling up with business diners. They scurry from the taxi to the door. Luckily, Cheryl has brought an umbrella.

Despite the awful weather, she's buoyant; it's the relief of the pitch being over, plus the fact she asserted herself. She'd made it clear to these money people that she wasn't to be railroaded. She thinks of her sister; Lorna would be proud of her.

'It's a pity Nat couldn't join us,' says Cheryl.

Hannah just smiles. 'What can I tell you? The man's a workaholic. He doesn't do lunch.'

Nat and Xan had horse traded over the shape of the deal. HDZ had upped its offer of pre-seed capital for a six percent stake in the new company. Xan seemed satisfied with that. Everyone shook hands, and now Hannah was taking them for a celebratory lunch. But it's just the three of them.

Cheryl is relieved that Freddie also had opted not to join them. Maybe he didn't like being snubbed.

In the short taxi ride to the restaurant, Hannah did most of the talking. To Cheryl, she seemed an open and friendly girl, and not unlike many of the postgrads Cheryl teaches. She buzzed with energy and enthusiasm, and left Cheryl feeling embarrassed by her earlier suspicions about her and Xan. Clearly absurd.

'Okay,' said Hannah. 'I'm going to come clean. I don't have Freddie's expertise in biotech.'

'Doesn't matter,' said Cheryl. 'I don't think we need a scientist in your role. Do you Xan?'

He seemed miles away; staring out of the window again.

But he beamed and said, 'Absolutely not.'

A young man in a long apron escorts them to their table, which is in a cosy alcove, and as soon as they're settled with menus, Xan stands up and excuses himself. He heads for the loos. Cheryl watches him go with dismay.

She's done what he wanted. Why isn't it enough?

She wonders how long he'll be absent. Who will he call? The PR girl? She's being neurotic.

Hannah is scanning her. 'You okay?' she says.

Cheryl sighs. 'Oh, I'm worried about Xan. He's not himself.'

'He looks pretty banged up,' says Hannah. 'How the hell did he get mugged?'

'The problem is,' says Cheryl, 'it becomes about male pride. He had to fight back. Why didn't he just give them the damned phone?'

Hannah nods. 'Yeah, blokes can be ridiculous.'

'You're lucky,' says Cheryl. 'Being with a woman, you don't have to put up with this stuff.'

'No,' says Hannah. 'But, hey, we're celebrating. We need a bottle of something sparkling and delicious.' She waves at the server.

Cheryl watches her. She's like Lorna. No problem getting attention and asking for what she wants. It's that confidence and ease. Even though she's so young, she's comfortable in her own skin. Cheryl can't imagine being like that. But it fills her with envy.

Turning to her, Hannah grins mischievously. 'What's your favourite champagne? Bearing in mind this is going on the Amex card and Nat's paying.'

'I don't know,' says Cheryl. 'Dom Pérignon?'

'Yeah, good choice.' She smiles at the server. 'You heard the lady.'

He nods and departs.

'You remind me of my sister,' says Cheryl.

'I don't know your sister, but I'll take that as a compliment.'

'She's good at dealing with people.'

Hannah opens her palms. 'That's my job, essentially. People.'

'I should imagine the City is a tough world for a woman.'

'If you mean, is it still one big, dick-swinging boys club, well yeah?'

Cheryl laughs. 'I like your turn of phrase.'

Hannah gives her a serious look. 'Listen,' she says. 'I appreciate you backing me in there. Particularly since Freddie is far more qualified for this job than me. It wasn't what I was expecting.'

'I could see that. But I found Freddie a bit—'

'Of a knob? He is. But he knows his stuff. Nat will rely

on him to analyse your data. But you can rely on me to keep them out of your hair.'

Cheryl smiles. 'I think everyone has to understand the complexity of this process, scientifically. It's two steps forward, one step back.'

'Our investment is in you and your potential. You keep me in the loop, I can manage expectations.' She beams. Cheryl smiles back. It's a relief. Having a woman as a go-between will be easier.

The server returns with the champagne. Hannah inspects the label. 'Yes,' she says. 'That'll do nicely.'

As he pops the cork, Xan returns to the table. His handsome face looks haggard, and with the eye patch, vaguely disreputable.

But he grins. 'I see you didn't hang about.'

The flutes are filled and Hannah raises her glass. 'Well, here's to, I don't know. What do you think?'

'Saving lives,' says Cheryl.

'And making a few quid in the process,' says Xan as he chinks her glass. They all drink, but Xan drains half his glass.

He picks up his menu and, as he peruses it, he says, 'So what've you girls been talking about?' There's a sourness to his tone.

Why?

Cheryl looks at him.

Is he jealous?

'Chit-chat,' says Hannah.

'Yes,' says Cheryl. Both women look at him. Female solidarity. Why not?

He empties his glass and waves it at the server for a refill. 'What? You mean handbags and lipsticks? You two?'

'What's wrong with that?' says Cheryl.

'Nothing at all, my darling,' he says. He looks at her and then across at Hannah. And his smile is more of a sneer.

Cheryl catches Hannah's eye and looks away. She's embarrassed. The fact this lovely young woman they're going to work with is glimpsing the seedy and fractious underbelly of their marriage is deeply distressing.

She stares down at her menu. Her chin quivers.

41

Friday, 3.10pm

Hannah returns to the office, mellow with booze, having put a sizeable dent in her company credit card.

What she needs is coffee, strong and black, to get her through the rest of the day. There's no sign of the barista, and she's staring at the massive Gaggia, trying to decide what to do first, when a voice behind her says, 'Who's a clever girl then?'

Freddie.

She spins round and smiles as she wonders how big a prick he's going to be about this.

'Lunch was nice,' she says. 'You should've come.'

'I don't think Dr Woodward is my biggest fan, and anyway, Nat wanted me to dissect their presentation.'

Oh shit. Here we go.

'And?' she says.

He folds his arms and chuckles. 'You really are flying by

the seat of your pants, aren't you? Nat told you to go to Cambridge, make contact and report back.'

She shrugs. 'Which is what I've done, isn't it?'

'You've got balls, I'll give you that.'

She grins.

Rattle his cage. Why not? She's won this round.

'But surely balls are what you like, aren't they, Fred? Nice big ones.'

'Don't be so bloody cheeky. You're still a rookie in this office.'

'Sorry. I've never been that good at knowing my place.'

He huffs and shakes his head. 'There's nothing wrong with ambition. In your shoes, I might've done the same. But don't let your impatience to succeed cloud your judgement, Hannah.'

'You sound like my dad.'

He tilts his head. 'Yes, and I've heard that Sir Brian is a smart bloke, so let's hope you take after him. You may've been born with a silver spoon up your arse—'

'Oh, come on, Freddie. I mean duh! I'm a girl! I'm not supposed to take after him; my brothers take after him. I'm supposed to marry a clone of him and have four kids.'

'No, you c'mon, Hannah. It's 2022. This poor-me feminist shit is way out of date.'

'You think so? You haven't met my family. And if you want to look at the bloody data, which you all seem to rely on, how many female partners are there in this fucking firm? Exactly zero.'

Heads are turning. Colleagues are tuning in. An office row is exciting enough to drag them out of their Friday afternoon stupor. She catches some smirks and the schadenfreude.

Is she being that loud?

Freddie glances over his shoulder and says, 'Can someone

find the bloody barista and get this stupid woman a coffee to sober her up?'

'I'm not bloody drunk,' snaps Hannah.

Well, not that drunk.

'I think we'll assume that you are,' says Freddie. 'So let's go into the meeting room and continue this in private, shall we?'

As if that fools anyone.

But she follows him. And, if she's honest, she is a little wasted. Witnessing the Woodwards trying to pretend that they didn't hate each other was quite an experience. They all drank too much.

He holds the door open for her, patronising git.

Walking in, she slumps down in a chair. She left the restaurant on a high, now this. Freddie is about to put a spanner in the works and tell her it's all rubbish. Cheryl's research is rubbish.

It's like hurtling towards a brick wall at a hundred miles an hour. Time slows as you see the crash coming.

Breathe. Focus.

She knows she can't afford to alienate Freddie. Nat listens to him. A lot.

Let it go. They'll be other chances.

'I'm sorry if I was rude,' she says.

'Oh, don't talk bollocks,' he says. 'I don't need an apology.'

There's a tap on the glass door. The timid barista is standing there holding a mug of coffee. Freddie waves her in. She puts the coffee on the table in front of Hannah. 'Sugar?' she mutters. Hannah shakes her head. The barista leaves.

Freddie takes a turn round the room. Even though he got drenched en route from the airport, he's back to looking neat and precise, from the pristine trainers to the hair gel. How does he manage that? It's annoying.

'You're very young,' he says with a sigh.

Here we go. So predictable.

'I'm twenty-four,' she says.

'Exactly,' he replies. 'And you've worked here for what? Three months?'

'Three and a half.'

'Here's the deal,' says Freddie. 'We work together, or you go back to daddy with your tail between your legs.'

She raises her eyebrows and sighs. Since he's gay, she can't even play the girly card. Still, it occurs to her that if Freddie wanted her out, she'd already be heading for the lift with her stuff in a cardboard box.

'Okay,' she says.

'I've been through the material they submitted. We've offered pre-seed capital, and that buys us the option to get a proper look at what they're up to.'

'Yeah, I know that.'

'Good. There are at least a dozen labs globally doing this work. They're just the ones I know about. And that doesn't include the Chinese. But I think Dr Woodward is on to something. Vasculature. Know what that is?'

'Yeah, like blood vessels and capillaries. I did listen to her pitch.'

'It's key. And her approach to the problem is quite different. Who knows if she'll breakthrough before anyone else? But it's certainly worth a punt. And Nat agrees with me.'

'Oh,' says Hannah.

Vasculature? Who knew?

'If she does, this could be huge.' He's staring at her. 'But managing these people is a delicate process. Lots of egos involved. You have to establish trust. Can you do that?'

Hannah meets his gaze. There's a seriousness she hasn't noticed before. It's unnerving.

This really could be big.

'Yeah. I think so,' she says.

'Dr Woodward likes you. Build on that. You've got your break. But this is a team effort. Do you understand that, Hannah?'

She nods.

'Talk to me about everything. I don't care what time you phone me. Keep in touch.'

She nods again. 'Yeah. I will. I promise.'

He smiles. 'Okay. Drink your coffee.'

Oh shit. She slept with the wrong Woodward.

42

Friday, 3.30pm

Boden's phone call to Dr Kayleigh Burrows went to voice mail. It's afternoon before she responds. Boden and Chakravorty go to meet her at the university laboratories where she works.

They stand outside in a chilly corridor. Dr Burrows, in a white lab coat, is rigid and radiating alarm. Her gaze darts back and forth between the two police officers.

'I'm sorry,' she says. 'I was working. When I'm buried in my work, hours pass. And I only just picked up your message.'

Speaking fast. Does she know what's coming or is she just nervous?

Boden hadn't wanted to tell her over the phone. The easier option, but never a good one in her view. 'I understand that a friend of yours called Arran may be homeless,' she says. 'Is that correct?'

Kayleigh Burrows stares back at them. The darting stops.

The eyes and the head roll back from a hit. She gasps, and a solitary tear rolls down her cheek.

'Where did you find him?' she says.

'I'm sorry to be the bearer of bad news,' says Boden. 'But we recovered a body from the river this morning, and there's a possibility it's him.'

Kayleigh swallows and turns away. Boden and Chakravorty wait.

Someone's girlfriend.

After several moments, Kayleigh shakes herself briskly like a wet dog. 'How did he fall in?' she says.

'We don't know. We're trying to determine that. And we still need to confirm that it is him.'

'You want me to identify him?' she says.

'It would help. If you feel able to.'

'I'll have to tell his mother. His father died last year. I think that's what tipped him over the edge psychologically. He thought his father was ashamed of him.'

Boden scans her. She gives the impression of a no-nonsense woman.

'I understand you know Hazel at the homeless shelter. She says he had some serious mental health issues,' says Boden.

Kayleigh nods. 'He did. We got him referred through the hospital once. But they wouldn't section him, so he just ran off.'

'Must've been very difficult for you,' says Boden.

'Difficult? It was impossible. No one would listen.' The bitterness is obvious, but Boden isn't surprised.

'I'm sorry to have to ask this,' she says. 'But did he ever get into any fights?'

'Fights? No. That wasn't Arran. He was the meekest of souls. Too bloody meek.' She sniffs and wipes her nose with the back of her hand. 'He got extremely paranoid, but he'd just run and hide.'

'We understand he got beaten up earlier this week?'

'Yeah, bastards put him in hospital.'

'Could he have known who they were? Had some kind of ongoing dispute with them?'

'I've no idea. I heard about it from someone. I went to the hospital. He had a nasty head injury. When they discharged him, I persuaded him to come home with me. He was very frightened. I think that's why he agreed.'

'Paranoia aside, did he seem frightened of someone specific?'

'I'm not sure. Impossible to tell with him.' She puts her face in her hands. Her shoulders shake. She seems in danger of toppling over.

Boden reaches out. There's a bench in the corridor. 'Come and sit down,' she says. She shepherds Kayleigh to the bench and they sit down together.

'Stupid thing,' says Kayleigh, between her tears, 'is I'd finally got him some help. Someone to pay for private psychiatric treatment. Maybe Arran overheard us talking last night? That might be why he ran? We tried to go after him. Well, my… friend did.'

'So last night, Arran was at your flat? And this friend came round?'

'Yeah. Arran was in the bedroom.'

'And who's the friend?'

'Well, not a friend exactly. He's… well, my boss's husband. I'd sort of persuaded them to help.'

She gives Boden a shifty look. Boden waits for her to say more. Chakravorty raises her eyebrows.

Sort of persuaded?

Kayleigh is exhibiting the discomfort of a person who's trying to dissemble but isn't any good at it.

'Your boss's husband had agreed to help Arran?' says Boden, pressing the point.

'It's just, well, super complicated.' Kayleigh is wringing her hands. 'Arran used to work here, too. And they owe him. Big time.'

More bitterness.

'What's the name of your boss's husband?' says Boden.

Kayleigh hesitates, she doesn't want to say, but she's snookered. 'Xan Woodward,' she says.

Xan? Not many of those about.

It takes Boden a couple of seconds to recall where she's heard the name before.

'Okay,' says Boden. 'Last night, Arran got upset, ran out of here. Xan Woodward followed him. Why?'

Kayleigh shrugs. 'To help him. To bring him back. I called Xan. He said he couldn't find him.'

'You called him when?'

'I don't know. I left several messages. He didn't get back to me until late. Sent a text. After midnight. Said he couldn't find him.'

Boden nods. 'Well, thank you for answering our questions. Are you going to be okay? Can we get you a drink or something?'

'No. I'll be alright. Thank you for… well, y'know.'

Boden gets up. She glances at Chakravorty. A body in the river just escalated into a more complex inquiry.

43

Friday, 4.20pm

The train journey back to Cambridge is slow and tedious. Outside, the rain is unrelenting. The afternoon light is fading. Cheryl sits opposite her husband, but he says very little. Closing his eyes, he dozes. She suspects this is a way of shutting her out. Her and the rest of the world.

Is he in pain? He must be.

The eye patch has left an indentation on his forehead and he's removed it to reveal a puffy and swollen eyelid, turning to a deep shade of mauve, which is spreading across his eyebrow and down his cheek. Over lunch they consumed two bottles of champagne between them, then he moved on to scotch. She wanted to stop him, but that didn't seem sensible. By then, they were all tipsy.

He's self-medicating. It's understandable. She still thinks he should see a doctor, but he refuses.

Why won't he let her near him?

Last night, once she'd agreed to come to London and do

the pitch, he withdrew from her completely, leaving her to prepare for the meeting. He collapsed into bed. But it was the exhaustion, and because he was hurt.

During the journey from Cambridge this morning, he remained detached. He instructed her on how she should present herself. The idea of them as a team, working together, all that enthusiasm and energy, seemed to have evaporated overnight.

It's not his fault. He thinks he has to be tough.

The rain streaks across the windows, almost horizontally, as the darkening landscape flies by. Cheryl is developing a headache. She's not a drinker. It always ends up depressing her. The buzz of alcohol, followed by the inevitable kickback; she hates it. The ticket inspector gives her a tepid smile as he checks their tickets. She needs some water, but there's no trolley service.

Xan is napping, but he can't get comfortable. He fidgets as he tries to rearrange his long limbs under the narrow table. Then his breathing slows to a steady rhythm. He sleeps.

She checks her phone. Lorna is taking care of the kids after school. Jordan will resent it. But Sasha loves her aunt.

Cheryl thumbs a text to her daughter. *What are you having for tea?*

Several seconds later, a picture pops up. Sasha is posing, slice in hand, over a frying pan of fish fingers. Lorna is next to her, hand on a saucepan of beans.

Cheryl reflects, not for the first time, how lucky she is to have Lorna.

As she sends back a stream of emojis, Xan starts in his sleep. He mumbles something and his face twitches. He must be having a bad dream.

She reaches out and touches his hand. His one good eye opens. He seems startled.

'What?' he snaps.

'Are you alright?'

'I'm fine,' he says, pulling away.

'Were you having a bad dream?'

'No.'

'Okay, sorry I disturbed you.'

He turns away. 'No, you're not. You and your bloody never ending anxiety. Drives me round the bend.'

'Sorry.'

He fingers his bruised cheekbone. She winces for him. It needs medical attention, but she bites her tongue. He'll just react.

He gives her a baleful look. 'It's no bloody wonder,' he says, 'that Jordan behaves how he does. You're always trying to baby him.'

His tone is spiteful. It stings.

She's encountered this with him before. Like a cornered creature, when he feels weak, he attacks.

Basic biology. Not his fault.

'It's not my intention,' she says. 'Sometimes I find it hard to get it right.'

He huffs. 'Tell me about it.'

A heavy silence settles between them. It's obvious he's brooding. But why? He's got what he wanted.

'The meeting went well, don't you think?' she says.

He shrugs and sighs. 'Well, you and Hannah seem to have become best buddies.'

'I think she's a nice girl.'

He chuckles cynically. 'Do you?'

'I prefer her to Freddie whatever-he's-called.'

'Sure that wasn't because he actually knows what he's talking about?'

Don't react.

But it's hard. The cruelty must be deliberate. She takes a deep breath. 'We went to London today. I did the pitch. I don't know what more you want from me, Xan?'

'Really?' he says. 'Now you're going to get all snippy? I'm doing this for you. Busting a gut doing all this for you. And yet it's like you don't even want it. I have to persuade you to go and talk to these people.'

'It's more complicated than that. Of course I want the work out there. But—'

'Why does everything come with a but? It's not complicated at all. You get in the lab and you deliver. That's what I need from you. I don't need your anxiety. Or all this fuss over a stupid black eye. This is not the first black eye I've ever had. It'll heal.'

'I'm just concerned about you.'

'Your concern is not what I need right now. Okay?'

'I'm your wife.'

'Yeah, don't remind me.' He folds his arms and turns away, the irritation pumping out of him.

Don't cry!

She swallows hard.

'I'm sorry,' she mutters.

He ignores her.

He's hurt. That's why he's lashing out. He doesn't mean it.

She can feel the tears welling. It's hard to stop them. She stands up.

'I'm just going to the loo,' she says.

44

Friday, 6.45pm

They take a taxi from the station and it drops them at the door. It's not that late, but the February darkness and the rain make it seem like the middle of the night. Cheryl hurries up the path to the house; Xan takes his time. Is he just finding a perverse pleasure in getting wet, or perhaps he wants to reinforce the gulf between them?

She lets herself in. Lorna comes down the hall to meet them. The interior is bright and warm. Cheryl's immediately cheered by the comfort of home and the hug from her sister.

But Lorna has the antennae of an ant. She holds Cheryl at arm's length and frowns. 'You okay?'

Cheryl shakes her head. 'Just a very long day. Dreadful weather. Alcohol at lunchtime.'

She has no time to say more because Sasha comes scampering from the kitchen, demanding her attention.

Greetings, the removal of wet shoes, the hanging up of coats creates a distracting bustle. Xan pats his daughter on the head and then disappears into his study. Lorna has heard about the mugging but not seen him since.

As the door shuts behind him, she says to Cheryl, 'That doesn't look too good.'

The sisters head into the kitchen. 'It isn't,' says Cheryl. 'He looks like he's been in a cage fight. Wouldn't go to the hospital last night, won't see the GP.'

Lorna sighs. 'Well, I can understand the reluctance to spend eight hours queuing in A&E for a black eye.'

'Don't side with him. What if his cheekbone's fractured?'

'He'd know about it. It would be far more painful. Broken nose? Heals itself. But, I agree, it looks nasty. Why didn't he just give them the phone?'

Cheryl shrugs.

Sasha has retreated to the long dining table, where she's doing her homework. Cheryl looks around.

'He's upstairs,' says Lorna in answer to the unasked question. 'He had two helpings of chips and beans. I think he's fine. But you, on the other hand, are not fine, are you?'

Cheryl perches on one of the kitchen stools and rests her forehead in her palms. 'I'm probably just being silly.'

'Oh dear,' says Lorna. 'I've heard that before.'

Cheryl glances in her daughter's direction, but Sasha has put earbuds in. She holds up her drawing and examines it with a critical eye as she jigs in her seat to the music.

'I agreed to do this today,' says Cheryl, 'because Xan was insisting. We don't want to miss the boat. That's his argument.'

'You did it because he wanted you to?'

'No, not entirely. And this venture capital firm seems like the kind of people we should be talking to.'

'You're evading the question. Did he persuade you you had to do it today? As opposed to tomorrow or next week?'

Such a bloody lawyer!

Cheryl smiles. 'It's more complicated than that.'

'It always is with you.'

'When he came home last night, he was hurt and upset. And I could see that he needed this. Needed me to agree with him.'

'No, babe,' says Lorna, shaking her head. 'That's placating him. Agreeing with him is when you do something because you think he's right.'

'Okay, well, we can argue about why, but I did it. I went to London. And I think the meeting was okay. But now he's being a complete arse. Makes me feel like I've done something wrong. I can't win.'

Lorna raises her eyebrows, but says nothing.

Cheryl rubs her face with her hands, then rakes them through her hair. 'What if he is right? What if we are in danger of missing the boat?'

Lorna goes to the kettle and flicks it on. 'How many years have you been working on this?'

'The question of vasculature, about three.'

'You're the expert, not him.'

'He's a businessman. I'm not a businessman.'

'You must've read every research paper on the subject that's been published. You know what the competition is up to as much as anyone does.'

'Well, yes, but…'

'But you still have to let your husband decide. Why?'

Cheryl sighs. Lorna has a knack of finding the weak spot in any argument.

It doesn't make her right.

'He's given up so much for me,' she says. 'I owe it to him.'

'Do you? What if he just wants to use you to get rich?'

'That's a bit harsh.'

'Somewhere in all this, you have to ask yourself that question. You know you do.' Lorna is staring at her. Implacable.

There's a knot tightening in her stomach.

First Xan, now her. Is everyone against her?

She says nothing. But Lorna is waiting her out. Expecting her to be the one to crack.

She's drained. She has a stonking headache. The dam bursts. 'You're being ridiculous,' she blurts. 'I know he's not your sort of person. But the truth is, you don't like men, that's why you're a lesbian.'

Lorna folds her arms. 'Oh, come on, let's not go down that road. You sound like the bloody tabloid press. I'm a lesbian because I fall in love with women. Men are not a problem for me. Xan would be fine with me if he made you happy.'

'How do you know he doesn't?' She sounds like a petulant child.

'Does he?' says Lorna.

She doesn't reply. In his way, he does. But her sister can never see that. He rescued her. He makes her feel safe. Mostly he does.

Lorna shakes her head in weary disbelief.

'Alright,' says Cheryl. 'We argue a bit. What couple doesn't? You and Amy argue.'

'Yes. About who's turn it is to take out the bins and where to go on holiday.'

Instead of who else he's shagging? Lorna doesn't say it, but she's thinking it.

'You just think the worst of Xan. You always have.'

Lorna sighs like a disappointed parent.

'Cheryl,' she says. 'You're the one who's come home saying he's being an arse.'

The atmosphere in the room is leaden. Sasha sits only metres away at the table, earbuds in, oblivious as she colours in her drawing with a felt tip. Cheryl looks at her child. She's his child too. And so like him. That's the part that Lorna doesn't get.

The kettle sings. Her sister unfolds her arms, goes to the cupboard, takes down two mugs and dumps tea bags in them.

It's horrible when they fall out. Cheryl hates it. For so much of her childhood, her big sister was her protector. The only bulwark she had against the chaos of boarding school, the loss of their mother, the complicated relationship with their father, not to mention his new family.

Contra mundum.

She inked this on her pencil case during a Year Seven Latin class. It was a posh, old-fashioned girls' school. Her and Lorna against the world.

She didn't make friends at school. Even the other maths and science geeks avoided her. When Lorna left school for university, she spent every hour she could alone in the library. The teachers didn't bother her. She got top grades and won a scholarship to Cambridge, where she got a double first. Being a social outcast had some benefits.

Lorna fills the mugs with boiling water and adds a splash of milk. She places one in front of Cheryl.

'Listen, I'm sorry,' says Cheryl.

'I can see it's been a tough day,' says her sister. 'Awful weather doesn't help.'

'No,' says Cheryl, cupping her hands round the mug.

They look at each other, letting the dust settle. Her sister smiles.

'I've always tried to like your girlfriends,' says Cheryl.

Lorna chuckles. 'Yeah, but I've only ever introduced you to the good ones. There are several that you definitely wouldn't have liked. We all do stuff we later regret.'

Cheryl meets her eye. She's still having a little dig. Lorna likes to have the last word.

Is that what she thinks? Xan is a mistake.

'I was stuck in the States,' says Cheryl. 'Lonely, far from home, trying to work and bring up a kid on my own, and Xan came along and rescued me. He took me on and accepted Jordan. I can never regret that.'

'I know,' says Lorna. 'And I wasn't saying—'

The doorbell rings.

Cheryl grimaces and frowns. Lorna looks at her, then adds, 'But we've discussed this enough. I'm sorry if I've upset you.'

'Doesn't matter.'

The bell rings again. Insistent?

'Xan must have headphones on,' Cheryl says.

She gets off the stool and heads out into the hall. Lorna follows.

Cheryl turns on the porch light at the wall and opens the front door.

And there they are. The police. Again? The same two who came on Wednesday afternoon to speak to Jordan. It's like déjà vu.

'Oh,' says Cheryl. 'Have you brought Jordan's phone back?'

'No,' says the tall one, holding up her ID. 'Sorry to bother you, Dr Woodward. This is not about Jordan. We were wondering if we could speak to your husband.'

'My husband?'

'About an incident that took place last night.'

Cheryl beams. 'Yes!' she says. 'He was mugged. Little

hooligans tried to steal his phone. I'm glad you're going to do something about it. You'd better come in.' She glances at her sister. 'Did you report it?'

Lorna shakes her head. Cheryl stands back for the two police officers to enter. Some action from the police. Maybe Xan did report it himself in the end? This will cheer him up?

45

Friday, 7.05pm

Lorna goes to fetch Xan while Cheryl leads the police into the kitchen.

'I do apologise,' says Cheryl. 'I don't remember your names.'

'DS Boden,' says the tall one. 'My colleague is DC Chakravorty.'

'Of course. Can I offer you a—'

Xan appears in the doorway, eye patch on. He looks disturbingly like someone attending a fancy dress party as a pirate. Feet bare, shirt loose with the sleeves rolled up. 'What's going on?' he says. His tone is abrupt.

'Sorry to bother you, Mr Woodward,' says the cop. 'We just want to ask you a few questions about your movements last night.'

'As you can see,' says Cheryl. 'He was mugged.'

Xan raises his hand to silence her. 'Why do you want to know?' he says.

He's moving slowly into the room, like a wary cat sniffing out the terrain. Cheryl can sense his jitteriness. This is not her husband; Xan is not a man who suffers from nerves. He's a man with breezy confidence and the assumption everyone will like him.

'We're investigating a suspicious death,' says the cop. 'Were you in town last night, Mr Woodward?'

He stops in his tracks. 'A death? Oh, I see.' His shoulders sag. His whole body seems to deflate like a punctured balloon, and his gaze scoots across the room to Sasha. She's sitting, wide-eyed, felt tip still in hand, watching the adults.

'Darling,' he says, turning to Cheryl. 'Perhaps it's time you took Sasha up to bed.'

Cheryl looks at their daughter. But Lorna steps forward and says, 'Don't worry. I'll take her. Come on Sash. I'll read you a story.'

While Lorna shepherds Sasha from the room, Xan pads across to the sink, picks up a glass from the draining board and fills it with water.

Cheryl watches the two police officers watching him. She has a nasty, fluttery sensation in her belly.

A suspicious death! Who? One of the muggers?

He turns to face the police, and taking a sip of his water, he smiles. 'Please, come and sit down. You must excuse us. We've just got back from a business meeting in London. Overcrowded train, couldn't get a seat. You know the sort of thing.'

They had a seat. And a spare next to them.

'Yes,' says Boden, smiling. 'That happens to me. It can be a nightmare.'

The smile is bland and polite. But this is not how she was when she came to talk to Jordan. She's scrutinising Xan intently.

The two detectives follow Xan over to the table. He scoops up their daughter's felt tip pens. But Cheryl can see his hand shaking.

'I'm sorry,' she says. 'I'm forgetting my manners. Can I offer you a cup of tea or coffee?'

Boden turns and smiles, but her eyes are opaque; they give nothing away. 'We're fine, thank you, Dr Woodward. This shouldn't take long.'

'Can you say who's died?' says Xan, as he pulls out a chair and sits. The two officers sit down opposite.

'We've yet to do a formal ID,' says Boden.

Xan opens his palms, lifts his chest and smiles. This is what he does when he's preparing to do a pitch. He's morphing into salesman mode, confident and easy-going.

'Ask away,' he says. 'Anything at all I can help with.'

'Your wife said you were mugged. Tell us about that?'

He tilts his head and chuckles, adjusting the eye patch. 'Okay, my wife's going to tell you I'm an idiot.' He shoots a brief look in Cheryl's direction. 'And, of course, she's right.'

'You don't mind if we record this. Makes it easier for us,' says Boden.

'Absolutely not,' says Xan with a flourish of his hand.

The other cop, the young Asian one, gets her phone out. Xan smiles, waiting as she presses record.

Cheryl is standing at the edge of the kitchen area. She has a sense that something momentous is about to happen. Xan has gone from sullen and uncommunicative to bright as a button. He's about to give a performance, and one which he regards as crucial.

Did he hurt the mugger? He can't be blamed for defending himself!

He takes a breath and meets Boden's gaze directly with

his one good eye. Not staring. Easy and comfortable. He's tried to teach her how to do this several times.

'Okay,' he says. 'Well, I was in town, parked in the multi-storey. I'd played a game of squash. Got back to the car, bloody thing wouldn't start. The garage man told me it needs a new battery a couple of weeks ago. But, y'know how it is, we put these things off, don't we?'

Boden smiles. 'We do.'

'Rain's sheeting down. I'm knackered. And, okay, I lost three games to five, so I'm not happy. I try to call a cab. Nothing for half an hour. Because the rain's sheeting down. So I decided to walk. I figured, brisk walk, twenty-five minutes.'

'In the rain?' says Boden.

Xan chuckles again. 'Well, y'know, I like to pretend I'm a hard man. What's a bit of rain, y'know?'

He's smiling at the cop, trying to charm her.

'Which way did you walk?' says the other one. It's the first time she's spoken.

Xan makes a point of smiling at her, too. 'I cut through the turnings from Lion's Yard and made for the Fen Causeway. There was a lot of spray from passing cars, so I walked back from the road. I tried to jog a bit. And they came at me from nowhere. Three, I think. Hoodies, y'know. One shone a light in my face. Phone, wallet. That's what they wanted.'

He turns to glance at Cheryl and gives her a sheepish look. 'You're right. I should've handed them over.' He turns back to the police officers. 'But one of them mumbled *hurry up granddad,* and I just saw red. I took a swing at him. He took a swing at me. The others piled in.' He removes his eye patch with a flourish. 'I think we can conclude from the result, they won.'

The eye is closed up, worse the earlier. Xan turns his head, displaying it like a proud war wound.

'You should get some medical attention for that,' says Boden.

He laughs and points at Cheryl. 'Yep, I have been told.'

'They stole your wallet and phone?' says the other one.

'Phone. Luckily, not the wallet. I managed to hold on to that. I think the phone was what they were after. They grabbed it and ran off.'

Why is he lying?

'You decided not to call the police?' says Boden.

'Well, they had my phone, so I couldn't. And by the time I got home, I was really pissed off. They were long gone. I couldn't identify them. And we had an important business meeting in London today.' He shrugs. 'So, I decided to let it go.'

Boden nods. She seems to be allowing the silence expand to see if he'll say more. But Xan smiles and waits.

Finally, she says, 'A horrible experience.'

He sighs. 'Yes, it was. But, y'know, I get it. You guys can't be everywhere, all at once.'

Boden smiles. 'It's true,' she says. 'Many people think we should have more officers on the beat.'

Xan grins. 'Especially in the pouring rain.'

'Yes,' says Boden. 'Especially in the rain. Just one other thing, Mr Woodward. Before you returned to your car, and found it wouldn't start, did you visit Kayleigh Burrows?'

Xan frowns and shrugs. 'Kayleigh, who works in my wife's lab?'

How is this about his visit to Kayleigh?

'Yes,' says Boden. 'She lives in town. Quite close to the multi-storey.'

Xan shakes his head. 'Nope. I think I saw her at the

party we had for my wife's birthday on Monday.' He turns and smiles at Cheryl. 'She was at the party, wasn't she, darling?'

Oh my God, another lie.

'Umm, yeah,' says Cheryl.

'Are you sure about that, Mr Woodward?' says Boden. 'Because Kayleigh says you did go round there.'

He huffs. 'It's not something I'd forget.'

'You didn't follow a friend of hers when he ran out of her flat?'

Arran?

He furrows his brow and throws up his hand. 'What friend? I don't know any of her friends? She's a girl who works for my wife. I hardly know her at all. Do I, darling?'

The two cops and Xan all stare at Cheryl. Her chest tightens. Panic floods through her.

What the hell has happened?

'No,' she says. But her voice is a whisper. She can feel Boden's gaze on her, boring into her.

'Any idea why she might say that?' says Boden.

Xan shakes his head. He looks genuinely mystified.

The cop turns to her. 'Do you know, Dr Woodward?'

'No,' says Cheryl more firmly.

Boden stands up, somewhat abruptly. 'Thank you for your time,' she says.

Cheryl remains rooted to the spot, while her husband shows the police officers out.

The front door slams. He returns to the kitchen with a thunderous expression.

'Xan, what the hell was that about?' she says.

He ignores her, goes straight to the cupboard, takes down a bottle of scotch and a glass tumbler. He pours a hefty measure.

'Xan?' she says. 'Last night you told me you went to see Kayleigh. Why did you lie to them? And about the phone.'

He takes a large mouthful of his drink.

'Stop asking bloody silly questions. I need to think.'

'But won't they find out?'

He ignores her. Taking his glass, he strides out of the kitchen and disappears down the hall. She hears the door of the study slam.

Cheryl can't move. She's shaking. Her husband is lying to the police and someone is dead. A suspicious death. That's what they said. Could he have harmed someone? A friend of Kayleigh's? Who? She's exhausted. Her head is throbbing, and it's impossible to order her scrambled thoughts.

Lorna appears in the doorway. 'What was all that about?' she says.

'I'm… not sure. Something and nothing. Hard to tell,' says Cheryl, forcing herself to move. 'Is Sasha alright? I should look in on Jordan.'

'I just did. He was texting away, possibly to some girl. He got very bashful.'

'Oh dear. Do you think I should be worried?'

She's saying this to fill the space. Inside, her brain is howling with panic.

Xan has done something terrible!

Lorna sighs. 'No. He's being a teen. I need to go. I told Amy I'd be back by eight.'

'Sorry. We've held you up.'

Lorna scans her, a small crease between her brows.

How is it her sister can always tell?

'Sure you're okay?' she says.

'I'm fine,' says Cheryl. 'I just need some paracetamol and an early night.'

'Okay.'

She escorts Lorna to the door, receives a peck on the cheek, and finally she's alone. The study door is shut. She wonders about tackling her husband again, but decides to wait until the morning. They both need time to think.

But her brain is frozen and a dark sense of foreboding is seeping through her. Witnessing her husband lying to the police was an alarming experience.

Why didn't she tell Lorna?

It was impossible. Her sister already has enough reasons to dislike Xan. No sense in adding to the list. Whatever he's got himself into, he's still her husband. It's her job to be on his side, isn't it?

46

Saturday, 9.20am

Hannah drives up the M11, heading north to Cambridge, under a louring February sky. She's borrowed a Range Rover Discovery from one of her brothers. He lives in Fulham, so why he needs a tank like this is a mystery to her. He uses it to ferry children and dogs. He has several of each, and it has a faint aroma of damp fur. But it's Saturday morning, and she's moving into her new temporary home from home, the better to follow Freddie's instructions and mind the Woodwards.

She made an early start, packing various necessities, like a flat screen TV, an Eames chair, and a box of kitchen utensils and groceries from her waterside apartment in Limehouse. The porter was very helpful, so she gave him a decent tip.

Once she sobered up, she realised she was in a far stronger position than she thought. If she'd known what Cheryl Woodward's response to Freddie would be, she might not have needed to twist Xan's tail to secure his co-operation. But it got the Woodwards to London. The deal was going ahead; she was on the ground and on point. Freddie would have to rely on her.

She can work with that. Plus, she has a new strategy for dealing with the Woodwards: become friends with all of them.

Last night she started chatting by text with Jordan Woodward; a teenage boy, pumped full of hormones, with one thing on his mind. Hooking him is crucial to her plan. If she can position herself as his new big sister, fun but also dispensing sage advice, then his mother is going to be grateful, isn't she? Also, having his son around will put pay to any of Xan's romantic ideas.

She's parking in front of the apartment building and wondering about the chances of a little chap with a trolley appearing, when Xan comes roaring up behind and stops inches from her tailgate.

He gets out of his cheap four-by-four and comes striding towards her. She lowers her window. He slaps the side of the door and leans towards her. 'We need to talk!'

'Good morning to you too,' she says. She opens the door of her vehicle and steps out. He's got his hands on his hips; he can't keep still, circling like a jackal.

Definitely got a bug up his arse.

'You and your bloody schemes!' he says. 'You have got me into so much trouble.'

'Sorry?' she replies. 'I have got you the kind of deal—'

'Shut up! SHUT UP! SHUT UP!' he shouts.

The outburst shocks them both. He glances around, has the grace to look sheepish and huffs.

She scans him. He's a wreck and stinks of alcohol. The eye patch is askew; it makes him look like a pantomime villain, striding around, trying to be menacing.

Why did she ever sleep with him?

'Are you drunk?' she says. 'Whatever your problem is, shall we talk about it inside?'

She skips up the steps to the front door of the building. He has no option but to follow. In the entrance hall, there's an empty concierge desk.

'Listen—' he says.

She raises her finger to silence him, glances around and sighs. 'Someone's supposed to be here to give me my key.' She finds a bell and dings it several times.

Xan paces like a caged panther.

Has Cheryl somehow found out she slept with him?

A cleaner in overalls appears. Turns out he has the key but no trolley, and little inclination to help unload her stuff.

'That your car?' he says to Xan. 'She can park while she's unloading, but you can't. You'll get a ticket.'

'Fuck off!' says Xan with a chilly smile.

They walk to the lift and travel up to her new apartment in silence.

She unlocks the door and opens it. Even on a dull winter's morning, it's flooded with light. Not a patch on her London home, obviously, but it'll do.

He follows her inside.

The agent has been as good as his word and furnished it. It's a bit John Lewis, but she can live with that.

'Well,' she says. 'What do you reckon? Not bad, eh?'

'Considering my company's paying for it,' he says sourly.

'Out of our investment, buster. Let's not forget that. And I have to say I don't find your manner this morning all that professional.'

'Really?' he says. 'Well, here's the thing Hannah.' He spits her name at her. 'When I got back from our meeting last night, I had the police knocking on my door. Two detectives investigating a suspicious death.'

'Oh dear,' she says, chuckling. 'Have you been a naughty boy?'

'You think this is some kind of fucking joke? It's not a joke.' Flecks of spittle fly from his mouth.

She stares at him. He's a big bloke, and he's steaming. As he does several circuits round the room, he radiates pent-up rage. It occurs to her he may be dangerous. And they're alone.

'Xan,' she says softly. 'Why don't you just calm down and explain to me what's happened? I'm sure we can sort this out.'

He stops, rakes his fingers through his hair, adjusts his eye patch. He reeks of desperation, which is worrying.

'Are you?' he says with a sigh. 'Because, I'll tell you one thing, they take me down for this, you're coming with me. I'll make bloody sure of it.'

She raises her palms. 'Whoa!' she says. 'This is getting surreal. Let's start with who's dead.'

'The cops wouldn't confirm it, but my guess is it's Arran Patel.'

Shit! Kayleigh's bloke?

'Who?' she says.

'Oh, don't play the innocent. We had a conversation about him, here, in this room, two days ago. You said he was a problem. You told me I had to sort it out.'

'Who're we talking about? Kayleigh's boyfriend? The one she wanted to get private psychiatric treatment for? All I said is the company should pay for it. Are you sure it's him? What happened?'

His arms are folded. He stares out of the window, over the Cambridge rooftops.

'I went round there to her flat on Thursday night,' he says. 'To do just that. To buy them off. But, I dunno, he must've heard us talking. He bolted out of the flat. It was dark, it was pouring with rain. I chased after him. I caught up with him down by the river. And he attacked me. Punched me in the face.' He pulls the eye patch down. His eyelid is a swollen pinky mauve mass. 'How d'you think I got this?'

'You weren't mugged then?'

'No, but I was attacked. By this mad sod I was trying to help. I had no choice but to defend myself.'

'Did you explain this to the police?'

'No course I didn't. Don't be ridiculous.'

'But if it's the truth.'

'They're not going to believe it, are they? They're just going to think I killed him. Particularly if I explain he used to work for my wife and you told me he could be a threat to your company's investment.'

'I never said that.'

'Yes, you did. That's exactly what you said. You said Freddie had an agenda to oust me, and he could use the problems with Arran to side-line Cheryl in her own lab and put Kayleigh in charge.'

'No, you must've misunderstood me. That's not what I said. I would never have said that.'

Freddie can't find out about this.

He stares at her. 'You lying cow. I went round to see Kayleigh that evening. Why else would I do that, eh? You and I made a deal. I'd sort that out and get Cheryl to come to London the next day to do the pitch.'

'Well, yes, that part's true. We agreed you'd persuade your wife to come to London to do the pitch. But anything else was just talk.'

'What d'you mean talk?'

'Speculation. Just things that might happen. I never suggested for one moment that you should harm Arran Patel.'

'I was trying to help him. He practically took out my eye. What am I supposed to do now?'

'I don't know. Have you discussed it with Cheryl?'

'No. Of course not.'

'Well, why are you telling me? She's your wife.'

He turns on her. She takes a step backwards, putting the kitchen island between them.

'Aren't you the fixer, Hannah? Isn't that your job?'

'Xan, you're crazy. I can't fix something like this. What did you… I mean, did you actually fight with him?'

He turns away. 'No, not really. I didn't think I'd hurt him. He just sort of stumbled. Somehow, he ended up in the river. Must've drowned. It's not my fault. It was an accident.'

'Shit!'

They stare at each other. He's right about one thing: this is a disaster. Any whiff of scandal, Nat'll dump the Woodwards like a hot brick. The contracts are still being drawn up, but nothing's been signed yet.

Xan knows all this. She can see the panic in his eyes. But also the calculation. 'Look,' he says. 'I told the police I was mugged. They seemed to accept that. Okay, it's a bit of a co-incidence.'

'Just a bit.'

'I need you to do something for me.'

'What?'

'Talk to Freddie. Get him to speak to Kayleigh. Persuade her to say that I never went round there.'

'Xan, I don't think he'll agree to—'

He takes a step towards her. 'He will. Because you'll persuade him. Come up with a convincing story. You're a cunning little minx, aren't you? You persuaded my wife you're a lesbian. That was clever.'

'That's different. I just didn't want her to be upset unnecessarily.'

He seems to be smiling at her, but it's more of a sneer.

'A lie? A story? Whatever you want to call it. You do this, it could all go away. I was never there. The police have got no evidence. We carry on. Build the company. Surely that's in both our interests?'

What planet is he living on? He must know how mad this sounds.

He wags a finger at her. 'But if they put me in the frame for this, you'll be there with me. I'll tell them you told me to shut Arran up. To do whatever it took. You're an accessory. You came to Cambridge because my wife's work is groundbreaking. There's potentially billions at stake here. You wanted to make a deal with us at any price. You seduced me to make sure I'd want to work with you.'

She can feel her heart thumping.

A splinter of truth. But he's twisting it.

She watches him, and it's unnerving, the zeal and the conviction he has. He's beginning to frighten her.

'Then you lied to my wife,' he says.

'It's your word against mine,' she says. 'No one'll believe you.'

He laughs, more a cynical cackle. 'Oh, they will. Juries love this stuff. They know about City types like you, Hannah, with your rich daddy.'

How does he know who her father is?

He chuckles again. 'What? You think I don't do my homework? It'll be obvious to them that you're the villain. They've seen plenty of TV shows about people like you. I'm just a poor fool who was weak and fell for this gorgeous temptress who waved money and sex under my nose.' He grins. 'Hey, maybe I was even falling in love with you. I would've done anything you suggested. And now I'm really sorry.' He clutches his hands over his heart, pulls a meek Jesus face.

Would anyone believe him?

Men like him always get away with it.

She's calculating. Even if the cops bought it, Nat would certainly want to distance himself. At the very least, she'd be out of a job.

He moves towards her and his tone softens. 'C'mon,' he says. 'We can do this. Okay, it's a shitshow. But, be honest, you helped create it. You know you did. We can be allies or enemies. It's your choice. Don't think you can beat me, Hannah. I'm a better liar than you. I've had loads of practice. Youth can make you over-confident.'

She scans him, and she feels sick. In some ways, he's like her dad. Big, solid, with that total conviction he's right.

'What if I agree?' she says.

'Then life will be sweet.'

He reaches out, takes hold of her hand and lifts it to his lips. 'We could be an amazing team,' he says.

His touch makes her skin crawl.

Suddenly she feels adrift. Small and scared. When she was little and got up to some mischief, her father would come looking for her. She'd get her telling off, a sharp slap round the legs. Then he'd scoop her up in his arms, and she'd be daddy's girl again. The relief was enormous.

But it taught her how to manage men, how to get what you want from them. She could do it then and she can do it now.

47

Saturday, 9.30am

A restless night has left Cheryl tense but enervated. She woke up after eight, late for her. Xan's side of the bed was smooth and empty. Maybe he crashed out in the study? She went downstairs and found Jordan in the sitting room with a bowl of Coco Pops, watching a Spiderman movie, and Sasha out in the garden feeding lettuce to her pet rabbit, Nesbit. Neither had any idea where their father was.

Cheryl prowled the house in her pyjamas, looking around for clues, but clues to what?

In the early hours, her febrile brain had cycled through every possible scenario. But one thing remained; the ghostly presence of her former researcher, Arran Patel. He'd ended up homeless, living on the streets. She and Lorna had found him bleeding on the pavement. He was taken to hospital. But what had happened since then, and how was Xan involved? Because it's clear that the police do think he's involved.

She wants to help her husband, to protect him. As his

wife, that's her natural reaction. But he lied to the police. Why? What's he trying to cover up? He would never hurt anyone deliberately. Violence isn't in his nature. He's the type to joke his way out of a tight spot. Despite his angry boast on the train, she's never known him with a black eye. Nor has he ever spoken about having one. Can he even throw a punch? He came home with a bruised knuckle; he must've been forced to defend himself.

But against Arran?

Round and round it all goes. She makes a coffee and toasted bagels with marmite for her daughter. Sasha is subdued; her eyes scanning Cheryl and looking for reassurance. She's too young to understand, but old enough to sense that something bad is going on. It's unusual for her not to ask questions. Normally, her chatter is incessant. Why this? Why that? She soaks up information like a sponge. But this morning she says nothing and doesn't mention her father at all.

Cheryl is at a loss. She struggles with these kinds of conversations with the kids. Talking about emotions and fears, and explaining grown-up behaviour that she can't even explain to herself. Ironically, Xan excels at this. He always has the right words to make their daughter smile again.

She sips her coffee as she watches her daughter eat.

'It'll be alright, y'know,' she says out of the blue.

Sasha nods and says, 'Can I take Nesbit some carrots?'

'Put some clothes on first,' Cheryl replies. 'It's too cold out there in your pyjamas.'

Sasha smiles and scampers off upstairs. Cheryl has a dismal feeling.

Jordan wanders in and heads for the fridge. He takes out a litre bottle of coke, unscrews the top.

'Glass!' says Cheryl.

He shrugs. 'Why?' And gives her a combative look; this happens now every time she tries to tell him something.

She softens her tone. 'Isn't it a bit early? Coke for breakfast?'

He chuckles and says in a posh, mocking voice, 'You mean like, darlings, no G and T before five? No coke before noon.'

He's a good mimic. It is amusing.

She smiles. 'You're cheerful this morning.'

He shrugs. 'Is that a problem?'

'No,' she says. 'Don't be daft. I'm glad to see you with a smile on your face. Relieved even.'

'That mean I can go out later? That I'm not under house arrest any more?'

'Of course you can go out. Who said you couldn't?'

'You did. Unless I'm with you or Dad.'

She sighs. 'No one wants to keep you prisoner, Jordan. Where do you want to go?'

He hesitates and frowns. She can see he's torn. Why do kids have to be so secretive?

'Nowhere,' he says. 'Forget it.' He takes the bottle of coke and heads for the door.

'Jordie, if you just tell me, then perhaps I'll say yes. Lorna says you've been texting a girl. Is that who you want to see?'

He blushes, his shoulders hunch, and he turns away. 'Oh for fuck's sake! What does she know?'

'C'mon, language!'

He waves his hand dismissively and disappears.

That went well.

Cheryl sighs. She picks up her phone from the counter.

She selects Xan's name and clicks on it. It surprises her when he answers on the second ring.

'Cheryl,' he says. 'You're probably wondering where I am.'

'Oh,' she says drily. 'It wasn't stolen then.'

'C'mon, look, I had to say something to the police. Let's not get melodramatic. I'm sorting this out. I'll be home soon and I'll explain.'

'Sorting what out? Listen, Xan, we need to—'

'I'll be home soon.' He hangs up. Cheryl watches the screen return to black.

She should've talked to Lorna about this last night. Foolish that she didn't. But it was out of loyalty to her husband. She has a fist of tension in her chest that's turning into a solid lump.

What does he expect her to do? Sit here and wait, like a good little wife, until he *sorts this out?*

Is that who he thinks she is? Maybe he does?

48

Saturday, 10.15am

Boden sits at her desk, turning a pen over end to end. She has the phone in front of her and for the last ten minutes, she's been on hold.

Finally, the pathologist comes on the line. 'Dr Cole, here,' says a brisk female voice. 'Sorry to keep you.'

'Not a problem. This is DS Boden. I'm investigating the death of Arran Patel, and I was wondering when you'll be doing the postmortem.'

Dr Cole sighs. 'We're waiting on his hospital records with details of his recent injuries. It's Saturday, so I doubt we'll get that until Monday now.'

'Can't you access them through the computer system?' says Boden.

'Not directly. Apparently, he was admitted under another name, so someone in admin has to sort it out. You know what it's like.'

Boden does. Not enough staff. Everyone's working flat

out. She can hear the weary resignation in the pathologist's voice.

'I can tell you the other name was Mohammad Rafiq,' she says hopefully.

She hears the doctor sighing. Boden's frustrated, but she also knows that hassling an overworked doctor won't get her very far.

'I've got a full schedule today,' says Dr Cole. 'Back to back until six. I don't know when I'd have time to even look.'

'I appreciate that. And I hate to press you. But this is a suspicious death, and it could be murder.'

Another sigh. 'I had a preliminary look earlier. The head injuries are extensive, so whenever it happened, it was a violent attack.'

'If they were pre-existing, the hospital wouldn't have discharged him, would they?' says Boden.

'Sergeant, I can't confirm that without the records to make a proper comparison.'

Boden knows she's on a hiding to nothing. She's fairly certain Xan Woodward is lying. But until it's confirmed that the victim was assaulted and didn't just fall in the river and drown because of his previous injuries, there's little she can do.

'Monday, then,' she says. 'Thank you.'

'We'll do our best,' says Dr Cole, and hangs up.

Boden glances round the office. It's Chakravorty's day off. And she takes them because, unlike Boden, she has a family and a life. She's also a keen, competitive runner; that's probably where she is today, out somewhere in the mud and rain having fun. Boden's envious.

The analysts are working through the CCTV; but on a dark, wet night, it's hard to identify anyone. Mackie is around somewhere. She gets up and walks down the corridor to the boss's office. As SIO, if they have a case on the go, he always checks in.

He's wearing a polo shirt and chinos, so he's not planning to stay. Glancing up, he waves her in. 'Well?' he says.

'It'll be Monday,' she replies.

He blows out his cheeks. 'Alright,' he says. 'You think Woodward's lying?'

'He's got a black eye. Okay, coincidentally, he could've been mugged. His story's plausible but convenient. But his wife looked freaked out.'

'It's still his word against Kayleigh Burrows,' says Hepburn.

'There's tons more going on here than meets the eye, boss. She works for his wife.'

The DCI rubs his chin. 'Right, let's get out in front of this. He says his phone was stolen? Let's see if he's telling the truth. Find out if the phone's been used since the alleged theft. Who it's called?'

'Burrows said he sent her a text after midnight. Which would be after the supposed mugging.'

'Okay, well, if we can confirm that. If he is lying, and the pathologist confirms the assault, we'll bring him in for questioning on Monday.'

Boden nods. It means a weekend in the office for her, talking to service providers and analysing phone records. It's not her favourite job but if gets the result, it's worth it.

49

Saturday, 11.25am

Cheryl stares at the three doorbells. The top one is marked *Burrows.* Taking a deep breath, she presses it. Kayleigh may not even be at home. She should've phoned. Now she's here, she feels ridiculously nervous. But she needs to look the researcher in the eye. She knows that much at least, although she knows little else.

Xan didn't come home. She tried calling again several times, but he didn't pick up. She showered and dressed, then paced and drank too much coffee. She thought long and hard about calling Lorna. But she didn't need her sister to tell she was being a fool.

Finally, her scientific brain kicked in. She concluded it was her emotions that were getting in the way. Loyalty mixed with fear, not to mention love for the man she married. What she needed was more data. Raw data. To get that, she had to speak to Kayleigh.

Jordan couldn't be relied on to take care of his sister. So

she called the mother of Sasha's best friend, Alicia. She didn't lie, but said it was a family emergency, which is true. She had no idea where the car was; possibly still stuck in the multi-storey car park in town. Or was that a lie, too?

She called a cab, delivered a dejected Sasha, clutching her backpack, to Alicia's house, and headed into town.

The last part, she walked, following directions on her phone, to a narrow back alley behind a restaurant. This is the oldest part of the city, a tiny warren of lanes and snickets, the vestiges of its medieval bones.

Is this really where Kayleigh lives? It occurs to her she's forgotten what it's like to be a broke, post-doctoral researcher, struggling to publish and make her mark.

The alley stinks of burnt cooking oil and rotting garbage. She suspects if she stands there long enough, she'll see a rat. In most city centres, rodents are seldom more than a few metres away.

She has to ring a second time before the door opens. Kayleigh freezes in the doorway.

'Oh,' she says.

'Sorry to bother you at home, at the weekend, but I was wondering if we could talk?' Businesslike and brisk. She adds a polite smile.

Kayleigh hesitates. Her jaw is slack, her eyes puffy and red-rimmed. She's wearing check pyjama bottoms and a sweatshirt from the university hockey club, and she smells of whiskey.

'You'd better come in,' she says.

They trudge up three flights to the top-floor flat. As she follows Kayleigh, doubts bubble up in her mind.

Shouldn't have come.

Kayleigh leads her into a compact, book lined sitting room. It's what Cheryl would've expected, precise and well-ordered. The laptop on the small glass coffee table is open. Kayleigh swoops down and shuts it. There's a glass beside it and a half-empty bottle of scotch.

'Can I offer you a cup of tea?' she says with polite formality. She hasn't forgotten she's talking to her boss.

Cheryl feels awkward. 'Look,' she says. 'Perhaps I shouldn't have come round like this. But the police came to see us. About a suspicious death, they said. And I'm wondering if they were talking about Arran.'

Kayleigh sways on the balls of her feet, buffeted by an invisible shock wave. She takes a moment to respond.

'Probably,' she says. 'They're supposed to be contacting me about the formal ID.'

'Oh Kayleigh, I'm so sorry,' says Cheryl. 'Do you know what happened?'

Kayleigh sways a bit more. The whiskey? Her eyes are glassy, the pupils dilated. Abruptly her body seems to crumple, and she drops into the armchair; it shudders from the impact of her weight.

She shakes her head, as if she wants to erase some awful memory. Then she glares at Cheryl.

'Why are you really here? To shut me up?'

'No. I came to find out about Arran.'

Kayleigh tosses her head. 'This is such bullshit,' she says. 'You're asking me what happened? Why? Your bloody husband is the one who went after him. He said you'd sent him round, that you wanted to help Arran.'

Cheryl can feel the sweat prickling the back of her neck.

'We talked about it…'

And Xan shut her down.

Tears well in Kayleigh's eyes. 'Y'know, I thought he'd turn up,' she says. 'I know Arran. He just runs away and hides. And Xan sent me a text, said he couldn't find him. I believed him. But then the police came looking for me at work yesterday afternoon, said they'd pulled a body out of the river.' Her chin trembles. 'Even then, I hoped… it didn't make sense. I didn't think Xan would actually hurt him.'

'Xan wouldn't,' says Cheryl. 'No way.'

Wouldn't he?

'This is all a stupid mix up,' she adds.

The two women stare at each other. Cheryl is staggered and dismayed. She wants to apologise. But for what? For being an awful boss? For being married to Xan Woodward?

'Listen Kayleigh,' she says. 'If Arran has died, then that's just terrible. I gather you two were, well… close. I can't imagine how you're—'

'You never gave him a chance,' blurts Kayleigh, wiping her nose with the back of her hand. 'You're so buttoned up. So inaccessible. He was ambitious, and he had a lot to prove. But you should've told him to just slow down. Not to drive himself.'

'Yes, but I wasn't aware that—'

'That's the trouble with you. You're stuck inside your own bubble. This brilliant one-woman show. Dr Woodward, the solitary genius back from the States. With the Silicon Valley husband who's going to make them rich.'

What's she talking about? Genius? Failure more like.

'That is not how I see myself,' she says.

'Everyone's frightened of you. Of your disapproval. That's why everyone in the lab is trying to do their own thing. Prove their worth. We get it. Once the company's set up, you'll be picking the top performers and everyone else will be out on their ear.'

Cheryl sighs. She hasn't even considered that. Is this really how people at the university see her? Remote and inaccessible. If only they knew.

'You seem to have a very definite view of me,' she says stiffly. 'I had no idea.'

Kayleigh says nothing. She pulls a tissue from the box on the table and blows her nose.

'What I was going to say,' says Cheryl, 'is perhaps you could assume that I know nothing, and tell me exactly what happened on Thursday evening?'

Kayleigh blinks at her. Her face is blank. She's beyond caring. She unscrews the top on the whiskey bottle and pours a hefty measure.

'I spoke to the woman from HDZ about Arran that morning,' she says.

'You mean Hannah? Why didn't you come to me? I told you on Wednesday that I wanted to help Arran.'

Kayleigh shrugs and sips her drink. 'I suppose I didn't trust you. Sounded to me you were just feeling bad about booting him out.'

'That wasn't my decision. The university has procedures—'

'C'mon, Cheryl. If we're going to be honest, let's be really honest. It all comes down to who gets to make money out of this work. Serious money. And your husband was always going to make sure it's you and him. The rest of us, no matter what our contribution, don't get a look in.'

'No, that's not true. I always intended—'

'He runs it. You stay tucked away in your bubble. I talked to Hannah because I knew she could use the money to twist Xan's arm. Get him to act. Pay for proper help for Arran.'

Kayleigh stands up. Bitterness and resentment drip from her. She towers over Cheryl. But she seems sad rather than threatening. Still, Cheryl takes a step back and away from her.

Why is everyone always fixated on the money?

'I don't care about the money,' she says. 'I care about moving this work forward and changing lives. I thought you did too.'

'That sounds very pure and noble when you already live in a fancy house in the best part of town.'

'There'll be enough for everyone, Kayleigh.'

'You sure about that? With your husband in control? I doubt it. That's why we decided to talk to Freddie. Make sure we get our share of the pie.'

Cheryl frowns. Her head is spinning. More things that don't make sense.

Who does she mean? That awful individual at the meeting in London.

'What are you saying? You told HDZ about our research? That's a breach of confidentiality.'

'Freddie Turner and I were undergrads together,' says Kayleigh. 'I thought with them at least we'd have some leverage. Better them than someone else chosen by Xan.'

Cheryl can't believe she's hearing this. All these machinations in her own lab.

'Who's we?' she says, although that hardly matters.

'Me and some of the others. I even hoped we'd get Arran his job back. But I'm a complete idiot, aren't I? You and Xan, I underestimated you. I had no idea the sort of people you really are. Just how ruthless.'

'Kayleigh, you've got this all wrong.'

'Have I? After the police spoke to me, it was obvious. Xan must've chased Arran. And killed him.'

She's crazy. This is grief talking. And booze.

Cheryl is shaking. She has to get out of there. What the hell is happening? In a few short days, everything that matters in her life has unravelled.

'You're drunk and you're talking utter rubbish,' she says.

'I can't believe you would betray my trust in this way. And to accuse my husband…'

Turning on her heel, she heads down the narrow hall to the front door. Kayleigh's voice follows her.

'What are you going to do, Cheryl? Get the university to boot me out too for breach of confidentiality? So you can enjoy your millions in peace. Is that Xan's plan?'

Cheryl hurries down the narrow staircase. She erupts into the stinking alley, and she runs.

50

Saturday, 11.30am

Hannah looks at Xan across the restaurant table. Getting him out of the flat and into a public place, with other people around and a solid object between them, is a huge relief. It took a good deal of wheedling and cajoling. It helped that he's been up all night drinking and was hungry.

She watches him devouring his bacon and egg bap in gulps like a ravenous dog. The yolk drips and runs down his fingers. He licks them and smiles at her. She smiles back.

Nightmare!

This has been the worst morning of her life. She's ticking with irritation, but also anxiety. All she wants is to escape this madman, get out of this damned place and back to London. She doesn't care what Nat says. She'll talk him round. He can't blame her for this.

Xan gives her a quizzical look. 'So we're on the same page?' he says.

'Course we are,' she replies.

Keep him calm.

'When are you going to call Freddie?' He's wiping his sticky fingers on a napkin.

She's fighting her nerves. She wants to fold her arms; it's an instinctive reaction. To protect and comfort yourself. She turns her coffee cup round on the saucer instead.

Be casual.

'Don't hassle me, Xan. I need to think, figure out the best way to tackle it.'

Xan waves at the server, holds up his beer bottle for another. He belches.

Disgusting.

He chuckles. 'Do I disgust you?' he says. 'See, I can read your mind.'

Hopefully not.

'Don't you think it would help the situation if you stopped drinking?' she says. She wants to sound flippant, remove any impression that she's intimidated by him.

Stay cool.

'How?' he says.

He's peering at her with his one good eye, and giving her that roguish grin. But there's a steeliness in his manner; this is a man determined to get his way. She glances at his right knuckle; the yellow bruising. The fact she had sex with him makes her feel sick. The way he's looking at her now, still with a hint of lust, makes her sicker.

How did any of this happen? It's mad.

'Isn't Cheryl going to wonder where you are?' she says.

He shrugs. Takes another bite of his bap. 'Probably. But she can wait. The priority is to get this sorted.'

A threat. But she refuses to let him see she's scared.

She sighs. 'Xan, I cannot guarantee that Freddie will agree to this.'

The server delivers his beer. Xan seizes the bottle and takes a swig.

'Well, you need to persuade him. It's not that complicated. He puts pressure on Kayleigh. She denies that I ever went round there. The police can't connect me to Arran's death.'

It's a crackpot idea. The notion that Kayleigh will lie because Freddie tells her to? Or even that Freddie would tell her to. Why can't he see that?

'I need to just pop to the loo,' she says.

'You went before we left the flat.'

She glares at him. 'Really?' she says. 'You want me to piss myself?'

'No,' he says. 'But there's no need to take your bag or your phone, is there?'

Smug bastard is grinning at her. He can read her mind.

'Call it a gesture of goodwill,' he says. 'We've got to be able to trust each other. That's the only way out of this for both of us. Bottom line, we're both responsible for what happened. I go down, I take you with me. Remember that.'

She stares at him; her heart pounds. Can she be blamed, too? It's her word against his that they even talked about Arran. One of her brothers is a lawyer. She wishes she could call and ask him. She can imagine how her family will react, how they'll mock her for getting into a predicament like this. Yet more proof of what a silly girl she is.

She glances across the restaurant. The toilets are in the far corner, miles away from the door.

She runs, but then what?

Getting up, she dumps her bag on the table and gives him a surly look. As she walks across the room, she senses his eyes on her back. She's shaky, but she needs to hold it together.

The toilets are unisex; round one corner is the separate section with the urinals. She glimpses the back of a man pissing.

Ask him for help?

No. She's overreacting. She needs to calm down and think. If she can play Xan along, eventually she'll get the chance to slip away. She'll get in her brother's car and drive back to London. It'll be fine. She's just been doing her job, doing what Freddie told her to do. Nat and Freddie will sort this out. She'll simply deny Xan's ridiculous story. They'll see it for what it is: the lies of a desperate man.

As she rinses her hands and face in the wash basin, and dabs away some streaks of mascara with a paper towel, she reminds herself who she is. She's Hannah Blakeney, her father's daughter, and she refuses to be intimidated by a broken-down hustler like Xan Woodward. This man is not going to ruin her career. No way.

She strides back across the restaurant, holding her head high and swinging her mane of hair. Xan watches her approach; he has that lecherous expression on his face again. What a fool he is if he thinks she'll let him touch her ever again. He's the pawn. She's playing him. This is what she needs to remember.

'Right,' she says. 'Let's go. I need to call Freddie.'

51

Saturday, 11.40am

Despite a blustery drizzle, the centre of town is bustling with Saturday morning shoppers. Cheryl soon finds herself being buffeted by passersby; shoved off the pavement, poked with umbrellas. She hates crowds. The press of other bodies always disturbs her; she needs distance and breathing space. She knows these streets so well, yet she's feeling disorientated and lightheaded. She finds herself outside McDonald's. This was the very spot where she and her sister saw Arran Patel lying injured on the pavement. She called an ambulance and tried to talk to him.

The coffee shop she and Lorna had just left that day is only a couple of doors away. She staggers towards it. It's familiar. A haven. And there are toilets in the back. The place is busy with a line snaking from the counter to the door; people are eager to get in out of the wet. But with uncharacteristic rudeness, she pushes her way past and gets inside.

The interior is long and deep; it opens into a large, unexpected cavern behind the narrow shop front. Raw brickwork, exposed pipes crisscrossing the vaulted ceiling and a fashionably mismatched array of second-hand furniture. Cheryl scoots between the tables to the back, but both the toilets are occupied. She tugs the handle of one. And then she notices a surly woman glaring at her from under a bright red woolly hat.

'There's a queue,' the woman says in a belligerent voice.

'Sorry,' Cheryl mumbles.

She wants to say that she's desperate. Her head is swimming with panic and nausea. She needs to escape from the world and bolt the door behind her, if only for a few minutes.

Instead, she turns away and slides into the banquette of a nearby booth. Sitting down helps. Red woolly hat is still scowling at her. But she doesn't care. She moves further along the banquette towards the wall until the sides of the booth conceal her. She checks the pulse in her neck with two fingers; it's racing. From the adrenaline? From the stress? She cups her face in her hands and focuses on her breathing.

The encounter with Kayleigh has unmoored her completely. The realisation that there's such hostility against her. Such resentment in her own lab. From the people she works with every day. And trusts.

She should never have gone round there.

Stupid stupid stupid.

She wonders where Xan is. Why hasn't he returned her calls? He must know she's worried about him. She cannot believe that he's responsible for the death of Arran Patel. And yet, a thought gnaws the edge of her consciousness.

Is it just that she can't accept it?

Her racing heart slows. The body returns to stasis if it can; all the studies show this. These are the things she knows about, the knowledge in which she has confidence.

Xan? Such a desperate longing for him.

But what does she know about her husband? His determination is often the thing that drives his actions. When his mind is made up, he's hard to deflect. In the nine years of their marriage, she's never felt physically threatened by him.

Not until the row on Tuesday night.

But did she imagine that? He's not the sort of man who would hit a woman. That's not in his DNA. He's a gentleman; he opens doors, fetches drinks. But it's also true that he always gets his way, and when charm doesn't work with her, he becomes sullen and dismissive. He's definitely a sulker.

Lorna says she doesn't stand up to him, that she's too meek. But why is it meek to want to avoid a row with your husband? And squabbling parents is not a role model she wants to show her kids.

He entered her life like a whirlwind. They bonded as fellow Brits in America. She couldn't believe that such a witty, beautiful man would look twice at her. But he did. He had such confidence, such ambition. He'd come to the States to get filthy rich, he told her. When he proposed, he said 'Marry me and we'll have such adventures.' It hadn't worked out like that. Not the money, and certainly not the adventures. He was the one who went off and did things. Business trips to Hawaii. Opportunities he couldn't pass up. She worked in various labs, focusing on her research, and did her best to juggle this with the care of one, then two children.

But it didn't start like that. The first year they were together, he took her on a magical mystery tour in an open top Chevy from Big Sur to the vineyards of Napa Valley. His optimism was infectious. Marrying him was like winning the lottery. She'd never been in love before. But it was more than that; it was a consuming passion. A fever. They couldn't keep their hands off each other. The desire they had for each other overruled everything.

Where did all that go? Did it just burn out?

Their return to England wasn't what he wanted; she understood that. But he made the best of it. He did consultancy work and made contacts. He decided it was all meant to be, because the biotech company they'd set up together would be a world beater. He'd make sure of it.

In the last year, it's all they'd talked about. The start-up. It was going to make them rich; he was convinced of it. He'd ask about her research, how it was all progressing. It was the most interest he'd ever shown in her work. She tried to explain it in lay terms. She made it clear to him it was a slow process. Most things they tried didn't work. But Xan was impatient. He wanted to get her out of the university into a privately funded lab, where throwing money at the problems would make them easier to solve. He believed that. But she was never convinced. She enjoyed the academic side of her work as much as the pure research. Teaching students was one area of her life where she felt confident dealing with other people. She didn't have his drive or sense of urgency.

That's why this is her fault.

She's let Xan down. If she'd shared his enthusiasm and got behind him sooner, this could've all been different.

Now she doesn't know what to do. She thinks about calling Lorna. But what would she say? Her big sister is always supportive on the surface, but she can also be just as stubborn and determined as Xan. Lorna is a woman who goes her own way and gets what she wants. She and Xan are polite to each other, but they've never got on. Cheryl's loyalty has always been torn between them.

She becomes aware of two people looming over her. A man and a woman, elderly, bundled up in anoraks. He's holding a tray, loaded with cups, a teapot and plates with pastries.

'Have you finished with this table?' he says in a plummy, authoritative voice.

She looks up and meets his gaze. His tiny eyes are dark pinpricks surrounded by wrinkles, his jaw is set. It's clear he expects her to move.

'No,' says Cheryl firmly. 'I'm waiting for a friend. She's just in the queue.'

A barefaced lie. But who cares?

He stares at her. He doesn't believe her. She stares back.

'When it's busy, people should order first, before occupying a table,' he says.

'Really?' says Cheryl. 'You're the man in charge, are you?'

His wife is tugging at his sleeve. She doesn't want a scene. But he continues to glare at Cheryl. The naked hostility in that look is chilling. Is she imagining it? What has she done to deserve it?

Don't back down.

He stands there for a moment longer, then he turns away, mumbling, 'so rude.'

Cheryl wants to run. Escape. Hide. But she laces her fingers and holds them tightly in front of her on the table. Staring at her hands, she swallows hard; she's determined not to cry.

52

Saturday, 11.45am

Hannah steps out of the lift on the fifth floor. Xan is close behind her, breathing down her neck. She can smell the booze on him and the sweat. But she's keeping her nerve.

They turn a corner and sitting on the floor, with his back against the front door to the apartment, is Jordan Woodward, scrolling on his phone.

Xan stops dead. 'What the fuck?' he mutters under his breath.

But Hannah's heart soars. The relief! This is the distraction she needs to turn the tables in her favour. It's her way out.

Jordan scrambles to his feet, giving his father a sheepish glance. Neither was expecting to see the other.

'What are you doing here?' snaps Xan.

'Hannah texted me. Invited me over,' says Jordan, defensively.

Xan turns to Hannah. 'Did you?' he says.

'Last night,' she says breezily. 'It's not a problem, is it?'

That strategy—make friends with all the Woodwards—is ancient history. She faces a very different situation now.

Xan is having to curb his temper. He glares at his son.

Jordan shifts from foot to foot, awkward and embarrassed. Hannah knows she has to use this. She smiles at the boy as she unlocks the door.

'Glad you came,' she says.

'Does your mother know you're here?' says Xan sourly.

Jordan is blushing; he shakes his head.

Hannah strolls into the flat. Father and son follow behind. She can feel the tension between them. Her ploy of connecting with Jordan, hoping to make him fancy her, has obviously worked, but exposure of this to his father is excruciatingly embarrassing for the boy. Xan, for his part, is annoyed and doing little to conceal it. None of that matters, though. This is the diversion she needs. She has to use it.

'So what do you think?' she says to Jordan brightly. 'Cool, huh?'

He nods, but it looks like he's about to bolt, and she needs to prevent that at all costs. He's her shield against Xan.

'And it's great you're here,' she adds. 'Because you can help me and your dad unload the stuff from my car. If that's okay?'

He shrugs. 'Yeah, sure.' He's avoiding his father's eye.

She beams. 'Two strong guys. Just what I need.'

She's aware of Xan scowling at her. 'What about the phone call?' he says.

'Yeah,' she replies. 'I'm about to do it.'

Xan rubs his face and adjusts the eye patch. The unexpected appearance of Jordan has thrown him off kilter, and the stress is getting to him. He glances at his son with some hostility. Yet another glimpse of the man he really is behind the facade.

Poor Jordan.

Hannah opens her bag and pulls out the car keys. She dangles them in front of Xan. 'There's not that much,' she says with a guileless smile.

Reassure him.

Reaching out, she brushes his arm with her fingertips. 'And don't worry,' she says. 'I'll get Freddie onside. Promise.'

Big smile.

Xan is frowning, but he takes the car keys and gives Jordan a curt nod. The two of them head for the door. Hannah pulls out her phone.

'Oh, and be careful with the Eames chair,' she says.

'Talk to Freddie,' says Xan. 'We need to get this done.'

The door closes behind them. At last she can breathe. It's a cold day, but sweat prickles down her spine. She goes to the kitchen tap, flicks it on and dipping her head, drinks straight from it. She wipes her mouth with her hand.

Concentrate.

She only has a few minutes to do this. And Freddie had better be answering his phone.

Scrolling to find his number, she heads out on to the balcony. The breeze is sharp, the day heavily overcast. But if they come back, she can't risk being overheard.

Freddie answers immediately, which is a relief.

'Hey,' he says. 'How's it going?'

'Listen, Fred,' she says. 'We've got big problems, and I don't have long to explain.' He needs to hear the urgency in her voice. But she doesn't need to fake it.

'I'm listening,' he says.

'Xan Woodward is...' she sighs. Where to begin? 'He's a

total liability. There's a former researcher of Cheryl's from the lab, who may have been able to challenge one of Cheryl's patents.'

'There's always someone who fancies their chances, but the lawyers'll—'

'Yeah, but this person has ended up dead in suspicious circumstances. And the police are knocking on Xan Woodward's door.'

'Shit.'

'Exactly. And Xan got his black eye on the night it happened.'

'Do the police think he's involved?'

'I don't know. But he came looking for me this morning, when I arrived at the flat, and I have to say, his behaviour is scary and threatening.'

'Scary how?'

'Look, I'm not being melodramatic.'

'Okay, then you should get out of there. Immediately.'

'Believe me, I'd like to. But he's got some crazy notion that we're going to concoct an alibi for him. I've tricked him into going and getting some stuff from my car. But he's fixated on me doing this. On us doing this. I don't think he'll let me just walk away. Seriously Freddie, I'm bricking it.'

'Has he threatened you?'

'Not explicitly. But it's his whole manner.'

'Okay, you need to keep calm. Tell him whatever you need to tell him. I'll speak to Nat. We'll handle this. And I'll be there as soon as I can.'

'Thank you!'

'You think his wife's in on this?'

'I doubt it. The guy's a piece of work. He's obsessed with the money. And as far as I can make out, he lies to everyone, including her probably.'

'It's going to be okay, Hannah. Just hang on in there. I've got this.'

The line goes dead. Hannah gazes out over the rooftops. She should feel relief, but she doesn't. London is an hour and a half away by car. In the meantime she's stuck here with an unhinged Xan Woodward.

She hears the main door to the apartment open. Xan appears, carrying a box of kitchen utensils. He dumps it on the kitchen counter.

As she walks back into the main room, he says, 'What the hell have you got in here? Weighs a ton.'

'Just a few essentials.'

No Jordan!

'Where's Jordan?' she says.

'I sent the little bastard home.' He glares at her. 'He showed me a couple of the texts you sent him. And I have to say, I don't appreciate you grooming my fourteen-year-old son.'

What?

'Don't be ridiculous, Xan. The kid's been having a rough time, and I was just being friendly.'

Xan leans on the counter and gives a hollow laugh. 'C'mon Hannah, a girl like you? Just being friendly? Every male you see, you think you can manipulate.'

'What's that supposed to mean?' she says indignantly.

Xan takes a step towards her. He towers over her and she can feel the menace. 'He's not your concern. Okay? Your job is to help me.'

She raises her palms and steps back. 'Fine. No problem.'

He roots in the box and pulls out a cafetière.

'What did Freddie say?' His tone is matter-of-fact.

She watches him, the detached calmness as he sorts through the utensils and groceries. He doesn't seem that bothered about his situation. Why did she never see this before? His unwavering belief he can get what he wants. It makes her blood run cold. Yet it's weirdly admirable.

'He's agreed to get in touch with Kayleigh,' she says.

'When?'

'I don't know, Xan. As soon as he can. We'll just have to sit tight and wait.'

She feels shaky. Why didn't she run from the restaurant when she had the chance? Or tell them to call the police? She's handled this all wrong. He just seemed like another middle-aged lecher. It never occurred to her he'd be dangerous.

He unearths a packet of ground coffee. 'Ah, here we go,' he says. 'Fancy a coffee?'

She nods. But what she said to Freddie was true; she's bricking it.

53

Saturday, 11.50am

It's in the waiting that the frustrations of the job weigh most heavily on DS Jo Boden. Waiting for calls to be returned, waiting for records to be traced through the system, waiting for forensic evidence to be analysed and reports to be written. And waiting for a post mortem to be completed to find out if a crime has actually been committed.

She knows there's nothing to be done. The technology available now to do the job can be amazing. The bottlenecks always involved people: staff shortages, mistakes due to lack of training, individuals who can't be bothered.

Telephone inquiries on Xan Woodward's phone are in hand. The Communications Data Application has been signed off. Woodward's phone account is with one of the larger service providers who, theoretically, should have procedures in place to deal with such a request quickly. But it's Saturday, and it's February, so absentee rates due to sickness are high.

They'll get back to her as soon as they can; that's what she's been told.

Boden has asked for a full billing, including a calls list, starting at midday on Wednesday, in order to cover the period when he says the phone was out of his possession, but also to establish his pattern of use in the period immediately before.

As she waits for the information to come through, she's been doing some digging. A trawl through the archives of the Police National Computer has produced a fifteen-year-old conviction for insider dealing for one Alexander Mark Woodward. He received a three-month prison sentence, a fine and a ban from working in the UK financial sector. The date of birth would make him a similar age to Xan Woodward. She's requested a mug shot from the City of London police, who prosecuted the case, to see if it's the same person.

Dr Cheryl Woodward crops up way more on the net than her elusive husband. There are numerous links to her academic research papers, several online lectures and conference appearances.

However, Boden does unearth a picture of the couple's wedding at a winery in Cupertino, California nine years ago. Cheryl Woodward, in a lacey, flowing dress, is a surprisingly girly bride beside her tall, handsome husband. A small boy stands beside them, beaming and clutching a bunch of dusky pink peonies. Boden thinks of the forlorn teenage boy in a Cambridge car park, a mass of unruly limbs and confused emotions. It seems the Woodwards were a happy family once; she doubts they are now. Digital forensics are still probing the contents of the boy's phone, although, as she told the boss, she still thinks that's a waste of time.

She gets up, stretches, and wanders across the room to where the civilian analysts sit. Two of them are working their way through the CCTV. One male, one female, both ridiculously young; the speed with which their fingers skip across the keyboard never ceases to amaze Boden. It would drive her crazy having to stare at a computer screen all day. But they seem to love it, and their sharp eyes miss very little. They belong to the online generation who've been glued to a phone screen since they were tots; they make Boden feel old. The girl is called Amber and Boden knows her slightly.

'Anything of interest?' she says.

'We've got a possible sequence,' says Amber. She clicks through several tabs and brings up a short video clip on her computer screen. Boden peers over her shoulder. The footage is very dark; a figure is stumbling along.'

'We think this is Arran Patel,' says Amber. 'We picked him up earlier in town when he emerged from the building where Burrows' flat is. We've been trying to map his route.'

She glances at her colleague. He grins.

'This is now the area close to the river?' says Boden, pointing at the screen.

'Yeah,' he says. 'It's the path that leads to the bridge. Watch here, in the background. We've enhanced it as much as we can.'

Amber moves her cursor across the screen to the lefthand side.

The video is hard to decipher. It's grainy, parts of it inky black, but with dancing shapes. A wild night with trees and bushes being lashed by the rain. Brief patches of illumination flare from the odd streetlight. Boden stares at the cursor and sees a figure take shape. There's definitely a second figure. Both figures are running. But the second figure is moving much faster and gaining on Arran Patel.

'Someone is running after him?' says Boden.

'Yeah, we think so,' says Amber. 'And they get pretty close before this camera loses them.'

'That's brilliant,' says Boden. 'Well done.'

The two analysts beam and glance at each other. Another tiny potential piece of the puzzle. But will they be able to ID the pursuer from any of the footage?

Boden returns to her desk. She opens her notebook and picks up a pen. Arran Patel was chased. Kayleigh Burrows says it was Xan Woodward who went after him. Would she lie? If so, why? She writes out the names and connects them with arrows.

Woodward is injured; he's been in a fight. He alleges he was mugged. Does he still have his phone? His account contradicts Kayleigh's story. Even if he chased Arran, he might not have attacked him. But then why lie about it? Because his wife didn't know?

How did Arran Patel die? Accident? Drowning? Or the result of a violent assault?

Boden goes over the lines with her pen, thickening and broadening them. As she doodles, the repetitive action helps her think.

Her encounter with Xan Woodward the previous evening, when she and Prisha went to his house to speak to him, is niggling her now. There's something about him that's quite disturbing. She's pretty sure he's lying, although she can't prove it yet. What's bothering her is the fluidity and confidence with which he did it. He seemed completely at ease, almost flirtatious. This is not typical. Most people in his situation would not react in this way. They may try to lie their way out of it, but their nerves or guilt would surface in some small way. A nervous tic? Even just a look or tone of voice?

Woodward's performance was flawless. His wife was the

jittery one. In Boden's view, this gives rise to two possibilities. He's either a man who's telling the truth, or, under the easy charm, he's a far more dangerous and psychopathic individual than he appears to be.

54

Saturday, 12.35pm

Hannah is rigid with fear, but keeping it in check. She sits on the sofa, fingers tightly interlaced in her lap. They've drunk their way through a cafetière of coffee. Xan can't keep still. He paces up and down. The eye patch has been discarded; his battered face looks sweaty and malevolent. He still has her car keys in his hand—no exit route there—and he's flicking the fob back and forth obsessively.

The time trickles by with excruciating slowness. Her phone is beside her on the sofa; occasionally she nudges it to check the time.

Forty minutes since she spoke to Freddie.

Without any preamble, Xan disappears into the bathroom. The door remains open and she can hear him pissing. But it gives her the opportunity to pick up her phone and scan her messages.

Don't worry. Cavalry on the way. Also spoke to Dr W.

She quickly tucks the phone back under her thigh.

Spoke to Dr W?

It's hard to imagine what Freddie might have said to Cheryl Woodward. Or how she would've reacted.

Xan comes out of the bathroom and stares at her.

'This is not my fault, y'know,' he says.

He's got a bruised knuckle and a black eye. Hannah wonders what would be his fault. She doesn't reply.

He drags his fingers through his hair and adds, 'I have worked my butt off for this deal. You knew that. And you manipulated me.'

Does he expect her to feel sorry for him?

He wanders across the room. But he's wound up like a spring and she can feel his impatience.

'Aren't you going to say anything? You going to sit there all innocent as if butter wouldn't melt?'

Her heart is hammering.

Be careful.

'Xan, I know you're upset—'

'Too bloody right. I've been thinking this through. You set me up. It was a pack of lies. Question is why? What was in it for you?'

'I don't know what you're taking about.'

'Why did you tell me Freddie had plans to sideline us, to put Kayleigh in charge?'

'I only said that might be a possibility.'

'You didn't. You said he'd pack the board and then use the question of Arran to oust us.'

'I was just speculating.'

'It was a fairy story, wasn't it? When you think about it, it doesn't even make a lot of sense. Why would Freddie do that? But you're so good at this, aren't you, Hannah?'

'You've got this all wrong.'

'No, I've finally got it all right. You think you're so smart. You wiggled your cute little arse, and you reeled me in. Women like you are toxic.'

The way he's glaring at her, the anger and the hatred, is terrifying. He's loading all the blame on her. But it's not her fault.

What did she actually do? She was engineering the deal in her favour. In the cut-throat world of finance, it's what everyone does. You have to in order to build a career. And as a woman, it's ten times harder, so you use any leverage you've got. In her position, Freddie would've done the same.

Okay, the sex was a mistake. She's certainly learned her lesson on that front. But she was hardly the seducer.

He's standing over her, hands on hips, with a look of utter contempt on his face. It's a struggle not to burst into tears.

'I didn't set out to seduce you,' she says. 'It was just sex after a party. We were both pissed. You wanted it as much as me. But that's a separate issue. And you're right, it's unprofessional. But I didn't tell you to go chasing after Arran and attack him.'

She didn't!

He's not listening. 'You set me up. Cause that's the kind of conniving little bitch you are.' He spits the words at her.

'I'm sorry you think that.'

'Thing is, are you still playing me? I reckon you are.'

'No, why would I? You said it yourself. I'm in the frame too.'

'But clever little Hannah probably thinks she can lie her way out of that, too.'

'Believe me, Xan. I don't.'

'So why hasn't Freddie called back?'

'I don't know. Maybe he can't get in touch with Kayleigh?'

'And you've got me waiting. Stringing me along again. What are we waiting for, Hannah?'

'For Freddie to sort this out with Kayleigh. Make sure you have an alibi. He'll call as soon as he's managed it.'

'Show me your phone.'

'What?'

He looms over her, holding out his hand. 'Show me!'

'Xan, listen to me—'

He grabs her arm and drags her off the sofa. His fingers bite into her arm. She had the phone tucked well away. But it gets knocked on the floor. Xan lets her go, reaches down and picks it up.

'That wasn't so hard, was it?' he says. 'You going to open it for me?'

What choice does she have? She takes the phone and places her thumb on the button. The screen lights up with another text from Freddie.

Just getting to M11 turnoff. There in 30?

Xan grabs the phone and looks at it. 'Well well,' he says. Then he scrolls to the earlier message and reads it out. 'Don't worry. Cavalry on the way. Also spoke to Dr W. What does this mean? Why's Freddie been talking to my wife?'

'I don't know.'

'What's the plan, Hannah? Cut me out of the loop? He doesn't even mention Kayleigh.'

'I don't know. He's probably trying to contact Kayleigh through your wife.'

'You mean he's mislaid her number?'

'I really don't know. He'll have a reason. And we've just got to—'

'No. No more lies. You think you can hang me out to dry?

You think I'll let you do that? What a truly stupid little bitch you are.'

There's a righteous indignation burning off him, laced with pure hate.

He's going to kill her. The realisation sweeps through her body like a howling wind. How does she know? It's an eerie sensation. And she resists it. The very idea is absurd, isn't it?

His eyes are diamond hard as he tilts his head and gives her that roguish smile. It could almost be a come-on, a precursor to sex. The smile is to lure her. To throw her off guard.

Time slows from a trickle to the spiralling descent of each individual grain of sand.

Is this how it ends? His choice. His decision. Has she lost all agency completely?

Her lips part to speak. But no words come. What do you say? Do you beg? Do you bargain?

Her heart thumps in her chest.

She's underestimated his rage. His spite and need for vengeance. As he steps forward, the smile fades. His eyes narrow to dark pinpricks of fury. He blames her. He's making it her fault that he has to do this.

She glances around. For a way out? For a weapon?

Will it be quick? Will it be painful?

A deep and visceral compulsion to survive kicks in. She'll fight. She'll claw the eyes from his face. Tear his flesh with her teeth. If she can just get past him and make it to the door…

She balls her fists. But her voice must beguile and seduce. Make him remember how connected they are, what it feels like when they make love. She must rescue him from the terrible rage that's consuming his reason. He can't be this man. She must make him see that.

‘Listen,’ she whispers. ‘Let’s just try and—’

He seizes a hank of her hair, twisting it round in his hand and yanks her towards him. The brutality and shock of it paralyses her. She inhales but before she can scream, he clamps his hand over her mouth.

55

Saturday, 12.40pm

Cheryl frets and fidgets in the back of the taxi, as it crawls at a snail's pace through the centre of Cambridge. This is taking way too long. She leans forward in her seat to speak to the driver.

'Isn't there another way?' she says.

'Road works, love. Not much I can do,' he replies. 'Saturday morning makes it worse. And the weather.' He huffs and shakes his head.

'Can't you turn round and find another route?'

He throws up his hands. In both directions, the road is choked by creeping, belching columns of traffic. The rain is falling steadily.

Her anxiety has been rising since she got the call. Now it's going through the roof. It must be nearly thirty minutes ago now.

She was in the cab, heading home, when the phone rang. For a moment, she hoped it might be Xan.

Unknown caller.

'Dr Woodward,' a strange male voice said. 'I'm afraid we have a situation.'

'Sorry? Who is this?'

'Freddie Turner from HDZ. I've just spoken to my colleague, Hannah Blakeney. I'm concerned that your husband may be threatening her.'

'What? That's ridiculous.'

'Please don't hang up, Dr Woodward. I'm on my way to Cambridge and I hope we can sort this out.'

'Why would he even be with Hannah?'

'She's moving into a flat today. Just temporary accommodation. I think she told you.'

Cheryl's mind was blank. Still full of Kayleigh's spiteful accusations. Whatever she was told, she couldn't remember.

'If you could just go round there,' he said. 'I'm sure Hannah would be reassured.'

'I don't understand.'

Is this where Xan's gone? Why?

'Once I get there,' he said, 'we can sort out any misunderstandings. I've spoken to my boss and we're very anxious that this shouldn't escalate. If it ends up in the media, none of us are going to look good, are we?'

Cheryl felt at a loss. Why would her husband be threatening Hannah? It made no sense.

'I really don't think—'

'Dr Woodward, let me be blunt. If you won't go there yourself to reassure Hannah, I'll be forced to call the police. And I think they already have an interest in Xan, don't they? This could only make things worse for him. I think you'd agree. It's in both our interests to de-escalate this.'

'Yes,' she said. 'You're probably right.'

'I'm texting you the address. Please do this.'

'Okay,' she says.

'Thank you.' He hung up.

The taxi driver was only too willing to turn around and head back into the centre of town. And now she knows why. The meter is ticking. Stuck in traffic, it's a fat fare for him.

Her thoughts are scattered and without focus. She's trying to put together the pieces of a puzzle. But they just don't fit. How does Freddie Turner even know the police are interested in her husband?

A dangerous question has infiltrated her mind.

If Xan isn't with Hannah, then where is he?

She leans forward again towards the driver.

'I'll have to walk,' she says. The directions on her phone say it's less than a mile. Maybe ten to fifteen minutes?

She pays off the cabbie and steps out into the pouring rain. She has no umbrella, only a light jacket, but at least it has a hood.

The earlier drizzle has turned into quite a downpour. It's drumming the pavement, which is awash with puddles. The curious thing is she doesn't mind. The cuffs of her jeans soon become sodden, but she walks at a fast pace and that keeps her warm.

The map on her phone guides her to an imposing stone-faced building near the Fitzwilliam Museum. It's old. She has no memory of what it was before, but a large sign at the front announces that it's recently been converted into luxury apartments. Work is still ongoing because there are builder's hoardings still in place on one side.

As she crosses the road towards it, she sees that a police car is parked across the lane at the other side of the building. The rain is teeming down and two uniformed officers are struggling to attach police tape to the railings on either side of the narrow street. They seem in a hurry to cordon it off. Then she hears a siren, and an ambulance comes tearing down the road towards her. It turns abruptly into the lane and stops beside the police car.

Cheryl walks forward. She's soaking; water rolling down her face and dripping down her neck. But a terrible sense of dread is seeping through her. She approaches the young PC who's winding the tape round the wrought-iron railings.

'What's happened?' she says.

'There's been an incident,' he replies, intent on his task. 'I'm afraid you can't come down here.'

The paramedics are running from the ambulance, lugging their medical bags, past the police car and down the lane.

'What sort of incident?' she says.

But the PC is in a hurry. 'Sorry, madam. I can't tell you any more. But you'll have to move back.'

She peers over his shoulder through the foggy blur of rain. But it's difficult to make anything out. The paramedics are twenty or thirty meters down the lane, and now they're bending over something. Someone?

The building has a large portico surrounding the main entrance. Two people, a man and a woman, are standing in the shelter of it, watching what's going on. They're dressed in identical green cleaning overalls. Cheryl trots up the steps towards them.

'Do you know what's happened?' she says.

The man has his arms folded and a grim look on his face. 'Woman moved into the top-floor flat this morning,' he says. 'And she's just taken a dive off the balcony.' He shakes his head. 'Five floors up. Bam! We heard it.'

Cheryl's jaw slackens, but she manages to say. 'Do you know her name?'

The cleaner shakes his head again. 'Came up from London this morning. She said the number, I gave her the key. She had some bloke with her, helping her move in. He left here like pretty damned quick. I reckon the cops are gonna want to speak to him.'

Xan?

Cheryl feels her body swaying. 'Thanks,' she mutters. She turns and walks away. It's all she can do to put one foot in front of the other. Her mind is as frozen as the icy rain. The only thing she can think of is *Go home now. Just get yourself home.*

56

Saturday, 1.05pm

Although it's miserably wet, Jo Boden is still relieved to get out of the office. She lets Mackie drive. The centre of town is snarled with Saturday morning traffic, made worse by road works. But Mackie loves this sort of thing, putting on the blues and twos and bulldozing his way through.

They're headed for a lane close to the Fitzwilliam Museum. Uniforms have already cordoned it off, and as they pull up, the ambulance is just departing with the victim.

Boden gets out, pulls her hood up and walks towards the young PC on the cordon. He looks damp and forlorn.

'Morning, Sarge,' he says. 'This looks like one for you. Woman went off a fifth-floor balcony, landed down the side lane here. But suspicious circumstances.'

'Dead?'

'Paramedics worked on her. She's gone to hospital, but she was a mess.'

'Nasty situation,' says Boden. 'You alright?'

The PC nods. Boden wonders if he's seen anything like this before. He looks shaken, so probably not.

'Okay,' she says. 'What else?'

Mackie is surveying the front of the building.

'Place has just been refurbed,' says the PC. 'Made into posh apartments.'

'Wish I could afford somewhere like this,' says Mackie.

'Hardly anyone's moved in yet,' says the PC. 'She arrived this morning. Some bloke with her. Cleaner saw them come and go a couple of times. Two of them were working in the building, doing a builders' clean. Basically, they heard her hit the deck. Came out to look. Saw the bloke legging it from the building. Got in his car, drove off. They called it in.'

'Don't suppose they got a reg number?' says Boden.

'Don't think so.'

'Right,' she says. 'Extend the cordon. No one in or out of the building. Once the CSM gets here, they'll take charge. Where are the cleaners?'

'Inside,' says the PC. 'Keeping out of the rain.'

'You're doing a grand job,' says Boden with a smile.

Mackie is on the phone, calling in the forensic team.

Boden looks around. There's a Range Rover Discovery parked near the front of the building. She walks over to it and peers inside. There's a chair crammed in the back and a flat screen TV. It has a parking ticket on the windscreen. She turns to Mackie.

'CSI are on their way,' he says.

'Find out who this belongs to,' she says, pointing to the car.

Boden walks into the building. The two cleaners are sitting on the floor sharing a flask of coffee. They're both wearing green overalls. There's a vacuum cleaner and several black sacks of rubbish next to them.

Boden holds out her ID. 'I'm DS Boden,' she says. 'Quite a horrible experience you've had this morning.'

The man stands up. He's small and balding and seems quite anxious. 'Pavel Kaczdowski,' he says with a deferential dip of the head. 'This is Lena. She don't speak much English.'

'Don't be nervous, Mr Kaczdowski. Just tell me what happened and what you saw.'

He nods. 'We hear this sound. Like a thump, but sort of wet. Looked out of the window and she's there, in the road.'

'And what did you do then?' she says.

'We run out to look.'

'Straight away?'

'Yeah, we just in the ground-floor apartment. Close. I get on my phone to call ambulance, and we see him run out. The man that was with her. He gets in his car and drives off.'

'This man, how did you know he was with her?'

'They arrive together. I give her the key.'

'Tell me about that,' says Boden.

'The penthouse flat. My boss give me the key, said the lady would be coming from London this morning.'

'Do you know her name?'

He shakes his head. 'Maybe he tell me. But we got ten apartments to clean this morning. So I forget. But I know it's her when she arrives. Very posh.'

'Is that her vehicle out there?'

'Yes.'

'They didn't come in the same vehicle?'

The cleaner shakes his head again.

Mackie joins them.

'But she arrived with a man?' says Boden.

'He came in another car. I told him. She can park to unload, but he can't. He was rude.'

'Rude how?'

'I was only trying to warn him he'd get a ticket. And he tell me to f off.'

'That was rude,' says Boden.

The cleaner shrugs. 'I seen the parking guy come later. He wrote tickets for both. So I was right.'

Boden glances at Mackie and smiles.

'I'm on it,' he says. He moves away and gets his phone out.

'Tell me more about the man,' says Boden.

'He's tall. And he's got like a black eye. When he come first, he has like an eye patch.'

'An eye patch?' says Boden. That's interesting.

She's about to ask another question, but she becomes aware of an altercation outside. Someone is shouting. Turning, she can see that the young PC on the cordon is trying to restrain a man, who's shouting at him and trying to get past. Mackie runs out to help him.

Boden heads outside after him.

The man is screaming. 'No! Let me by!' Parked next to him is a red Ferrari.

Mackie weighs in. He grabs the man by the shoulders and holds him, as Boden catches up.

'Calm down, mate,' says Mackie. 'Just calm down. What's the problem here?'

The man seems to crumple. Mackie has to support him. The man has tears running down his face. 'That fucking bastard,' he says. 'What's he done to her? What's he done to Hannah?'

57

Saturday, 1.10pm

It takes a while for Cheryl to realise she's in shock. Her body is on autopilot, her brain is flickering between random thoughts, snippets of memory. She's in survival mode. She called for a cab, but there was a thirty-minute wait. She tried Xan again. He still isn't picking up.

Somehow she ended up on the bus, which drops her at the top of her street. She sets off along the familiar route towards her house. The rain has eased back. The air is sharp and damp; the pavements slick with water. But the cloud base remains low, the sky is threatening and dark; this is just a respite between downpours.

Nearly home. Nearly there.

She trudges on. When they moved into this place, she told her husband that this was it. She'd never move again. That's how much she loves this house. He'd just laughed and said he'd find her something better. That's Xan, always has his eye on something better. Something more.

She once asked him why money was so important to him. He'd shrugged and replied, 'It's how you keep score. It's how people judge you. If you're rich, you get different treatment. Basically, in our society, what you're worth financially, is what you're worth.'

This seems obvious to him. But it's never been her approach to life.

Her father wasn't rich in Xan's terms, but he was well off. He owned an engineering business, inherited from his father, but which he'd improved and expanded. It provided a large detached house in Surrey and an expensive boarding school education for his daughters. But her childhood fell into two distinct phases: before her mother died and after.

Don't think about all that. Not now.

As she walks, Cheryl's scampering thoughts flit back to an early row she had with her husband. He'd accused her of being spoilt and overprivileged. His argument was that because she'd never been without money, she didn't appreciate the value of it. He insisted that he'd worked for every penny and was proud of that fact. However, it seemed to Cheryl that his pride was tinged with resentment at having to do it.

But what has he done now? What has he done to Hannah?

These questions must be answered.

Not now. Not yet. Get home first.

She retreats into her musings. His assumptions about her were always unfair. As a post-doctoral researcher in the States, she'd lived on an extremely tight budget. When she became a single parent on top of that, she often found it hard to make ends meet. On a couple of occasions, her sister had stepped in and paid off her credit card debts. She knows the value of money.

When they argued, and his charm evaporated, his spite and envy surfaced.

And when he's angry…

His accusations could be vicious. She was the lucky one with a posh education. He never went to university. He started in a lowly office job in the City and worked his way up. Learned about business and finance the hard way. But his efforts were never rewarded. His firm booted him out through no fault of his own. That's when he abandoned London for the States. She'd heard this tale from Xan frequently. And when he'd drunk a bit, it would turn into a rant about how he'd prove the bastards wrong. Eventually he'd get the respect he deserved.

As she approaches the house, Cheryl sees a car double parked outside. A Volvo? She stops. It takes a moment for her to recognise Teresa, Alicia's mother, hurrying back to her vehicle. She waves to someone on the front doorstep. Cheryl moves forward; only then does she see Xan standing there with a fatherly hand on their daughter's shoulder.

He's come home.

She glances round and sees that their car is parked in a slot further down. Everything is a terrible mess. But now it can be straightened out. This Freddie was lying. Whatever's happened to Hannah, Xan can't be involved.

Cheryl crosses the road. Teresa is about to get back into her car, but hesitates when she sees Cheryl.

Teresa tilts her head and paints on a smile. If anything, she looks pissed off.

'Cheryl,' she says. 'I'm so sorry. I had to bring Sasha home. She was getting rather upset.'

'Upset about what?' says Cheryl. She's well aware that she must look a bedraggled mess, and Teresa will be judging her.

'Oh, you know what these girls can be like,' Teresa says with an exaggerated sigh. 'She and Alicia had a squabble, and it got a bit out of hand.'

Cheryl can see Alicia sitting in the front passenger seat of the enormous Volvo and giving her a baleful look.

'Well, thank you anyway for helping out,' says Cheryl with as much dignity as she can muster.

'No problem at all,' says Teresa. 'I hope you've managed to… well, do what you needed.'

She climbs into the car and drives off.

Snooty cow.

Cheryl tries to suppress her uncharitable thoughts as she walks up the path to her own front door.

Xan scoops their daughter up. Sasha flings her arms round her father's neck, legs round his waist, and buries her face in his shoulder. He rocks her like a toddler.

'It's alright, baby,' he whispers. 'Daddy's here.'

This irritates Cheryl.

'Shall we go inside?' she says.

'Where have you been?' says Xan. 'You're drenched.'

'I've been looking for you.'

'Why? I told you I'd be home soon. I just needed to sort a few things out.'

He carries their daughter into the house. Cheryl is left to pick up Sasha's abandoned backpack from the doorstep and follow.

58

Saturday, 1.20pm

Cheryl kicks off her shoes at the door. She's wearing trainers with socks, which are also soaking wet. She peels them off. Xan has disappeared into the kitchen with Sasha. She hurries after them, her bare feet leaving a damp footprint on the polished wooden floor.

Xan sits their daughter on the kitchen counter, holding her gently by the arms, as if she's still a five-year-old who's come home from school distressed. It's ridiculous him babying her like this. And he knows Cheryl disapproves. Sasha's legs hang down, foot tapping the cupboard door. She knows she has to play along.

'So what's happened?' he says softly. 'No one's going to be angry.'

Sasha gives him a mournful look. 'I didn't want to go. But Mummy said I had to.'

'I'm sure Mummy had her reasons,' says Xan. He gives Cheryl a side-eyed glance.

'Alicia's a pain. Going on about her new phone and her new iPad. She's always getting new stuff. I hate her.'

Cheryl ought to pick her up on this, but she doesn't have the energy. And Alicia is a spoilt brat. She doesn't mention that either.

'Here's what we're going to do,' says Xan. 'Go upstairs and put your stuff away and read quietly, while Mummy and I talk. And later, there'll be treats.'

'What treats?' says Sasha, giving him a coy smile and touching his cheek.

Cheryl watches her daughter with a sense of unease. She knows how to please him. She's Daddy's girl.

Only eight years old.

Is it her fault Sasha's like this with her father? She's never wanted her daughter to be like her. To always need to please a man and put him first. But where has she learned this behaviour if not from her mother? It leaves Cheryl with a horrible feeling.

Xan lifts Sasha off the counter and pats her on the head. 'A big treat. You'll see.'

'Your backpack's in the hall,' says Cheryl. Sasha gives her a nervous glance, turns back to her father and beams, before skipping out of the room.

Xan frowns and shakes his head. He picks up the kettle, takes it to the sink and fills it. Now his manner has flipped. He seems weary and annoyed.

Sasha can be heard going upstairs.

He sets the kettle on its base, flicks the switch and sighs.

'Why the hell did you ship her off to Alicia's?' he says. 'Surely you know they've fallen out?'

'No, I didn't.'

'Last week. Chrissake, Cheryl. You need to pay more

attention to her. To both the kids. Then we wouldn't have such problems with them.'

What?

Cheryl's head is in a spin. He's accusing her of being a bad mother?

'What do you mean?' she says.

He folds his arms. 'You thought Jordan was in trouble before, well I can tell you, he's in much bigger trouble now.'

She stares at him. 'Jordan? What are you talking about?'

'You want to know where I've been? I've been trying to rescue our son.'

But she left Jordan at home.

'Xan, you're not making any sense.'

He takes two mugs down from the cupboard. 'Cup of tea?'

'Can you just explain what you're talking about?'

He drops a tea bag in each cup and says, 'Well, long story short, seems our fourteen-year-old son developed a crush on Hannah Blakeney.'

'How do you know?'

'I've seen the texts he's been exchanging with her. He went round there this morning. I followed him. Unfortunately, I didn't get there in time.'

'In time for what?'

'To stop him. There was obviously some kind of argument. Maybe he thought something was going to happen between them? They had a fight. He pushed her off the balcony.'

Jordan? No!

Cheryl is reeling. The kettle comes to the boil and switches off. Xan picks it up and fills the two mugs with hot water. He stares at her. There's a curious blankness in his expression, and a hardness in his eye. He gets a spoon from the drawer and prods the tea bags.

A wild panic seizes Cheryl. She turns on her heel, runs out of the kitchen into the hall and up the stairs two at a time. The door to Jordan's room is shut. She throws it open.

Jordan has his back to her. He's hunched over his laptop, playing a computer game. He turns and gives her a surprised look.

'Have you been out this morning?' she says. 'And don't lie to me, Jordan. I want the absolute truth.'

'Well, yeah.'

'Where?'

He's blushing. 'Dad told me not to say.'

'Why?'

'I dunno. Guess he doesn't want you to know what's going on.'

'What is going on?'

'I dunno.' He hunches his shoulders and stares at his feet.

'Jordan,' she says. 'Did you go round to see Hannah Blakeney at her new flat?'

He twists the toggle of his hoodie. 'Yeah, but she invited me.'

'Then what happened?'

'She wasn't there. I waited. She and Dad came back. She wanted us to help unload her stuff. But Dad got pissed off with me, told me to come home. And not to tell you about it.'

'Did you have a fight with her?'

He scrunches his face. 'A fi—? Course I didn't.'

Cheryl gazes at her boy. His soft cheeks are bright red. His downy beard. Tears are welling in his eyes.

'You sure? I want you to tell me the absolute truth.'

'Course I'm sure. I just left. Dad gave me money for the bus.'

'Dad says you've got a crush on her. Is that true?'

He huffs and seems even more embarrassed. Then he says sourly, 'Yeah, a bit, but I realised I'm probably not the only one. That's why he wanted to get rid of me.'

'What do you mean?'

He raises his head and looks at her, tears streaming down his face. 'I dunno. You're the scientific genius, Mum. You figure it out.'

59

Saturday, 1.25pm

When Cheryl returns to the kitchen, Xan is seated at the table, calmly sipping his tea. He turns towards her and gives her a blank look.

Who is this man? She's not sure she even knows any more.

'Jordan says you sent him home.'

Xan sighs. 'The boy's going to lie, obviously.'

'He's not the one that's lying,' she says.

He shrugs. 'After all I've done for you, you'd believe a lying teenager over me? You're a sad woman, Cheryl. You know that?'

The barb hits its mark. It always does. He's trying to bully her.

Not this time.

'Freddie Turner phoned me this morning,' she says. 'He said you were threatening Hannah. I didn't want to believe him. But he gave me the address, and I went round there. The police were cordoning off the lane at the side. A woman fell from the fifth floor. That's what the cleaner told me. I'm guessing it was Hannah.'

Xan shakes his head wearily. 'It's not fair. The way you leave all this to me. All the mucky business stuff. While you sit there like a queen in your lab.'

That's what Kayleigh said.

'Fuck's sake, Xan. Do you even know if Hannah's alive?'

'No. And I don't care. Because, y'know, that woman was devious. She tried to shaft us. You don't know the half of it. She lied about everything.' He chuckles. 'Even convinced you she was a lesbian, so you wouldn't think I was shagging her.'

Cheryl's head is spinning. She grasps the edge of the table and flops into a chair. Her son's innuendo is true then. She feels a fool. She is a fool.

Xan is watching her, scanning her face.

'Oh, c'mon,' he says, softening his tone. 'I play away sometimes. But I've told you before, haven't I? It means nothing.'

'Means nothing to you,' she says.

'Men and women are just different,' he says in a flippant tone.

'I've only ever wanted you to love me,' she murmurs.

'And I do. I always have. You know that?'

'No, I don't know it.' She feels sick.

My God! What has he done?

He reaches across the table and puts his hand over hers.

'Listen to me, Cheryl, there's a way out of this for us.'

Us?

He's holding her hand now, stroking her fingers. 'Let's suppose she is dead. And I think that's likely. If Jordan makes a full confession, what's going to happen to him? He's a fourteen-year-old boy, and she was grooming him. It's all there on his phone. He'll get some youth detention. His identity won't be revealed. By the time he's eighteen, he'll be out. And we'll have launched the company, with seed capital from someone else. Fuck HDZ, they're a bunch of crooks. We'll have made millions by then and we'll give the kids the life they deserve, the life we deserve.'

She pulls her hand away. 'You'd do that to Jordan? To your own son?'

'I agree. It's not ideal. But it's the least worst scenario for us. He'll survive. It'll probably toughen him up.'

Cheryl stares at him in disbelief. 'And how are you going to persuade him to confess?'

Xan shrugs. 'He's a smart lad. We'll just put the facts to him. Three, at most four years, he comes out, he'll have shares in the company. He'll be a multi-millionaire before he's twenty. I think plenty of kids would take that deal.' He sips his tea. 'I wish someone had offered me a deal like that.'

The horror of it hits Cheryl. He really thinks he can blame this on her son.

She slaps the table.'No!' she says. 'No way.'

He looks at her and sighs. 'C'mon darling, don't be difficult.'

Difficult? His tone suggests she's refusing to go to some boring dinner party with him.

'You expect Jordan to go to prison instead of you?'

'Don't be ridiculous. They don't send fourteen-year-old kids to prison. It's more like a strict boarding school.'

'But he's innocent.'

Xan exhales and shakes his head. He gets up and comes to stand behind her chair.

A frisson of fear runs up her spine.

He killed Hannah, and he wants to blame it on her son.

He puts his hands on her shoulders, leans over, and kisses her hair. 'Listen to me, my darling,' he says. But it's the soft cajoling voice he uses with Sasha. 'We're nearly there. All we have to do is keep our nerve. You have to keep your nerve. You're doing brilliant work—'

She pulls away from him and jumps up, sending her chair skittering across the floor. 'Forget the work,' she says. 'This is not about the work. I don't care if it never makes me a penny.'

He stares at her in disbelief. 'Well, you should. What have we been doing all these years? Came back from the States, all our sacrifices. What's it all been for? We stick together. We're a team, you and me. Trust me. It's a win-win situation. It'll work.'

She steps back from him.

'No, Xan. No way! It's not going to happen.'

He puts his hands on his hips and shakes his head, like a disappointed parent with a naughty child.

'Everything I've tried to do for this family, and you won't even meet me half-way on this.'

'Half-way? I've listened to your nonsense for too long. Have you any idea what you're saying? Or is it just another story you're telling? Another elaborate lie?'

He shrugs his shoulders, opens his palms; his expression is one of total mystification and innocence. 'Cheryl—'

'Don't Cheryl, me. It's over.'

She turns on her heel and walks out of the room. Every part of her body is shaking. She grasps the newel post at the bottom of the stairs to steady herself. She looks up and sees her two children seated next to each other on the top step. They're staring down at her with shocked looks on their faces. They must've heard everything.

'Put some overnight stuff in your backpacks,' she says. 'You're going to Auntie Lorna's.'

'What's going to happen?' says Jordan.

'Nothing's going to happen to you,' she says. 'You've done nothing wrong. He's not going to put this on you. I won't let him.'

Xan is standing in the kitchen doorway. He's staring at her. The eye patch has been discarded, but the swelling has gone down, leaving an ugly bruise.

He chuckles to himself and mumbles something. It sounds like *we'll see.*

60

Saturday, 1.26pm

The cleaner has unlocked one of the unoccupied flats for them. There's some furniture shrouded in plastic covers. Boden perches on the edge of an enormous white leather sofa. Ferrari man sits opposite in a bucket of an armchair, his face cupped in his hands. He's identified himself as Freddie Turner. The victim, he says, is Hannah Blakeney, who works for him at HDZ, a City investment firm. And another name has been mentioned, which has got Boden's attention.

She waits. She's seen a lot of men cry. They try to suppress it, swallow it down. But not Freddie, he sobs, which, in Boden's opinion, is a much healthier response.

'You okay?' she says.

He wipes his face with a hand and takes a deep breath. 'I didn't know what to do,' he says. 'Hannah can be a bit of a drama queen, if you get what I'm saying. I wasn't sure if she was exaggerating.'

'But she told you she was being threatened by Xan Woodward?'

He nods.

'Why?'

'She said he was involved in the death of a researcher who used to work for his wife and he wanted an alibi. It sounded… I don't know, outlandish. How was that going to work? I thought, I need to get here, see the lay of the land. Potentially we've got a lot of money tied up in this deal.'

'What sort of deal?'

'We're putting seed capital into a biotech start-up run by Xan Woodward and his wife, Dr Cheryl Woodward.'

This is about money, thinks Boden. It often is. When you follow the money, it all makes sense.

'I did call Cheryl and try to persuade her to come over,' says Freddie. 'I hoped she might calm her husband down. I don't know if she did.'

Boden watches him. In shock, and speaking quickly. But there's something else; he's blaming himself. He thinks he should've acted differently.

'I should've just called the police,' he says. 'But I didn't really think… oh God.' He puts his face in his hands.

Mackie comes in with a plastic bottle of water. He catches Boden's eye and shakes his head.

Boden takes the bottle. 'Have a drink,' she says, handing it to Freddie.

He unscrews the cap and takes a swig. 'Which hospital have they taken her to?' he says. 'I should get over there. And I need to call my boss. He'll tell her family.'

'I'm afraid we've just heard,' says Boden, 'that Hannah has died. I'm so sorry.'

'Oh Christ!' he says, clamping his hand over his mouth.

'I'll stay with him,' says Mackie. 'DCI's just arrived.'

Boden nods. She walks towards the door.

Freddie Turner is keening. Grief and guilt, never a good combination. Mackie squats down beside him and rubs his shoulder.

Out in the foyer of the building, more officers are arriving. Members of the CSI team are carrying their gear in. The flat is on the fifth floor. But the lift could contain evidence. It'll be a long walk for them up the emergency staircase.

DCI Hepburn is over in one corner, talking to the CSM.

He turns as Boden approaches. 'Right,' he says briskly. 'We've checked it. A parking ticket was issued outside here to a vehicle registered to Xan Woodward. So it's definitely him.'

'The cleaner saw the man who'd been with her run from the building a few minutes after they heard the impact. He got in that car,' says Boden.

'That's about how long it'd take him to get from the fifth floor down to the ground,' says the boss.

'Perhaps we'll get lucky with CCTV,' says Boden, pointing up at the tiny cameras tucked in the architrave above the entrance. 'The building is supposed to have state-of-the-art security, including cameras in the lifts. If it's up and running, it should give us the entire time frame.'

Hepburn turns to the CSM. 'Put that top of your list, Kev,' he says. 'What's his connection with this woman?'

'She worked for the venture capital firm that's investing in the Woodwards' business. A colleague of hers has turned up. Says she phoned him and alleged Woodward was involved in the death of a researcher. Sounds like it could be Arran Patel. Woodward wanted her to give him an alibi.'

Hepburn absorbs this. 'I saw the Ferrari outside.'

'Belongs to this colleague,' says Boden.

The DCI shakes his head. 'So we think money is at the root of this? Both cases?'

'Still need to join up the dots, but it's looking like that, boss,' says Boden.

Hepburn sighs. 'Okay, bring him in.'

Boden nods. 'Yes, sir.'

61

Saturday, 1.35pm

Cheryl is a bundle of jangling nerves. Who knows what her husband might do next? She has one priority: protect the children. She's standing in the middle of her daughter's bedroom when her phone rings. It's Lorna.

'You okay?' says her sister. 'I just got your text.'

'Can you come? I need to get the kids out of the house.'

The text had contained a simple, hastily typed message: *Help!*

'I'm on my way,' says Lorna.

Lorna hangs up. She gets it, thank God. But the relief is momentary, because Sasha doesn't. Of course she doesn't. She's sitting on her bed crying, and she won't budge.

'I don't understand,' she wails. 'Daddy said we'd have a treat. Why can't we do that? I don't want to go to Auntie Lorna's. I want to stay here with Daddy.'

Cheryl is at her wit's end, stuffing pyjamas and a change of clothes into the bright pink backpack. She doesn't know how to answer her daughter. Sasha can be obdurate and Cheryl has never coped with that effectively; the truth is, she's left it to Xan.

For years, she's left too many things to Xan. With the children, with her work, she's let him set the agenda. Has he controlled her? That's what Lorna thinks. All she wanted was to please him and to keep everyone happy. And they have been happy, haven't they? Until now.

A deep sorrow is engulfing her, threatening to suck her under and down into the abyss. It would be a relief. But she can't let it, not yet. She must focus. For the sake of the kids.

She sits down beside her hysterical daughter. 'Sash, I know this is hard—'

'Why don't you and Daddy just make up? Like you usually do.'

'When you're older—'

'Don't you love Daddy anymore?'

Cheryl is at a loss. Her head is swimming, her limbs are leaden. 'I… I love you. And I love Jordan.'

Focus.

She looks up. Jordan is standing in the doorway, his back-pack hooked on one shoulder. His face is deadly pale.

'C'mon, Sash,' he says. 'Stop being a baby. Get your stuff and let's go.'

Sasha looks at her brother. 'I'm not being a baby.'

'Yeah, you are. You know you are.'

Her two children stare at each other. A rush of affection floods her veins. It seems impossible that she made these two people; each of them totally individual and unique. She knows the biological processes and has recited the facts, the proven details in numerous exams, but it's still a total mystery. And the drive to protect them is hard-wired, she knows that too. In this moment, all that matters is getting them away from Xan.

Sasha is still wearing her sulky face. Cheryl realises she might have to haul her up and drag her out.

But Jordan comes and sits beside his little sister. 'When we get to Auntie Lorna's,' he says. 'I'll teach you how to make a video. Cool edits and effects. Better than anything your mates can do. I guarantee it.'

'Will you?' says Sasha.

'Promise,' says Jordan with a smile. There's more than a bit of Xan in him, even though Xan is not his real father.

Sasha stands up. In a couple of minutes, her bag is packed. Cheryl shepherds her down the stairs. Jordan follows. They walk down the hall; the study door is wide open.

Xan has his back to them. He's standing at the desk, laptop open, typing something.

Will he try to stop them?

He turns and looks at them. 'What are you doing?' he says.

'The kids are going to Lorna's,' she replies.

He smiles. 'I don't see any need for that. Don't you want your treat, Sasha?'

Her daughter is close to tears. She'd probably run to her father if Jordan wasn't clutching her hand.

'Leave her out of this, Xan.'

'Out of what? You've clearly scared them. Now you're hustling them out of the house as if there's some kind of problem. There is no problem. Jordie, take your sister into the kitchen and get the ice cream out.'

'I don't want ice cream,' says Jordan.

'I bet Sasha does. C'mon, mate, help me out here. Your mum and I need to have a chat. Don't look so worried, Sash. I promise you, everything's going to be fine.'

Jordan is staring at Xan, with a mulish expression. How much of her previous conversation with Xan did he overhear?

All of it?

Sasha's lip is trembling. This stand-off is no good.

'You two go into the kitchen,' says Cheryl. 'Don't worry. We're just going to talk. I'll only be a minute.'

Jordan looks at her. What's he thinking? His gaze dips and he nods. 'C'mon, Sash,' he mumbles. 'Ice cream.'

As the two children disappear down the hall, Xan holds open the study door and invites her to enter. He closes the door behind her.

How scared should she be?

But he walks over to the desk, where his laptop is open. 'I'm booking a flight to San Francisco,' he says. 'I figure it's sensible to have a Plan B.'

'You can't just run away, Xan.'

He shrugs. 'Says the woman who's spent her life running away. Because that's the truth about you, isn't it?'

He's trying to provoke her.

'The police will catch you, extradite you,' she says in a matter-of-fact tone.

'I've been thinking about the States. It's always puzzled me why you chose to go there. For me, it was like the promised land. I was drawn to it.' He has a wistful, faraway expression. 'But you were never that comfortable. You never seemed that happy there.'

'I was a single parent trying to care for a small child and do post-doctoral research.'

'I know all that. But why did you go in the first place? What were you running from?'

'I wasn't running from anything. Berkeley was a great opportunity to do cutting edge research and to learn.'

'You can't have been there even a year, when Jordan was born.'

'I never intended to get pregnant. It was an accident.'

'Yeah, I've heard the story you tell—'

'It's not a story.'

She feels a tightening in her chest.

'Isn't it?' he says. 'The idea of you rocking up at Berkeley and immediately going to frat house parties doesn't make a lot of sense to me.'

'I was trying to fit in.'

'Be honest. The party on Monday, your fortieth, you didn't even want to come. In the nine years I've known you, you go out of your way to avoid most social gatherings.'

'Xan, why are you going on about this?'

'Makes you nervous, doesn't it? I can see it from your face. You're frightened.'

'Yeah! Because of what you've done to Hannah. Of course I'm frightened.'

He frowns and shakes his head. The look is one of exasperation.

'You think I would hurt you? Don't be ridiculous. You're my wife. I've taken care of you, haven't I? I've done everything I can for you. Bought this house. Set up this biotech business for you. Hannah was a problem, a glitch. I dealt with it. For us.'

A glitch?

'Don't put this on me, Xan.'

He has that look in his eye. Pure spite. She knows what's coming next. He's going for the jugular.

'I think you were pregnant before you went to the States. You went because you were running away.'

'That's ridiculous.'

'Is it? Who's Jordan's real dad?'

'I don't know. It was a one-night stand. I was drunk. I never knew his name.'

Xan shakes his head and smirks. 'Oh, I think you know his name very well.'

'I went to Berkeley in the summer of 2007. Jordan was born the following summer. 2008.'

'I think you're fudging the dates. But you probably didn't even know you were pregnant when you left. You were just desperate to get away. And I get it. Berkeley was your way to escape.'

Cheryl stares at him.

He's guessing. How can he know?

He smiles. 'I understand why you've lied about it all these years. I really do. And I don't blame you. Because sometimes lies are necessary to protect the ones we love, aren't they?'

Hold it together. He's fishing.

'I've no idea what you're talking about.'

'Yes, you do. You've shielded Jordan from the truth for his entire life.'

'I can't tell him what I don't know. I went to a party. It was drunken sex. I didn't even know his name.'

Xan strolls round the room, as if he's on a podium giving a lecture. He loves the sound of his own voice.

'I've got to admire you, Cheryl,' he says. 'I'm pretty good at this, telling a good story. But you, my little scientific genius, you outshine us all. You've been telling the biggest lie of all. And you've stuck to it without wavering. Only trouble is, you let your guard down just the once, and I got a glimpse of the truth.'

'Xan, this is all a distraction from what you've done. You may think—'

'It's not a distraction. You want me to keep your secret, you've got a choice.'

He stops a few feet away; his face is implacable.

Don't let him see you're shaking.

She stares right back at him. 'There is no secret.'

'Let me take you back to your father's funeral. Five years ago, was it? And there we all were in some dinky little churchyard in the Cotswolds. And there's his grieving widow, your stepmother, and your two step brothers who you never see. I never even met the old guy.'

'We'd only just come back from the States.'

'But it's still a bit strange, don't you think?'

'The heart attack was sudden, there wasn't time—'

Xan raises his hand to silence her. 'Let's go back to the funeral. There's you and Lorna, side by side. His two daughters. And she glanced at you, and you glanced back at her. What was that look about Cheryl? Relief? Vindication? Escape?'

She takes a breath. It feels as if she's walking along a narrow ledge above a precipice. One wrong step and she could fall.

Mindset.

'Lorna and I have never made any secret of the fact that after our mother died—'

'Cheryl, you don't need to repeat the tale. He sent you off to boarding school, where you had a shitty time. But here's my alternative. Because Lorna left straight away, didn't she? But you didn't.'

'I was only eight. I went the following year.'

'Only eight. Left at home with your poor, grieving father. What happened then, Cheryl?'

'Nothing.'

'Nothing at all?'

She can feel the sweat gathering on her upper lip.

'I don't remember details.'

'Yeah, you do. Because I reckon that's when it all started. He wanted someone to comfort him, didn't he? Lorna was gone. Just you and him. He'd lost his wife, and he wanted someone to take her place. And you stepped into your mother's shoes, didn't you?'

A shudder runs through her. Xan reads people, identifies their weak spots. But she buried this so deep.

Not deep enough.

He's relentless. 'What choice did you have? He was your dad. Of course, you wanted to comfort him. So you were a good girl, and you did the things he asked you to do. A hug, a kiss, a cuddle on the sofa. But he wanted more than that, didn't he? Nowadays we'd call it grooming. Back then? Was there a word?'

Grooming? He has no idea what that means. What it involves.

Xan shrugs. 'But he was your dad. What could you do?'

He makes it sound so simple.

She forces herself to speak. 'I don't see where you're going with this.'

'I think your father started to sexually abuse you when you were a child. But it never stopped, did it? School holidays, whenever you went home. Whenever you were alone.'

'He remarried when I was twelve.'

'Come on, Cheryl. That makes no difference. Paedophiles don't stop. They're addicted to the power. Your solution was to put as much distance between you and him as you could. It was the only way you could escape him. But before you left, he insisted on one last time, didn't he? That's how you got pregnant. He's Jordan's father.'

The words hang in the air.

He's Jordan's father.

She feels herself swaying. Xan grasps her arm and guides

her to the old leather armchair in the corner. She slumps into it. Her palms rest on each arm as she tries to steady herself. The leather is cool to the touch. Her thoughts slide and drift. She knows the process: disassociation. The brain's mechanism to defend her from the effects of trauma. She's read all books, but she still can't stop it. Her husband is leaning over her, but she finds it hard to focus.

'Listen to me,' he says in a silky voice. 'What's going to be worse for Jordan? Knowing that his grandfather is his father, or a few years in youth detention? Incest is a terrible stigma. On you. On him. He'll blame you and he'll hate you. You know that. You'll lose him. You've kept this secret his whole life to protect him, and to protect yourself. That's what you need to do now. You have to do it for Jordan.'

'I don't understand.'

'It's simple. You persuade Jordan to confess, and he'll never find out that he's the result of an incestuous relationship between you and your father. That's the choice.'

He's looming over her, waiting for an answer. She can't speak. She can barely breathe.

Abruptly, he moves away. She's only vaguely aware of a noise. The study has a bay fronted window that faces the street. Shafts of blue light flash through the slatted blinds and bounce off the walls. Car doors are slamming. Xan peers out.

The police?

He has his back to her. 'Okay,' he says evenly. 'What's it going to be? If you protect me, I'll protect you. Do we have a deal?'

He really expects her to persuade Jordan to take the blame?

He turns to face her; no panic, just blank indifference. He's waiting for an answer.

Her head is swimming. She forces herself to concentrate.

'Yes,' she says. 'But on one condition. Afterwards you use that plane ticket to San Francisco and you don't come back.'

The doorbell rings.

He's still looking at her. He blinks a couple of times. His jaw is set. But there's no hint of affection. It's as if she's talking to a stranger.

'Okay,' he says. 'Deal. Now let me do the talking.'

62

Saturday, 3.15pm

Cheryl sits at the table in Lorna's kitchen. It's compact and colourful, looking out over the small patio garden. It could be an ordinary winter's afternoon, chilly and damp, colours fading to grey outside, but bright and cosy within. Her sister is making tea. The children are in the sitting room with Lorna's wife, Amy. Except nothing is normal. Cheryl's life has been brutally upended. The raw horror underpinning it exposed.

Lorna had arrived, her little Fiat 500 steaming up the road, just as the police were arresting Xan. It was her suggestion that Cheryl and the kids should leave while the police searched the house.

Xan's line with the police was to turn on the charm. But as they put him in the back of a police car, he shot her a glance. She knew what it meant and what he expects.

Lorna places a mug of tea in front of her. Camomile. The fragrance of the flowers is soothing.

Cheryl looks up at her sister. 'You trying to calm me down?' she says.

'I thought you liked Camomile.'

'I do.'

Lorna pulls out a chair and sits down opposite her.

'He's trying to blackmail me,' says Cheryl.

'How very Xan,' says her sister drily.

'He thinks I should somehow make Jordan confess to pushing Hannah off the balcony. He's cooked up some story that she was grooming him.'

Grooming? That word again.

Lorna reaches across the table and places her hand over Cheryl's. 'Listen to me,' she says. 'The police are not stupid. If they've arrested Xan, then they have grounds for suspecting him. They'll be gathering evidence. They'll analyse phone data—'

'Jordan did go round there. But Xan sent him home.'

Lorna sighs. 'How is he trying to blackmail you?'

There's a fist clutching her guts and twisting. She tries to meet her sister's gaze, but it's impossible. She struggles to get the words out. 'He knows about…' The tears erupt. She can't stop them.

The shame engulfs her.

Lorna gets up and stands next to her, placing a comforting hand on her shoulder.

Cheryl weeps in short, breathless gasps as the fist tightens its grip. Lorna reaches for a box of tissues and hands her one.

For several minutes, neither speaks.

Finally, Lorna says, 'He can't know, he can only guess.'

'What if he tells Jordan?'

'Is that what he's threatening you with?'

Cheryl nods.

Lorna sighs. 'Well, it's always been my view that Jordan

should be told of his true paternity at the appropriate time and in the appropriate way.'

'But now? He's only fourteen. Will he understand?'

'I don't know. But hearing it from you, your story of what happened to you, that will help him understand.'

'I don't think I'm capable of doing that. It petrifies me. I can hardly explain it to myself. How can I explain it to him?'

'You keep it simple. But he's a smart boy who's grown up in a world awash with information. Kids nowadays have a different degree of sophistication to us. He knows what a paedophile is, and what incest is. He also knows that no matter what, you love him.'

Cheryl blows her nose. Lorna has always had a solid macro view of the world; she sees the bigger picture. Whereas Cheryl is happiest staring down a microscope. At that level, things are far more random and strange, a world you can lose yourself in.

'You know what he asked me a couple of months ago?' says Lorna. 'He said: why didn't Mum have an abortion?'

'Oh my god, what did you say?'

'I just said that you may not have intended to get pregnant, but once you discovered you were, you wanted to have the baby.'

'What did he say?'

'He made a flippant remark. Bet she regrets it now, something like that. But I think it answered some question in his own mind.'

'About if I really wanted him?'

'Yes.'

Cheryl picks up her mug of tea and cradles it in both hands. The warmth is comforting.

Xan and his lies have dominated their lives for too long.

He accused her of telling the biggest lie of all. But she did it to protect her son.

'Jordan has a right to the truth, doesn't he?' she says.

'I think so.'

'I just don't know how I'm going to tell him.'

63

Sunday, 10.30am

Boden walks into the interview room, flanked by Chakravorty. After some discussion, the DCI has concluded that Xan Woodward's narcissistic confidence is more likely to trip him up if he's facing two women.

But having compiled all the evidence, Boden is glad that the boss is giving her a crack at him.

As they enter, Woodward stands up and offers them a handshake. Boden ignores it. He's opted for the duty solicitor, which is interesting. He's trying to appear innocent.

This has been his stance throughout, expressing shock and sadness at what happened to Hannah and insisting he'll do everything he can to help.

Boden runs through the preliminaries, reminding him he's still under caution and informing him he's being questioned in connection with two murders. He doesn't flinch; listens attentively. His eyes never leave Boden's face.

When she's finished speaking, he opens his palms, smiles

and says, 'I know it looks bad, and I don't blame you for arresting me. But I'm an innocent man. I was trying to protect my son. What father wouldn't?'

Boden sits back. 'Tell us about that,' she says.

'You already know what happened last Monday, in the car park. Jordan's friend was killed. My wife and I did our best, but he was so upset. I think that's how he fell into her clutches. She exploited his distress and his emotional need.'

'Who's she?' says Boden.

'Hannah Blakeney, of course. I'm sorry to speak ill of the dead. But that woman was a piece of work. You must've found the texts she was sending to my fourteen-year-old son?'

'We have,' says Boden. She glances at Chakravorty, who opens her iPad and says, 'There were fifteen texts in all, back and forth.'

'There you go,' says Woodward. 'She was grooming him.'

'Ten of them involve a discussion of the technicalities of editing video footage for social media,' says Chakravorty. 'Hannah was asking for advice, Jordan recommended a couple of apps.'

'Yeah,' says Woodward. 'She was reeling him in.'

'Five sent on the morning of her death suggest that you and he should visit her at the apartment she was renting.' Chakravorty closes the iPad.

'Okay,' says Woodward, changing tack. 'But, c'mon, he's a fourteen-year-old boy full of testosterone, and he clearly thought something was going to happen with her.'

'What sort of something?'

'Y'know that she'd pop his cherry. But he's just a kid.'

'How do you know this?' says Boden. 'Did he tell you?'

'Hey, I'm his dad. I knew what he was up to. When I saw him leave the house, I followed him.'

'On foot?'

'No. I guessed where he was going.'

'Oh,' says Boden, glancing at her notes. 'Didn't you put a tracking app on his phone? Why didn't you use that?'

This wrong-foots him. But he recovers quickly. 'Yeah, I did. I drove into town. When I got there, he was helping Hannah unload stuff from the back of her car.'

'What did you do?'

'You can imagine he wasn't that pleased to see me. But I played it cool. Helped them carry stuff up to the apartment.'

'And what did Hannah do?'

'She seemed amused.'

'Amused by what?'

'The situation.'

'Is it true that you and Hannah Blakeney were having a sexual relationship?'

He chuckles. 'I slept with her once. After my wife's party. We were both pretty pissed. It wasn't a big deal. And that's why I think she was amused by the idea of having the father then the son. She was that kind of girl.'

Boden scans him. As he gets more into his tale, he's relaxing. Lots of smiles, lots of eye contact.

'You unloaded her car and took her things up to the apartment. Did you take all of her things?' says Boden.

He frowns, as if trying to remember. 'No,' he says. 'Because that's when it all kicked off.'

'What kicked off?'

'Well, we couldn't get all the stuff, plus the three of us, in the lift. So the two of them went ahead. They sent the lift back down. And I followed. When I walked into the apartment, I heard raised voices. They were out on the balcony and

Jordan was really upset. I rushed out there. Of course I did. But I didn't get there in time. He pushed her.'

'He pushed her?'

'Yeah, shoved her hard. He's a strong lad. She tumbled backwards, went head first over the balcony.' He shakes his head. 'Horrible.'

'And what did you do then?'

'Well, okay, this was probably a mistake. But I did what any father would do. I got my boy out of there.'

'But Jordan isn't your biological son, is he?' says Boden. 'He's your stepson.'

'Well, yeah. But that's never made any difference to how I feel about him.' He frowns, as if struggling with something. 'Listen, this is no good,' he says with a sigh. 'I think you should just talk to him. I've got a feeling he wants to tell you the truth.'

'You think he wants to confess?'

'He's basically a good kid. I think it'll come as a relief to him.'

'Okay,' says Boden. 'DC Chakravorty is going to show you a series of CCTV clips obtained from the bus Jordan took to travel home that day. You'll see that there's a time code on each clip. He boarded the bus in central Cambridge fifteen minutes before we received a 999 call reporting that someone had just fallen from the fifth floor balcony. Two minutes before the call was made, he got off at the bus stop near your house. We also downloaded the data on your phone. The tracking app? It confirms his route.'

Woodward shrugs. 'Well, yeah. I sent him home on the bus. I guess it just took a while before someone noticed what had happened.'

'What did you do?'

'I told Jordan to get the bus. Because I wanted to check what had happened to Hannah.'

Now he's busking it. This isn't part of the story he's planned.

'And did you?'

'Yeah, sadly, she was dead. I suppose I panicked. I had to get home for Jordan.'

Boden meets his gaze directly. 'Paramedics found Hannah Blakeney conscious at the scene and in considerable distress. Despite their efforts, she died in the ambulance.'

The temperature in the room seems to plummet several degrees.

He looks away and shrugs. His expression is blank.

'It's all a pack of lies, isn't it, Xan?' says Boden. 'We've also recovered CCTV footage from the foyer of the building and the lift. That shows you and Hannah coming and going together. It shows you speaking to the cleaner long before Jordan arrived. It shows his arrival. Then it shows him coming down to Hannah's vehicle with you, and him leaving the scene at that point. Did you push Hannah Blakeney over the balcony, Xan?'

He shakes his head, then gives her a stoney glare. 'No comment,' he says.

'We'll take a break,' says Boden. 'Give you a chance to talk to your solicitor about this.'

She and Chakravorty get up and leave the room. They return to the office. DCI Hepburn, Mackie and several others are standing in front of the monitors.

'Nicely done, Jo,' says Hepburn. 'Good team effort all round.'

'Thank you, sir,' says Boden. She looks at the screen. Xan Woodward is slumped in his chair, head dipped forward.

64

Sunday, 10.45 am

It's an overcast morning, but the rain is holding off. Cheryl and Jordan are following a winding footpath across the water meadows. Even with his shoulders hunched and his hands in his pockets, he towers over his mother. Sunday cyclists and a few joggers pass them; it's a familiar route and they've often walked it as a family.

Since Xan's arrest, Jordan's said very little, but he's been watching. He's also become wary. It's Cheryl's impression that he's searching for clues. Trying to work out what the adults are going to do next. In the last few days, he's had to cope with some harsh realities. The death of his best friend in a stupid accident. And that's about to get worse. Cheryl is terrified. It must show on her face.

Jordan gives her a sideways glance.

'You okay?' he says.

She sighs. 'I'm not even sure what that means anymore,' she replies.

Has she ever been okay? Certainly not since her mother died.

'I can't believe he wanted to blame it on me,' he says. 'I always thought he liked me.'

'Oh, Jordie, he just…' she sighs. How do you excuse the inexcusable? You can't.

'I get it,' says Jordan. 'He's a hustler. Back against the wall, he figured out I was the perfect scapegoat.'

The words her son uses, it's not the language of a child. But he'll be fifteen in two months. He's not a child.

'I need to tell you some things,' says Cheryl. 'But I'm scared, because frankly, I don't know how you'll react.'

He laughs nervously. 'You mean like Xan's also defrauded the tax man? We're losing the house and gonna end up on the streets?'

Cheryl smiles. He's using humour to diffuse the tension between them.

'I wouldn't put it past him,' she says. 'But it's not that.'

He dips his head and sighs. 'My real dad, then,' he says.

How does he know?

She looks up at him. He's avoiding her eye. 'Y'know when Ben died,' he says. 'And his dad went ballistic. Said Ben would've never done that. I must've made him, cause it couldn't be Ben's fault.'

Cheryl nods.

'Well, I thought if I'd died instead, would my dad be saying that about me?'

'You mean Xan? He would've been devastated.'

Can she even be sure of that anymore?

'I dunno,' he says. 'It's just how much his old man cared about Ben, believed in him. What have I got? Xan and some guy who walked away. Didn't want to know you or me.'

'It was my father.' The words are out of her mouth before she has time to consider.

Jordan stops in his tracks and stares at her.

'Your father?'

No going back now.

'Yes.' Her heart is thudding. He's going to want an explanation. Surely he deserves that? But how can she explain it? Her throat is constricted. It's hard to swallow.

He's looking at her in astonishment.

'It started with him not long after my mum died,' she says.

'How old were you?'

'Eight.'

A memory flashes into her mind. Her mother, skin and bones, like a corpse, but still breathing. She grasped Cheryl's hand, and she kept saying, *take care of your dad, won't you?*

'Then it carried on,' she says. 'It never really stopped.'

'Why not?'

'I don't know. I wish I could tell you a reason. He wanted it, and I never felt able to say no to him.

'He forced you?'

'No, that's not how it happened.'

'How did it happen?'

There's a bench next to the path a few metres ahead.

'I need to sit down,' she says. They walk to it, and she sits. He sits too, leaving a couple of feet between them.

On the river, a solitary swan glides by. It's checking them out, trying to decide if they could be a source of food. She looks at her son. She has to do this. Somehow, she has to make him understand.

'My father ran this engineering firm. I think I told you that?'

Jordan nods.

'But he was always into science. Would've preferred that as a career, but he had to take over the family firm. In the offices, in a separate room, he set up a little laboratory for me. He was always telling me how clever, how special I was. He bought a microscope. Not a kids' chemistry set thing. A proper scientific instrument, the sort that would've been in a university lab back then. And he showed me how to make slides, using my blood. All kinds of other things. And I wasn't even nine years old. What kid gets to do that?'

'So like, he was bribing you?'

'Well, yes, but he was… I don't like the word, but he was grooming me. Told me I was much smarter than my sister. Made me feel I'd been chosen because I was special. And I loved it there, in my little lab. It was amazing. It was also my escape. Does this make any sense to you?'

'Yeah. You got access to all that, but you had to do what he wanted.'

'Yeah, I suppose it comes down to that. But, I can't separate who I am now, who I've become, from that experience.' Tears well in her eyes; she wipes them away with her fingertips.

They sit, side by side, staring at the river. The water is fast flowing, turgid and brown, stirred up by all the recent rain.

After a while, Jordan says, 'I did wonder why we never saw him.'

'I told him about you in a letter from the States. Sent him a picture. He never wrote back. Later, when we came back to live here, I phoned and reminded him about the letter. He swore he never got it. Wasn't long after that, he died.'

Jordan folds his arms and shakes his head. 'My father is my grandfather. Fucking hell!'

'Jordie, I am so sorry.'

'Why? You were only a kid.'

'The reason I went to the States was to get away from him. I didn't know I was pregnant when I left.'

'You could've had an abortion.'

'I know. I'm glad I didn't.'

They sit in silence. She becomes aware of her hands. No gloves. Her fingers are freezing. Jordan is staring out across the water. She can't read his expression.

She scans him. 'Are you alright?' she says.

He shrugs his narrow shoulders. They rise up like angel's wings. 'Yeah, I dunno… it's weird. I dunno what to think. But I'm glad you told me.'

'Are you?'

'Definitely. But, y'know, incest. Doesn't that increase your chances of getting strange diseases or being a special needs kid?'

'Marginally.'

He looks at her. His cheeks are rosy from the cold. 'Does anyone else know?' he says.

'My sister. And Xan. He guessed.'

'You gonna tell Sasha?'

'No. That's a decision for you.'

'Maybe tell her when she's older.'

'Up to you, Jordan.'

He smiles. 'Yeah.'

EPILOGUE

Cheryl is lying on a sun lounger in the garden. The weather is hot for September. The kids have got the paddling pool out and Sasha is squirting her brother with the hose. He grabs it from her and sprays her back. She squeals. It's taken a while but her daughter is laughing again and playing. The puppy is gambolling about and trying to join in. A puppy was Lorna's idea. She's a black Lab, named Velvet. Sasha chose the name and is attempting to train her, with some help.

As Jordan chases his sister, she runs over to her mother for protection.

'Mummy! Help me!' she squeals.

She ducks down behind the lounger.

Cheryl laughs. 'Hey!' she says to her son. 'Don't you dare!'

He laughs and lowers the hose. He's grown so tall, close to six foot. She's bought him an electric razor, and he goes through trainers in no time. But he's changed in other ways too. He's taken on the role of protector of both his sister and his mother. He's watchful, and far more gentle with Sasha than he was before. When she torments him, he doesn't retaliate.

It's taken seven months for Xan's case to come to trial, and according to Lorna, this is quick. He was judged a flight risk and refused bail.

Media coverage has been extensive. The salacious details have been picked over. Hannah's father has taken out a libel suit against one tabloid newspaper and threatened several others. Cheryl has tried to discourage Jordan and Sasha from looking at any of this. But the reality is she's powerless to prevent it.

She's resigned as head of the lab and is taking a sabbatical from the university. Jordan has moved to a different school at his request.

At first, Sasha refused to go to school at all. So Cheryl spent days just reading to her daughter. They worked their way through every book they could find containing fairies and goblins, and demons and sprites. Sasha would curl up on the sofa with her head on her mother's shoulder. It was a slow process, coaxing her back to school. Cheryl gradually introduced some maths and science into the mix, making sure she didn't fall behind.

Then one day, out of the blue, Teresa phoned Cheryl up and suggested she bring Alicia over. This helped persuade Sasha to go back to school, and Cheryl makes sure she's at the gate to collect her without fail every day. Small steps for both of them, but it seems to be working.

A kind of normality has seeped back into their lives, except everything is different. The landscape looks the same, but it's full of shadows and mists. Each of them has to navigate this unfamiliar territory in their own way. But Cheryl has made it her absolute priority to be there every step of the way with them.

She gets up from the lounger. 'Come on,' she says to Sasha. 'You can help me make some lemonade.'

As they walk across the sunbaked lawn towards the house, Cheryl's phone rings. The call she's been expecting, and also dreading.

Sasha is skipping ahead of her. 'You get the lemons out,' she says, 'while I just speak to Auntie Lorna.'

She catches Jordan giving her a sidelong glance. He knows, but he turns away and fusses the dog.

She strolls down the garden as she answers the phone.

'Hey,' she says.

'What are you up to?' says Lorna.

'We're about to make some lemonade.'

'I hope you'll save us some.'

Lorna and Amy have been there every inch of the way, through the endless interviews with the police. It was only when Xan's case finally came to court that he changed his plea to guilty.

Cheryl would like to believe it was so neither she nor Jordan would need to testify in court. But Lorna pointed out that his lawyers will have advised him it was his best hope of reducing his sentence.

Today was the sentencing hearing, which Lorna and Amy had attended.

'Well?' says Cheryl.

'A life sentence with the judge recommending he serve a minimum of seventeen years. The plea in mitigation tried to hint at the idea he was being blackmailed by Hannah. But the judge slapped that down. I think that's why he said seventeen. The defence were probably hoping for fifteen.'

Cheryl absorbs this. She doesn't want to ask, but she has to.

'How did he take it?'

'Indifferent, I'd say. Like the shutters had come down.'

'What will happen to the other case?'

'He's sticking to his story that he looked for Arran but never found him. No chase. No fight. The CPS can't prove the person caught on CCTV is him.'

'He always gets away with something,' says Cheryl ruefully.

But part of her still wishes...

She turns to face the back of the house. Her beautiful home has become her sanctuary. The ivy on the back wall needs trimming; it's hanging down over the terrace, but the clematis laced through it is still flowering. The bi-fold doors to the kitchen are wide open. Sasha appears with a bag of lemons in a string sack.

She holds them up and shouts, 'How many, Mum?'

Jordan has his phone out. He holds it up and films his sister. 'Come on Sash,' he says. 'Let's see you juggle. Three lemons. Bet you can't.'

'Bet I can,' says Sasha, extracting lemons from the sack. She drops one and Velvet the puppy pounces on it.

Cheryl watches them. Her heart soars.

Focus on this.

'Are you okay?' says Lorna.

'Yeah, I'm fine,' says Cheryl. 'We'll save you some lemonade.'

LEAVE A REVIEW

If you'd like to write a review, I'd be most grateful. The choice of books out there is vast. Reviews do help readers discover one of my books for the first time.

Scan QR code to review Lie Deny Repeat.

A MESSAGE FROM SUSAN

Thank you for choosing to read *Lie Deny Repeat.* If you enjoyed it and would like to keep up to date with my latest book releases and news, please use the address below.

susanwilkins.co.uk/sign-up/

**Your email address will never be shared, and you can unsubscribe at any time.*

Scan QR code to go to Susan's sign up page

Do get in touch and let me know what you thought of *Lie Deny Repeat.* I love hearing from readers. You can message me at susanwilkins.co.uk/contact

Scan QR Code to go to Susan's contact page

BOOKS BY SUSAN

The Informant

The Mourner

The Killer

It Should Have Been Me

Buried Deep

Close To The Bone

The Shout + The Right Side Of The Line (Free when you sign up to Susan's newsletter)

A Killer's Heart

She's Gone

Her Perfect Husband

Lie Deny Repeat

See Me Fall

BOOKS CONT.

facebook.com/susanwilkinsauthor

twitter.com/SusanWilkins32

instagram.com/susan_wilkins32

ACKNOWLEDGEMENTS

Huge thanks to Colin James and Graham Bartlett for their expert advice on how the police would proceed. Some things have been altered slightly in the interests of drama.

In my career as an author, I've received the help and support of too many people to mention. The community of crime writers is friendly, welcoming, and nowadays global. Learning from those who have gone before is essential for any writer.

Big thanks to my Reading Team for their diligence and valuable feedback.

Last, but not least, thanks to Laura Wilkinson for her sharp editorial eye on the manuscript and her many suggestions for improvements.

But getting the books out into the world would be impossible without my partner in crime, Sue Kenyon. I just write the books. She does everything else.

Published by Herkimer Limited in 2022
Summit House
170 Finchley Road
London NW3 6BP

Scan QR code to go to susanwilkins.co.uk

ISBN 978-1-9169012-9-2

Printed in Great Britain
by Amazon

17251562R00203